TIME ASSASSINS

R. Kyle Hannah

Jumpmaster Press™
Birmingham, Alabama

Library Cataloging Data

Names: Hannah, Kyle, R. (Richard Kyle Hannah) 1967-

Title: Time Assassins / R. Kyle Hannah

5.25 in. × 8 in. (13.34 cm × 20.33 cm)

Description: Jumpmaster Press digital eBook edition | Jumpmaster Press Trade paperback edition | Alabama: Jumpmaster Press, 2018. P.O Box 1774 Alabaster, AL 35007 info@jumpmasterpress.com

Summary: Futuristic Assassins travel throughout time changing alternative timelines into actual history.

Identifiers: ISBN-13: 978-1-949184-03-7 (ebk.) | 978-1-949184-02-0 (trade)

1. Science Fiction 2. Time Travel 3. Action Adventure 4. Alternate History 5. Assassination 6. Politics 7. Presidents

Printed in the United States of America

TIME ASSASSINS

R. Kyle Hannah

Acknowledgments

I would like to extend my heartfelt thanks to the fans who kept insisting that I write another book. I could not and would not do this without your support!

I'd like to thank Glen, Caitlin, Brooke, Cheryl and Gene for stepping up and proofing the book. Your insights and suggestions really made it a better story!

Special thanks to Gene Rowley for designing the cover art. Another fantastic job, my friend!

And finally, to my wife and family who continually ignore me and my laptop so that I can put words on paper.

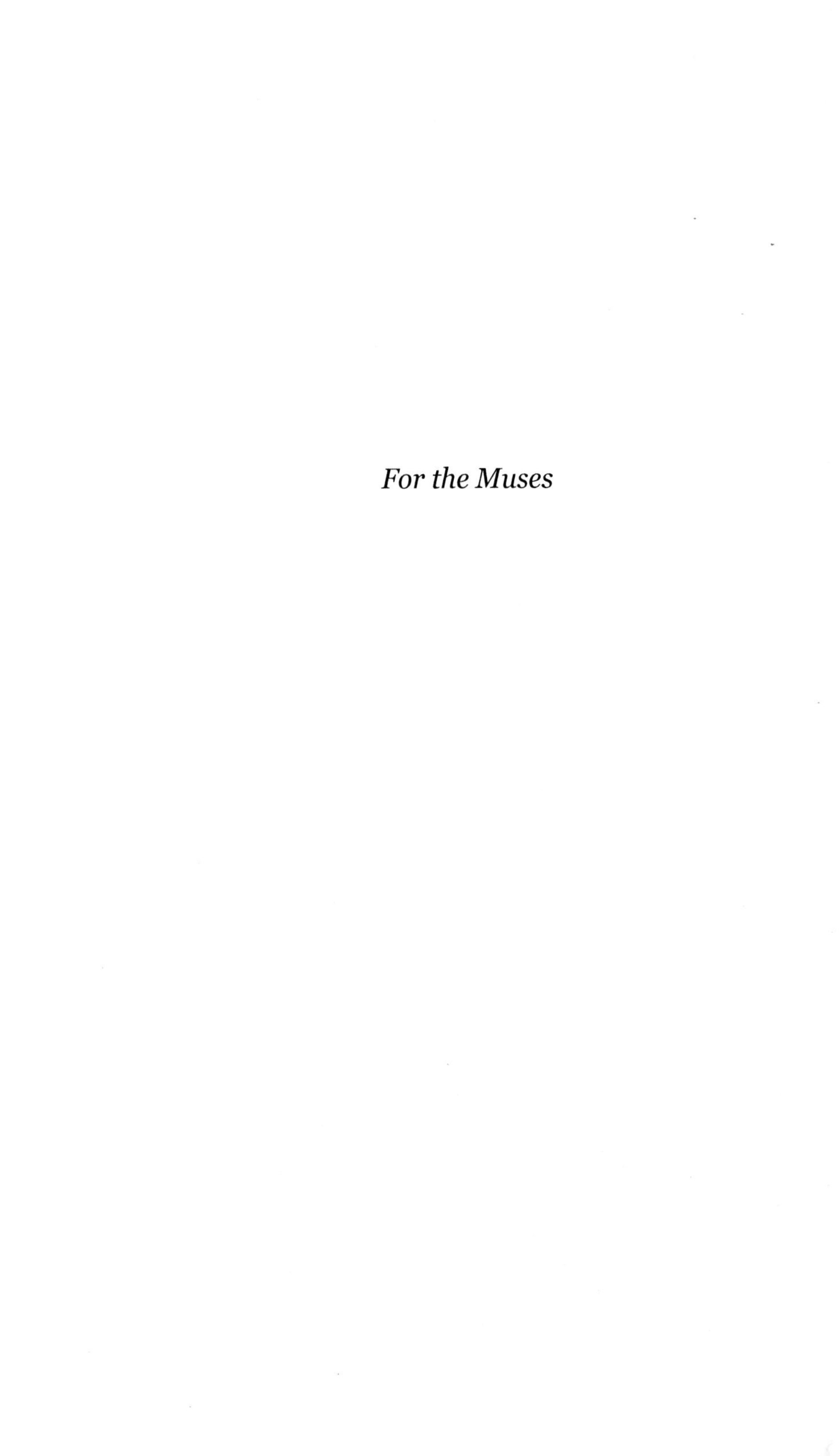

For the Muses

Prologue

THE COLD METAL OF the stunner barrel touched his neck, sending a chill down his spine.

"Do not move!"

Good advice, thought Apprentice 58, and did as ordered. He sat upright in his chair and stared straight ahead, past the holo-reader in front of him, at the far wall filled with books and holo-crystals. A rather complex diagram of interlocking gears and cogs, that supposedly represented the inner-workings of time, also filled his vision. Several black gloved hands crossed into his peripheral vision to remove the holo-crystals and books he had been studying. He almost breathed a sigh of relief as the barrel of the stunner left the nape of his neck. He steeled himself for whatever came next but still did not move.

Professor Jackson Donovan moved into his vision, pulled out the chair opposite the Apprentice and sat down. He placed his hands on the table, clasped into a single fist, and simply stared at the young man. The silence lasted a half minute but felt like a half hour to the Apprentice.

"Would you like to explain yourself?"

A gruff voice from behind startled him, but Apprentice 58 remained perfectly still. He did not need to turn around to know that Master Li, the Chief of Combat Studies, stood behind him. He felt the chair shift slightly as Master Li rested his hands on it. Still, he did not move.

The Apprentice kept his eyes on the Professor. "Sir?"

"You are not authorized to research faculty," Donovan said, leaning back in his chair. "Yet we find you doing that very thing. Would you care to explain?"

"No, sir...I mean, no, I'm not researching faculty." Apprentice 58 took a breath to calm himself and gather his thoughts. He felt the first pangs of nervousness creep into his system. *Was this another absurd test the Guild had devised for him?* he thought. He looked at his mentor and saw the determination and fear in his eyes. Apprentice 58 quickly realized that the Professor was not that good of an actor and thought that he might actually be in some sort of trouble. He rubbed his hands on his robes, but otherwise remained still. "I'm researching Presidents of the United States: weaknesses in security, best times to plot an assassination."

"That is a Cleaner's job. Not a potential Assassin's." Professor Donovan's voice held an edge the apprentice had never heard before.

"I thought it would be a good idea to know scenarios from a Cleaner's point of view. To...uh...enhance my...uh...perception of the mission." He stammered slightly as he searched for the right words and realized it made him sound like he was lying. He started to explain but the professor continued speaking.

"You talk to the Cleaners on the ground. You do not do unauthorized research." Donovan picked up a crystal and checked the target and date etched onto the top. His eyes widened. "Especially not for current missions!"

"But I saw you talking with one of the Cleaners before they left and I thought I could help."

Donovan jumped from his seat. "What did you overhear?"

"Nothing, sir!" Apprentice 58 replied, sliding his chair back by the sudden movement from his professor. The chair stopped abruptly as it hit Master Li standing behind him. "I didn't hear anything. You were too far away. I only saw you talking with the Cleaner before he left."

"What did you see, Apprentice?" Master Li asked as Donovan reclaimed his seat.

Apprentice 58 closed his eyes and recalled the scene in the corridor from the day before. Two men were talking outside the Skip Control Room. Professor Donovan gave the other man—a Hispanic looking man with dark skin and black hair—a small notebook and package. The two men argued for a couple of moments, although they kept their voices low. Once the conversation was complete, the Cleaner disappeared into the control room with an unhappy look on his face. Professor Donovan stood for another moment, deep in thought, before he turned and disappeared down the corridor. The Apprentice relayed his memory.

Master Li raised an eyebrow at Donovan and the Professor lowered his head to his hands.

“I'm very sorry you had to see that exchange, Apprentice,” Donovan said in a sad tone. He left his head lowered, unable to make eye contact.

Master Li grunted toward the door and two guards entered, stunners at the ready. “Take him to the Council.” He looked at Donovan who still had his head lowered to the floor. “The Apprentice was caught copying the historical archives.”

“What? No! I wasn't copying—” His voice trailed off as he was escorted out of the library and down the corridor.

Silence invaded the library, consuming the two that remained.

Finally, Master Li broke the silence. “You know you just signed that boy's death warrant.”

Donovan nodded. His head in his hands; he never looked up.

"You were supposed to be more careful about your identity!"

"I was careful—am careful," Donovan said, shaking his head dejectedly. "Only a handful of people know who I really am. I doubt the boy even knows."

“Maybe not,” Li said turning to the door, “but the Council will not take any chances. They will put that boy to death to protect your secret.” He left the Professor sitting in the now empty room, head still in his hands.

“I know.”

* * * *

Apprentice 58 stood, surrounded by several guards, Master Li, Professor Donovan, and a man he did not know, awaiting his execution. His trial, convened quickly after his capture, had been brief; guards escorted him into a large ominous chamber, he met the Council, the Council pronounced judgment and he was escorted out. His head was still spinning by the whirlwind chain of events: accusation, trial, verdict and sentence.

He absentmindedly fiddled with the metal that bound his hands behind him. Apprentice 58 almost laughed at the irony in the fact that the group huddled outside the Time Skip Control Room, almost in the exact spot that he had witnessed the conversation between Donovan and the Cleaner three days earlier.

He knew that his time was short and that he needed to do something fast if he wanted to stay among the living.

"Hold him here," the unknown man said. "There is a mission about to commence."

The young Apprentice peered through the partially open door and caught a glimpse of the Control Room itself. He had taken a tour of the room as a first year Apprentice, but he had never seen an actual skip in progress. An idea struck him, he stopped fiddling with the cuffs, and he put his training to use as the Guild personnel around him stood watch.

He smirked. Neither Professor Donovan nor Master Li could look him in the eye. They knew he was about to die because of their testimony to the Council. *False testimony*, he thought.

A technician poked his head from the control room. "Sir, Assassin 73 is skipping in one minute."

"I'll be right there, Joseph," the unknown man said. He turned to Master Li. "Excuse me. I'll be back in a moment." The man disappeared through the open door.

Apprentice 58 saw the open door, the time portal beyond, and knew he had to make his move.

The lock to the cuffs silently clicked open—Guild training was quite extensive when it came to lock picking—and the young Apprentice lashed out at his guards. A quick jab, a knife hand chop, a kick that sent one guard into Master Li, and he was free. He only had one true option available and he took it. He launched himself through the door and into the Skip Control Room.

He entered the Control Room at a near run and took in the scene in a glance: the unknown man talked with two technicians, several other technicians sat at their terminals monitoring the time flux, and Assassin 73 stood ten feet from the Skip Portal. Apprentice 58 adjusted his course and headed for the glowing opaque door to the past.

He crossed the twenty meters quickly as yells and shouts sounded behind him. One of the guards managed to get off a stunner shot. It missed the Apprentice but hit a technician that moved to intercept the fleeing man. The technician crashed to the floor, twitching, as Assassin 73 turned to grab the prisoner. Apprentice 58 was quicker. The younger man shoved the veteran Assassin out of his way as a stunner bolt hit the Apprentice in the back.

Electric currents ravaged his body as his momentum carried him forward. Apprentice 58 hit the edge of the time portal, bounced off the doorframe, spun lazily in a half circle and fell backward, disappearing through the door into history.

Chapter One

JASON LASSITER STOOD OUTSIDE the colossal double doors. Shivering from the near freezing temperature, he squinted against the gale force winds. He stood alone, hands clasped behind his back, waiting for someone to open the doors and let him into the training area. He grimaced slightly and wished he had known it was going to be so cold; he would have worn a few more layers. Ice crystals and blistering winds plastered his hair to his head. His trousers and weathered blue jacket whipped in the wind.

The teenager felt that he had not moved in days, even though it had only been about an hour. *When you're this cold*, he thought. *Hours can seem like days.*

He said nothing. He did not move an inch other than to squint. He knew *they* were watching. With that sobering thought, he steeled himself against the cold and stood in the blowing wind, his brown eyes squinting, but alert.

Jason had spent the last seventeen months honing his physical and mental skills as he progressed through the selection process. It had been a demanding and exhausting time. His first hurdle had been the application and a simple essay stating why he wanted to be an assassin. He wrote what any sixteen-year old would write. He wanted to fight the good fight, travel through time, and kill people (bad guys as he had originally written). The killing was tertiary. He was a student of history and Jason knew that by joining the Guild he would learn more by travelling, and doing, than he ever could by studying.

Jason had travelled the world with his archeologist father after his mother's passing before his tenth birthday. At the ripe age of fifteen, Jason had travelled to over one hundred countries and set foot on every continent on the Earth. He had seen so much, learned so much, but no matter where he had visited, he had wanted to know how those people had managed to get to that point. Why were some countries rich in wealth, while others were rich in history? He knew that only by travelling in time could he get those answers. He said so in his essay.

The next obstacle had been the physical endurance test. Not athletic as a teen, Jason had almost quit the running and climbing and other physical abuse. Three days of physical torture at a regional military recruitment center had been almost more than the teen could take, but thoughts of travelling to ancient cultures motivated him. The selection process ended with a series of mental trials, mostly puzzles and riddles, which proved to be no contest to the young man. Highly intelligent, Jason had maintained superior marks throughout his education. He had even set a new record for the fastest answers to the selection of riddles. Now, as he approached his eighteenth birthday, he would face the final challenge and be officially welcomed into the Assassin's Guild.

Or be dead and buried.

The creaking of the three-meter tall doors swinging open jerked him from his reverie. He stood quietly, literally frozen in place, as three men exited the temple. All three were bald, well built, wore loose, baggy light blue clothes and carried no visible weapons. Jason did not move, except for a small shiver from the cold. His eyes, however, followed the men intently as they quietly surrounded him.

* * * *

Training Master Ki Lon Li stood in a second story window, sipping coffee as he watched the scene develop below him. The steam swirled up into his face as he raised the folder and reread the applicant's essay and qualifications. He smiled slightly as he read the naïve "bad guys." It brought back his adolescent thinking from some forty years earlier. Being a student of history himself, Master Li could relate with the paragraph on learning about ancient cultures. He took a sip of coffee and turned his attention back to the four men standing in the snow. No one had moved. Another smile touched his lips as he opened the window a crack and grunted.

With the sound from above, the three men moved toward Jason in unison, presenting themselves as a clear threat. The would-be assassin mentally calculated his options and, remembering the explicit rules, remained perfectly still. The blue-robed men exploded into a flurry of punches, a series of kicks to the head and a continuous stream of loud screams. None of which connected.

Jason Lassiter stood perfectly still, unmoving, except for a slight shiver in the freezing snow. As quickly as it began, it ended, and the three assailants moved back to their original positions, surrounding the young man in a rough circle.

Training Master Li looked at the folder again and nodded his satisfaction. He looked out of the window, caught the eye of one of his blue robed assistants, and made a motion with his cup. The three men in blue quickly moved back to the door, entered the dark confines, and closed it behind them, leaving Jason Lassiter alone in the cold. The teen quietly breathed a sigh of relief.

* * * *

A half hour later, the doors opened again, and an older man exited. Bald and well built, he wore baggy clothes of an odd green color and no shoes. He moved quickly and quietly, almost floating across the snow, to a point directly in front of Jason. A few inches shorter than Jason, the young man ended up looking over the top of the Training Master's head. The boy still had not moved.

"Jason Lassiter," the Oriental man stated matter-of-factly, his English lightly accented. Master Li began to circle the teen as he continued. "I have read your application, seen your fitness score and reviewed your mental acuity results." Master Li stopped his circling and stared into the teen's face. "Are you ready for your final challenge?"

The young man started to answer, but something in the back of his mind stopped him. The odd tense in the bald man's voice sent a warning trigger to his brain. His mind went through the instructions again, and his brain zeroed in on the primary instruction: DO NOT MOVE UNDER ANY CIRCUMSTANCE! Therefore, Jason stood, stoically, staring at a point over the old man's head. He could feel his heart pound as adrenaline flooded his system. *What do I do?* he thought, unmoving.

The two men stood in silence, neither moving for almost ten minutes, in the freezing cold. The sun began to set, and the wind picked up. The temperature started to drop, and Jason shivered slightly. Finally, the door behind Master Li opened again and the three men in the light blue robes once again exited, each carried either a cup of coffee or a blanket.

"Master, he has stood here for the allotted time," one of the men stated, bowing and handing the old man a cup of steaming coffee. The other two men surrounded the boy; one draped a blanket over Jason as the other offered the nearly frozen teenager a second cup of coffee.

"You have passed the final challenge," Master Li said, passing a steaming cup to the now visibly shivering boy. "Welcome to the Assassin's Guild."

* * * *

The blast of heat hit Jason as they entered the training area. Pain immediately shot through his hands, feet, nose and ears as the heat began to battle the cold of his nearly frozen flesh. Without thinking, he began to lean on one of his former attackers as 'pins and needles' attacked his body. The man, as if expecting the sudden extra weight, adjusted immediately and the quartet continued to move inside the training facility. The giant double doors closed behind them with a solid boom that echoed through the chamber.

Although in pain, Jason studied the interior of the facility with keen interest. The foyer of the facility was a cavernous entryway that spanned at least one hundred feet across with a dome ceiling twenty foot high. Richly, yet sparsely decorated, it held only a dozen chairs, a few sofas and a gurgling fountain in the center of the room. Held in place by intricately paneled walls, the double doors gave way, on the far side of the room, to a wall of bay windows overlooking a domed courtyard.

With Master Li leading the way, the quartet exited the foyer into the bustling courtyard and continued their journey along a graveled trail, skirting the main training area. Jason stared mesmerized at the scope of the facility and by the number of people, divided into three distinct groups, in an area adjacent to the path.

The newest Guild member stopped for a moment and watched the hand-to-hand combat training. He saw several men and a few women, dressed in light green robes, standing between rows of students dressed in light blue. At a barked command, the row on the left assumed a defensive stance and the row on the right attacked with a series of kicks. The ferocious attacks were easily blocked and the two reformed after a few seconds. Jason stood awestruck at the sudden violence and at the ease the kicks and punches were blocked. Another command rang through the training yard and the event repeated, with the roles reversed.

Master Li allowed the procession to stop and he watched the new Apprentice as he studied the training. “You've never witnessed a training session?”

“No, sir,” replied Jason.

After a minute, the group started walking again. Jason continued to study the sparring as they moved around the perimeter of the training area. He stared, enthralled at the choreographed movements on the matted floor. “I've never seen anyone move that fast before!”

“Mr. Lassiter.” The teen turned to the Master. “There is a lot for you to learn now that you have been accepted into the Guild.” That brought an inadvertent smile from Jason. “So here is your first lesson:

“There are three distinct groups that comprise the Assassin’s Guild: The Assassins, the Apprentices, and the Cleaners.” Master Li pointed to each of the groups in turn. “There is a fourth and a fifth group, but that is not for this discussion. You will learn their functions as you progress over the next several years.”

Jason turned his attention back to the assembled factions; blue robed Apprentices and grey robed Cleaners stood in sparring lines, preparing to do mock battle. Scarlet clothed Assassins assisted green-suited combat instructors, insuring the Apprentices learned form and technique.

Jason looked at the man he leaned on and received a knowing smile for his trouble. “Assassin’s Apprentice 74 here is in his third year of training. He will soon be an Assassin ready for his first mission.” Jason looked at the other two men and each nodded their assurance. “Apprentices 84 and 87 are in their second year of study.”

The quartet continued their journey through the courtyard and Jason realized the color of the clothing dictated the course of study. The light blue robes were the Apprentices; scarlet robes identified the Assassins; and gray the Cleaners.

"Master?" Jason began, realizing he did not even know the man's name.

"Li."

"Master Li, why are there so many Cleaners? There seems to be three or four times as many?"

The three apprentices laughed softly, and Jason blushed slightly.

"Do not be embarrassed at your question, apprentice. They only laugh because they too asked that question." Master Li opened a door and led them down a long corridor with doors spaced at regular intervals. Rich mahogany paneling gave the corridor a warm, home-like feeling. "The Cleaners make up the majority of the guild because they are responsible for the missions even more so than the Assassins. Again, you will learn all about it as you progress through your studies.

"For now," the trainer said as he opened a door to a room, "you need to rest. Your training begins early tomorrow, Apprentice 101."

The door shut behind the young Apprentice, leaving him alone in the room. A quick survey left him little doubt that he had a roommate. Two beds lined the far wall, two desks and two dressers adorned the near wall. Jason sat down heavily on the unmade bed, pushing the stack of bedclothes aside. The feeling in his extremities had finally returned and he flexed his fingers.

Jason acknowledged the stark contrast between his untidy side of the room and his roommate's immaculate side. He moved his head slowly soaking up his surroundings. Aside from the bedclothes he had already moved he saw his new wardrobe on his dresser: light blue robes and sandals.

The Apprentice sighed heavily, removed himself from the bed, and got to work putting his side of the room together.

Jason Lassiter, now known as Assassin's Apprentice 101 by the Guild, rubbed his baldhead and stared at himself in the mirror. "It's not me," he said to no one, and finished his morning preparations.

For almost two weeks, he had been trained, taunted, and damn near tortured. His face held a slight scar from two narrow escapes with a katana—a Japanese short sword—and he had too many bruises to count. He could see in the mirror the fading remains of a black eye and his left ear was cauliflowered - bruised and disfigured from Jujitsu.

He shook his head and winced, reminded that every movement brought pain to his bruised and battered body. He buttoned the wooden toggles on his shirt and acknowledged the bruises masked developing muscles and that made him smile slightly. *The regimen may be tough, but it's effective,* he thought as he finished getting dressed.

His roommate, Apprentice 93, slapped him on the back, partly as a way to say good luck on the day, partly because he knew that Jason had a large developing bruise from a hit with a wooden staff. The young assassin-to-be flinched noticeably and his roommate sprinted out the door laughing. Jason followed a minute later, leisurely walking down the hall toward the academic wing of the facility.

In addition to his physical routine, Apprentice 101 had started his historical study of past missions for the Guild. He did not really enjoy the research that accompanied the case studies. He wanted to get out and experience the history.

Patience, he continuously chided himself.

Apprentice 97 met him in the hallway. She was one of only a dozen women in the academy. She wore the same light blue clothing and sported the same baldhead. The female apprentice was the same height as Apprentice 101, but more trim, and a year or so older. She was also full year ahead of the newest addition to the Guild. She sported her typical warm smile.

"Morning!" she said cheerily. She gave him a knowing smile. "I hear you've started the historical missions. Fun aren't they?"

"I think I'd rather take another beating from Master Li than sit through those things for another day," he replied.

"Don't say that too loud," she whispered conspiratorially as they walked down the paneled corridor. "You might get both!"

They laughed together and continued down the corridor toward the academic wing. "Lunch?" she asked, pausing before her classroom.

"If we get done with the Guild history class on time today," he said. "Last couple of days, the guy has just rambled on through lunch."

She nodded. “He did the same thing to us.” She opened the door a bit and held it with her foot. “If you can make it, I’ll be at the usual table.”

With a wave, she disappeared into the classroom. The two had met on his first day when he took a wrong turn and ended up at the entrance to the infirmary. Apprentice 97 had taken pity on the 'newbie' and escorted him back to the academic wing.

The new Apprentice had never seen a bald woman before and could not stop staring at her. Instead of being insulted she found it endearing because, in her brief time at the Academy, most of the boys did not even look at her. Their friendship was immediate.

Apprentice 101 had learned his way through the maze of corridors after that first day with the help of his new friend. She had escorted him through halls, showed him all of the hotspots, such as the cafeteria and the laundry, and introduced him to several of the other Apprentices. Now, two weeks into his regimen, he strolled down the familiar corridors, took the first right, then the second left and before too long he found himself in front of a wooden door marked ‘HISTORY’.

He opened the door and began his day.

* * * *

He did not make lunch, as usual. Professor Jackson Donovan, a skinny man of average height, with a large nose and unkempt hair, had another rambling episode about a Japanese Assassin in the 16th Century. The class went over by two hours.

The Apprentice wanted to pull his hair out. He would have, if he had any. Mentally exhausted, he held his head low as he sauntered back to his room at the end of the day. By muscle memory, Apprentice 101 moved his body away from the academic wing, his mind focused on the day's lesson. He kept reliving the last words of the Japanese Assassin; "Keep vigilant your surroundings." He missed the fact that he was the only person moving down the empty corridor. That is when the attacker struck.

His assailant came in high, from the second landing on the stairs and aimed a kick at the young man's head. The teen ducked, narrowly missing the foot as it brushed past his face. His fatigue forgotten, he used the only weapon he had at his disposal to defend himself. He threw his history book.

The book flew open as it spun through the air and nailed the unknown attacker in the face. He followed a half second behind the book and threw himself into the mid-section of his assailant. Both of them went down in a heap on the hardwood floor.

Apprentice 101 ended up on top, holding his assailant just below the throat with his left hand and raised his right fist to strike. His right fist paused in mid-air as the sound of laughter split the air: feminine laughter. His left hand rose and fell with the breathing laughter of his attacker as Apprentice 101 slowly lowered his right hand and unwrapped the light blue facial covering. The robes parted to reveal Apprentice 97; her green, mocking eyes, still laughing. His face reflected his shock.

Apprentice 97 caught her breath, reached up with both hands and grabbed his face, placing a wet kiss on his lips.

"At least you don't look depressed anymore," was all she said when she released him.

* * * *

Apprentice 101 had never seen anything like the weapons range.

He stood with a dozen other blue robed Apprentices at the edge of the weapons training area. The sheer scope of the complex and the sounds of weapons fire sent his adrenaline into overdrive. As a child, firearms were forbidden in his province. He had never even held anything other than a toy bow and arrow. A quick glance at this peers, told him that a lot of them had not either.

The range stretched for almost a half kilometer, all enclosed within a soundproof dome. Firing points were evenly spaced the length of the range, with targets as close as ten meters and as far as a thousand meters distant—or so the Apprentice was told. The only thing he could see in his vicinity was a series of firing points that stretched out to about fifty meters.

"Today, you will get your first lesson in firearms training," announced an Instructor dressed in forest green robes. He stood on a small platform about a half-meter high. It elevated him, leaving no doubt who was in charge.

"Do you hear that?" the Instructor asked, pointing a thumb over his shoulder toward the distant sound of gunfire. "You will get to fire those weapons only after" - he picked up an ancient cross-bow in one hand and longbow in the other - "you master these."

A silent groan echoed across the gathered students, but the instructor paid no mind. His bright, intelligent brown eyes had seen those disheartened looks a hundred times.

“My name is Master Gunsmith Hart,” continued the gruff voice, “and I have been instructing Assassins in the use and lethality of firearms for almost thirty years.

“You will visit my home”—he waved his hands around at the firing range - “twice a week for the next six months. You will pay attention. You will learn the rules. You will learn how to use these weapons properly and accurately, and,” he paused again, adding emphasis by eyeing each of the dozen students, “you will be safe.

“Each of these weapons, from these ancient crossbows to the most modern high intensity pulse rifle, *will kill you*!” He said the last three words with such vigor that several of the Apprentices stepped back. “So you will practice safety at all times. Do you understand?”

"Yes, Master Gunsmith!" answered the students.

Master Gunsmith Hart nodded absently. He had already stepped off his platform and moved toward rack after rack of ancient weapons. “You will be trained on these until you know them intimately.” He pointed to the racks of crossbows, daggers, bow and arrows, spears, and other assorted weapons. "Once you master these, you will move on to more advanced weapons, including grenades." That perked up the students a little. “You will continue this pattern until you master every weapon on this range.

“Now, gather 'round and allow me to introduce you to the medieval crossbow, Mark I.”

* * * *

The months continued to fly by, most of the days were the same: physical training, history lessons, hand-to-hand combat and physiology. Apprentice 97 would attack Apprentice 101 occasionally, keeping him on his toes. He had even surprised her on a couple of occasions. He lost most of those assaults, but he knew he was getting better with every encounter. Overall, his lessons went well, until his class experienced its first loss.

Apprentice 102, a young man accepted to the Guild a few days after 101, shot himself with a 9mm pistol on the range. It was ruled an accident by the investigation: Apprentice 102 had mishandled the weapon during a magazine change and shot himself in the leg. Unfortunately, the young man hit his femoral artery and bled out even as the medics tried to stop the bleeding. It was a sobering day for all of the Apprentices.

It got worse.

The day after Apprentice 102 died, the entire Guild turned out for the funeral. The Guild Council took the occasion of any accidental death to teach a lesson to the young Apprentices and Cleaners that their actions held deadly consequences. The death also served the Council as a hazing tool. Giving those not quite cut out for the life of an Assassin or Cleaner an excuse to leave.

The Assassins, Apprentices, Cleaners, Teachers and Technicians all stood in a rough formation. Their assorted colored robes created a rainbow as the formation took shape. Apprentice 101 stood in the middle of the Apprentice ranks, unmoving. The cemetery was near the training grounds, not far from the entrance to the weapons range, through a non-descript door that led to an exterior courtyard. Apprentice 101 had not even noticed the door before he had to step through it. After seeing this side of it, he hoped he never had to step through it again.

The snow, somehow, did not blow on this side of the mountain. The landscape was clear and the sun shone brightly on the cold, crisp day. The graveyard stretched for what seemed like forever. Small headstones, in neat rows, stretched to the horizon. There was no separation on the headstones between Assassin, Apprentice or Cleaner.

The ceremony was brief, moving, and sobering to the young masses. A few broke down and wept as the casket lowered into the burial vault. As the ceremony ended, an old man dressed in black robes stepped onto a meter tall platform and looked over the assembled Guild. A complete Guild gathering did not happen often, and the leadership wanted to take full advantage.

“This,” he began, waving his left hand behind him toward the graveyard, “is a tragedy. A tragedy that could have been avoided.” He paused, “Should, have been avoided.

"We must learn from this horrible event! This accident provides a valuable lesson to everyone in the Guild.” He paused, adjusting the voice amplifier he wore around his neck. “It proves to all of us that we must be aware of our environment. We must pay attention to all of those,” he paused again, unsure if the words were the correct ones, “little details. Because if we do not, we perish.”

The old man, with assistance from several of the Instructors, stepped down from the platform and made his way through the colorful formation and out of the cemetery, leaving the Guild sects—Assassins,

than Assassins." Mr. Donovan raised his right hand, looked and pointed across the room at another Apprentice. "Why the disparity?" He moved across the room as if following the question.

Apprentice 95, a short, dark skinned East Indian man from New Delhi responded quickly as Mr. Donovan settled before him. "The Cleaners are generally three-man teams sent back before the Assassin to set up the scene. Their job can be anything from setting up the initial meeting to scouting the kill-spot.

"The Cleaners are also sent back to review and record every major assassination in history, whether sanctioned by the Council or not."

"Why?"

"In case the Council decides that assassination is detrimental to the timeline. The Council will have the information necessary to send an Assassin or a Cleaner Team back to prevent the kill."

"Excellent," said Mr. Donovan and moved on to the next apprentice. "Who comprises the Council?"

A nervous Apprentice responded tentatively. "The Council is...uh...a group of...er... five Senior Assassins."

"Correct!" Mr. Donovan replied. "Where does the Council get its authority to exist?"

"The...uh...Directorate of Temporal Studies," the young man replied with a little more confidence. "It's an arm of the...uh...Government with a direct link to the Parliament. Parliament is...um...who directs, funds, and sanctions Guild Activities."

Mr. Donovan nodded his approval and moved back to Apprentice 105. "Who are the teachers?"

"A cadre of Senior Assassins and Cleaners that have completed at least six successful missions," she answered. "They are selected by the Council based on their performance from the time they are Apprentices to the completion of their final mission. Only the absolute best are chosen to mentor the next generation."

The questioning went on for two hours, with one fifteen-minute restroom break. No student was spared. Most knew the answers immediately. One unlucky Apprentice was asked to leave the class after failing to answer two questions in a row. Later, neither he nor his belongings were anywhere to be found. That was a sobering thought since the three-year training curriculum was not even half over.

Toward the end of the two hours, Mr. Donovan made his way back to Apprentice 95.

"What is the farthest back in time an Assassin has travelled, who was that assassin, and what was his mission?"

"The farthest back any assassin has travelled was to the year 1216, to stop an assassin from preventing the implementation of the Magna Carta. That Assassin was Assassin 22, who retired after that mission." The young man smiled, pleased with himself.

"Correct," Mr. Donovan replied, and then he smiled. "Why did he retire after that mission?"

The young apprentice's smile disappeared. He looked down, deep in thought, and paused for several seconds before looking up and looking the professor directly in the eyes. "I don't know, sir."

Without missing a beat, Mr. Donovan turned back to Apprentice 105. "Why did he retire?"

"Because of the time-skip."

"What about the time-skip?"

"The time-skip puts a lot of stress on the human body because you are travelling against the flow of time," she moved her hands to simulate the movement and aid in her description. "In theory, it takes one minute to travel ten years back in time, so Assassin 22 spent almost two hours travelling against the time stream, instead of the average skip time of twenty minutes. His body was so fatigued after he returned that he felt another trip of *any* duration would kill him."

Mr. Donavon moved in front of Apprentice 99, a tall black man with a scar on his left cheek. He had lost his left ear in an accident on the firing range early in his career as an Apprentice. He was at least ten years older than the other Apprentices.

"There is stress going back in time, what about returning?" asked the Professor.

"There is some stress, yes," the Apprentice replied in a heavy African accent. "But it is not as severe as flowing against time." He cut his eyes to the right as he recalled the textbook from memory. "Time is like a river, travelling against the current is much more difficult than flowing with the water. It takes much more energy to travel back in time. That's part of the reason for the stress." He looked back at the professor. "However, flowing with the current takes much less energy and creates less stress. Most Assassins report that the biggest stressor on the return trip is the deceleration to end back here in the proper time."

Mr. Donovan nodded his approval and moved in front of Apprentice 101. "Tell me about the Magna Carta mission..."

* * * *

The skip left Assassin 22 weak and disoriented. He stood alone in a sparsely wooded meadow in the dark of night. He absorbed the almost total absence of sound in the meadow: no electrical hum, no sound of hover cars or air cars. He could hear only natural sounds emanating from the meadow; see only the natural light of a crescent moon, and a billion stars. Assassin 22 collapsed onto the damp grass as the skip bubble disappeared behind him with a barely audible pop.

He awoke the next morning to a light breeze and a bright sun quickly warming the meadow. Assassin 22 stretched, ate a snack from his pack and began to hike in a generally easterly direction, toward London. He had not gone far when he joined a caravan. With their cover as traders, he entered the heavily fortified city that served as the capital of Britain.

Assassin 22 moved through the city for several days gathering information. He had no advance team to rely on and hoped he had given himself enough time to gather intelligence before he had to act. Even after four days in London, still weak from the time skip, he was exhausted, dirty, and hungry. His dirty clothing and weak limp on his left ankle served him well; he blended in with the dirty and hobbling citizens of the city.

Unfortunately, his drained appearance made him a target of opportunity from those who prey on the weak. In four days, he had defended himself seven times. The body count was mounting.

On his fifth day in the city, his luck changed. He found himself in a small tavern with a woman who liked to talk, as long as the drink kept flowing. He confirmed the date was September 27th, 1216 and England had been in a civil war for almost a year. The woman dipped her finger in her goblet, used a few drops to wipe some of the dirt off her face. She dabbed a little behind her ears and smiled at her companion.

"I'all started after those nobles made the King sign that document. Wot was i'called now?" She tapped her head in thought.

"The Magna Carta?"

"That's right, luv," she said, smiling and pointing at her new friend. Her accent slurred with the drink, making it even harder to understand her. "Well, the King told 'em to bugger off. That's wot started the war!"

Assassin 22 simply nodded, he knew the history of the Magna Carta, at least in his timeline. According to the Guild Archives, King John had caused the war with the nobles. The nobles compelled the King to sign the document that, in essence, established the principle that no one, including the king or a lawmaker, was above the law. Assassin 22 also knew that, by his history, the war ended in 1220 with the decimation of the nobility of England. That act had repercussions all the way to the 21st Century, when the British citizenry overthrew the Monarchy completely.

The Assassin's thoughts flashed back to the archive room at the Guild and the briefing before the skip. The Council had decided to prevent the nearly thousand-year turmoil in the United Kingdom based on information gathered from a returning Assassin. The Assassin's time-data crystal showed an alternate history where the King had died abruptly and his son, Henry III, re-implemented the Magna Carta. That act brought peace to the United Kingdom and ended the Civil War. Assassin 22 had succeeded in the longest time-skip ever attempted, but now had no idea how to reach the King.

"The King don't seem fazed none by the war with the nobles," his friend continued, taking another long drink. "He just keeps having banquets every week. Eating and drinking and whoring." She shook her head and belched. "While we sit here and starve. Well," she smiled, showing her blackened teeth. "At least I have you." She slumped out of her seat and passed out before she hit the floor.

Assassin 22 left the pub and made his way through the city to the castle. The next day, he took a job in the Royal Kitchen after one of the chefs suddenly disappeared. The Assassin had paid the chef ten gold coins to take a long vacation to France. The man left with his family on the next vessel out of Britain. It only took a few days for the Assassin to learn the political feel for the kitchen and rapidly moved up in the ranks, to the great annoyance to the Court Jester's nephew, Bolin, who took an instant dislike to the man known simply as Smythe.

Bolin hated everyone. The short, dumpy man with stubby, white hair had ambition of becoming more than a simple commoner. He wanted to make a name for himself and move up to the nobility. It was a rare feat, but it did happen from time to time. Now he had a new rival that threatened his advancement.

As the assistant to the assistant to the assistant Lord of the Kitchen, Assassin 22 found himself filling wine goblets at the Royal Court.

The sounds of music and laughter greeted Assassin 22 as he carried a jug of wine into the Great Hall. Immediately accosted for drinks as soon as he stepped through the door, he filled empty chalices as he made his way through the crowd and caught snippets of conversation as he weaved through the already inebriated guests. Careful not to pay too much attention to any of the conversations, he filed everything he heard away for future reference.

Guests packed The Great Hall as guards stood at uneven intervals along the outer perimeter of the room. The men stood tall, armed with swords, spears and crossbows. He paused to watch one guard as he spied an affectionate couple make their way toward the Royal Chambers upstairs. The guard caught the couple as they reached the door and turned them away to find another room to continue their amorous intentions.

"Watch what you're doing!" An angry voice brought Assassin 22's eyes from the guard back to the crowd. His eyes fell on a flamboyantly dressed man, in a silly hat, with a silver goblet in his hand. Wine dripped down his arm. The man changed the goblet to his left hand and shook his right, inadvertently spraying a nearby woman with wine. She half screamed and yelled a very unladylike obscenity at the man before moving away.

"My apologies, m' Lord," the Assassin said, bowing and producing a towel for the man. "Let me clean that for you."

"Get away, you bumbling fool!" screamed the man, drawing attention to the developing scene and flipping the towel at the Assassin's head.

Assassin 22 caught it without flinching.

Bolin appeared as the sounds of conversation died down in the room. "Smythe, leave Lord Warwick immediately!" He almost hid the smug, satisfied smile as he pointed back to the kitchen.

Having brought himself undue attention, Assassin 22 nodded and tossed the towel toward Bolin's face. The Assassin stood for a moment and then turned his head to look at the King. The throne sat on a raised dais, surrounded by sycophants and others courting the King for favors. The King simply sat, chalice in hand, and watched the drama unfold.

Assassin 22 knew he had only days in the palace and this would likely be the last chance he would have to finish his mission. Instead of heading for the kitchen, the Assassin headed straight for the throne. The room seemed to grow quieter before a collective gasp echoed through the crowd and several of the guards took aim at the man as he approached the King.

He produced a special flask of wine and bowed. "Shall I refill your chalice, Your Majesty?" There was an eerie silence in the hall as everyone held his or her breath to see the King's reaction to the entire scene.

The King laughed and slapped Assassin 22 on the back, spilling a little of the wine from the flask. "Yes, my boy!" he exclaimed and extended his chalice.

Assassin 22 filled the chalice, bowed again, took two steps backward, turned and walked back through the still silent crowd, past Lord Warwick and Bolin, down the stairs and into the kitchen. As the door closed, the crowd turned back to the King who was downing the entire chalice in one gulp. He finished the drink, tossed the chalice wildly behind him, smacked his lips and raised both hands in the air. “Jester!” he called, clapped twice, and the party continued.

Assassin 22 breathed a sigh of relief as the party began again behind him. He was in the process of taking off his serving apparel when Bolin entered the kitchen. The man stood before the assassin, clinching his fists and blushing with anger. “You bumbling clod,” came the accented tirade. “I told you to report to the kitchen, not go and have an audience with the King!”

The assassin said nothing. Instead, he simply continued to change out of the serving clothes. The rest of the kitchen staff turned to stare at the spectacle unfolding before them. It was likely the best entertainment they would be privy to all evening. Several of the more faithful to Bolin grabbed kitchen utensils, hoping for a fight.

The Assassin never looked at the screaming man, paid him no mind at all, until Bolin reached out and grabbed his shoulder. “Are you listening to me?”

Assassin 22 reacted without thinking, grabbed the Englishman’s hand, twisted the wrist, and sent him to the floor before the man could take a breath. Another twist and Bolin’s wrist snapped. Bolin screamed and fell to the floor writhing in agony. His sobs almost drowned out the music and laughter coming from the Great Hall beyond the door.

“I quit,” said the assassin, and silently slid into the night as the sounds of the Royal Hall continued behind him.

King John died two weeks later on October 18, 1216, at Newark Castle in Nottinghamshire. A mixture of steroids and other chemicals caused the dysentery that killed the King; ingredients not found in the 13th Century and introduced by the wine.

The timeline morphed to match the target timeline as the King's nine-year-old son, Henry III, who was next in line for the throne, was swiftly crowned. Henry's regents reissued the Magna Carta in November, streamlining the document by omitting several of the more controversial articles. That act ended the war and saved a thousand years of torment to the English people.

Assassin 22 waited until the King's death and Henry's coronation before returning to the 23rd Century.

* * * *

Mr. Donovan stood up from his seat as Apprentice 101finished the story. He had decided to sit when he realized that he was not going to get a quick answer to the question. He stretched and straightened his gray suit. "Excellent," was all he said to the young man. He patted the Apprentice lightly on the back before he moved back to the center of the room.

"Congratulations!" he exclaimed and spread his arms wide. "You have completed the first year of your training."

Chapter Two

REGINALD MAYWEATHER THE FOURTH was one of the richest men in the world. He had earned his money the old-fashioned way; he inherited it from his ruthless, business tycoon father. Reginald Mayweather III taught his son the tricks of the trade, both good and bad. Mayweather IV learned those lessons well and earned a long list of enemies around the world and beyond.

His business dealings had bankrupted corporations, toppled countries and in three cases, installed dictatorships loyal to Mayweather Enterprises. The slightest slip, the slightest hint of failure, and Reginald Mayweather would ruin you...and your family. He played politics, worked hard, and used his vast wealth to get what he wanted. Period. He paid for politicians, Presidents, Dukes and Kings; Mayweather's influence spanned the world.

Dressed in a garish dark red suit with a 17th Century Monet-style billowing artist hat, he stood before a set of gigantic double doors beating on them with his custom-made swagger cane. Anger burned his face red in the blowing wind. Not a patient man, Reginald Mayweather expected to get everything he wanted and right now, he wanted to get out of the cold. The sun cast long shadows as it peeked above the nearby mountain. The sun shone brightly in the early morning, but Mayweather felt like the temperature was dropping by the minute.

He paused from beating on the door long enough to look over his right shoulder, his eyes squinting from the blowing snow. His gaze fell across a young boy, nearly frozen from the cold, hands clasped behind his back, unmoving. "Still, I'm doing better than that poor sod," Mayweather whispered before resuming his incessant knocking.

The door opened a crack and Mayweather pushed his way inside, knocking the second year student opening the door aside. "Out of the way!" he exclaimed as he pushed his way into the Guild Training Area.

Apprentice 97 picked herself off the floor as Mayweather made himself a spectacle, shaking snow and brushing the powdery flakes off his red coat. She clenched her fist and started to move toward him when the door slammed open once more. The young man, who had been standing in the cold, charged in from the freezing twilight.

The door caught Apprentice 97 in the face, sending her back to the floor with a broken nose. She cursed as she landed on her rear, and grabbed her nose to try to stop the bleeding. "Son of a bitch!" came the muted cry as she held her nose.

Her two companions, who had been preparing to go outside and complete the last phase of initiation for the lad, pounced on the young man as he turned toward the voice. The young man paused at the sight of Apprentice 97 and the blood staining her robes. The two other Apprentices grabbed the boy just as Mayweather hit the nearly frozen teen with his cane, the metal tipped cane connecting with the recruit's head with the sound of a grapefruit hitting the pavement. The young man collapsed in the arms of the two Apprentices before they unceremoniously dropped the would-be Apprentice in a heap on the stone floor.

Master Li arrived with Apprentice 101 and two other Apprentices in tow. Apprentice 101 brushed past Mayweather and knelt to check on Apprentice 97, staring holes through the wealthy man as he went by. Mayweather stared at the boy and started to say something, but thought better since he was suddenly outnumbered six to one. The businessman had known not to use that door. He had been briefed about Guild protocol. Only students and Guild personnel were allowed in the academic wing, but he did not like being told what to do.

The businessman also did not like to lose control of a situation, so he went on the offensive. He looked at the still bleeding young woman on the floor. "What the hell took you so long?" Without waiting for an answer, Mayweather turned to the two male Apprentices assisting her. "Now, you," he pointed at Apprentice 101. "Close that damn door!"

Master Li immediately stepped in front of the portly trillionaire. "Mr. Mayweather, guests are not permitted in the training area. I'm sure you were instructed to enter through the—"

"You obviously know who I am," he interrupted. "So you should also know that I go where I want, when I want." He stared at the gathered crowd until several of the students looked away. Satisfied he was now firmly in control again, he turned his back on the group of young Apprentices. "Now, take me to the Council." He made eye contact one last time with Apprentice 101 and saw pure rage. Mayweather made a mental note to find out who that boy was and ruin him.

Master Li moved aside with a slight head bow and waved his left arm toward a door off to the side, away from the primary training area. As Mayweather moved toward the door, Master Li made eye contact with Apprentice 101 and nodded his head toward the double doors. The intent was clear: escort the unconscious young man to the outskirts of the training facility and ensure that Mayweather did not have an entourage waiting outside the door.

Apprentice 101 bowed in acknowledgement and Master Li turned and hurriedly walked to catch up with the Guild's guest.

* * * *

Reginald Mayweather followed the elder teacher through a maze of rich mahogany corridors that had him turned around and confused within minutes. Master Li attempted to make light conversation to change the tone of the initial encounter, but Mayweather simply maintained his gruff demeanor, secretly developing a modicum of admiration for his guide's sense of direction.

Mayweather ordered to be taken to the front entrance to meet his entourage. The detour was another of the trillionaire's tricks to establish his dominance. He had deliberately used the training entrance—against instructions—to establish his authority and his power. He hated to be told what to do.

Master Li proceeded to the guest entrance—a foyer, larger and more ornate than the trainee entrance—where Mayweather commented briefly on the busts of honored assassins from the past, but otherwise remained silent. Moments later, Mayweather's entourage joined the group and took the trillionaire's coat and cane. Mayweather kept the ridiculous looking hat and motioned for Master Li to lead on.

A quartet of Guild guards stood stoically in the foyer observing the guests. The guards, dressed in dark blue robes over a skin tight fighting uniform, carried stunners and continually scanned the entourage and the men with Master Li. The Guild guards fell in step behind the small formation as Master Li led the guests into the bowels of the Guild.

Even as he fought against it, Mayweather's admiration for the Master Li's knowledge of the maze of corridors grew. As the procession made its way along dozens of turns through more mahogany paneled walls, the businessman thought the corridors were strangely empty. The Guild security policy was specific; clear the corridors when guests were present.

Attempts to infiltrate the Guild in the past created the policy to minimize exposure to outsiders. Any information that might be released to the public about its activities, personnel or methods would be dangerous to the Guild, its Assassins, and its Apprentices. The world knew the Guild existed. That was enough.

Finally, the corridor widened considerably and opened into a large antechamber. The group came to a set of double doors even larger than those at the trainee's entrance. Twenty-five meters high and ten meters across, ornate figures of ancient mythology decorated the doors. Mayweather studied the antechamber with interest; it was the only room he had seen in the Guild not lined in rich mahogany.

The antechamber stretched thirty meters high, opening into angled windows that looked down upon the group. Mayweather squinted at the darkened windows and felt an ominous presence stare back at him. He thought he saw a shadow move within the darkened glass and shivered involuntarily. He made another mental note to install this type of foyer leading into his office. He would really set the tone of a meeting with this type of entrance.

Master Li smiled as his guest shivered. The elder combat instructor knew that there were indeed guards behind those windows. Each armed with weapons so advanced that many governments, even their own, would destroy the Guild and everyone associated with it to get them. That was another reason for the high security, to keep those weapons safely in the confines of the Guild. Master Li motioned toward the doors. "Mr. Mayweather, if you'll accompany me into the Council Chamber."

Mayweather motioned for his three companions to enter the door ahead of him, but Master Li held up his arm to block their path. "They come with me," Mayweather ordered. "Your Council is expecting us!"

"Sir," Master Li spoke softly but firmly. "The Council is expecting *you*. Your employees must remain here. They are not permitted inside the Council Chamber."

The small group began arguing among themselves about who was to go in and who would not. The conversation rose in tone quickly. Mayweather raised his right hand and the noise died instantly. He stood in silence for several moments before looking at Master Li.

"My staff will remain here," announced Mayweather. His tone made it sound like it was his decision and not the policy of the Council. "Take me to the Council."

Master Li opened the chamber door and Mayweather stepped through the gigantic wooden doors into a large circular chamber completely devoid of furnishings. No chairs, no tables, no windows, the only way in or out, that he could see, were the gigantic double doors. A walkway ringed the chamber about fifteen feet off the floor. Sitting on this raised dais, overlooking the barren room, sat four men and a woman, dressed in black robes. They towered over Mayweather, making the trillionaire uncomfortable. Master Li closed the door with a solid—and Mayweather thought, ominous—boom and then remained where he stood.

"Good afternoon, Mr. Mayweather," the female Council member began. "What can we do for you?"

The pleasant and businesslike tone of the introduction caught Mayweather off guard. He had been expecting a rebuke for his unorthodox entrance into the Guild facility and had steeled himself for the onslaught. It was several seconds before he could shift gears and respond. "I need someone killed," he stated matter-of-factly.

The silence in the chamber showed him how off balance he was and he silently reprimanded himself. *That was a stupid statement. This is the Assassin's Guild after all.* Mayweather took a breath and composed himself. He admonished himself a second time at how off balance he truly felt. Someone would have to pay.

"I have a business rival that has started underbidding my contracts. He recently cost me hundreds of millions." He grimaced at the thought of losing the business deal. He had already bankrupted the company that had gone to his competitor, but he wanted more. "I want the rival killed and out of my business."

"Mr. Mayweather," an old, gray Council member shook his head. "This sounds like a local matter. You have billions. You could attempt to buy him out."

"I've tried that," he replied through clinched teeth. "He won't sell."

"I'm afraid we cannot get involved in a simple business matter." The female Council member shook her head.

"Consider this, Mr. Mayweather," a third Council member chimed in. His bald head reflected light hidden from Mayweather's view and the businessman made yet another mental note to find the architect and have a chamber like this built for him. "Killing this man would bring undue attention to you and your business practices. You could stand to lose more than you might gain."

"You don't understand!" Mayweather spoke quietly and with more venom than he cared to acknowledge. "I don't want him killed in the present. I want him killed in the past. I want his whole *family* wiped out. His ancestors! His dog! His *dog's* ancestors!" Mayweather raised his voice with each statement.

The echoes of the word 'ancestors' died out in the oval chamber and silence fell over the Council. “Mr. Mayweather, we cannot get involved in a simple business dispute. I'm sorry for your troubles, but this is not within the purview of our charter.”

Mayweather looked at each Council member in turn. “I'm not a patient man. I always get what I want.” He turned and stormed out of the chamber.

* * * *

“That man is going to be trouble," Master Li began. The Combat Instructor had spent ten minutes escorting Mayweather and his entourage from the building. The businessman had been placing calls the entire trek out of the facility. Mayweather maintained an impressive list of contacts.

Master Li returned to the Council chambers to find the four male Council Members sitting patiently, waiting for the Master’s report. “He is too well connected to just walk away when he wants something,” Master Li concluded.

“We will deal with that when we have too. In the meantime -”

The female Council member interrupted the bald Councilman by appearing on the dais from a well hidden anteroom door that lead to a portion of the Guild that even Master Li was not privy to. She plopped unceremoniously into her chair and looked at her fellow Council members, ignoring Master Li. “It appears we may have to deal with Mr. Mayweather. I just got off the comm with our Guild contact in the government. Mayweather was making calls before he even got into his limo. The

Commerce Department is already writing up a letter to the Guild, threatening our Charter. We have received four different calls from the State Department, and the Commissioner of Temporal Exploration is threatening to fly out here tonight if he gets one more call."

"He appears to have some very powerful friends," said one of the Councilmen.

Master Li confirmed that with a nod.

The room quieted as the Council began weighing options.

It was several minutes before Master Li broke the silence. "No matter how we feel about the situation, I suggest that we begin preparations for a skip."“

The Council confirmed the course of action and the elder teacher turned and left the chamber.

Master Li took an indirect route to the Skip Control Room. His route took him past the combat arena where things were getting quickly out of control. Apprentice 91, with his two companions, had once again squared off against Apprentice 101. This scenario was playing out all too frequently and the elder instructor knew from experience that it would end badly.

Master Li noted Apprentice 101's foul mood and could sympathize after the day's events. Apprentice 101 had been the one to escort Apprentice 97 to the infirmary, and Master Li was certain that played heavily into the distracted match the Instructor witnessed. Master Li shook his head sadly as Apprentice 101 missed the attack from low and behind. The boy was on his back and pinned in less than five seconds.

He watched another few seconds before continuing with his task. *The boy will have to clear his mind or he was going to be in serious trouble,* Master Li thought. The Combat Instructor continued on his journey through the Guild: Mayweather would return shortly and if something was not set into motion, there would be hell to pay.

The Time Skip Control Room was a dull yellow painted room with four rows of control stations set into a rough crescent. The far wall was composed of over thirty digital holographic screens that displayed current mission data on every mission currently in progress or scheduled. An office sat on the right hand side of the room, overlooking the control stations, while the Time Skip Portal broke the solid wall on the left. Technicians, dressed in the same dull yellow lab-coat/robe combination, operated the stations and monitored the screens. Half a dozen supervisors, dressed in their white robes/coats, spread out across the room monitoring everything.

There were only three missions currently in progress, with four more in various stages of planning. Seven screens displayed information for everything the Guild had in the works. Master Li watched as one Assassin checked himself a final time, confirmed he had everything, and stepped through the Time Portal, vanishing into the opaque time stream. The veteran instructor nodded, wishing silently he were the one racing back in time.

Master Li bypassed the technicians, the controlled chaos of a mission execution, and headed straight for the lone office in the room. Painted a dull gray, the private office stood in contrast to the dull yellow of the Control Room and sported a great view of the workstations, the monitors, and the skip door on the far wall. The Control

Room Chief, Mr. Tomlinson rose from his desk as the combat instructor entered.

“Master Li.” Tomlinson greeted the older man with a slight bow before shaking hands. Tomlinson adjusted his glasses with his left hand as he shook with the right, then he offered a seat before retaking his place behind the desk. “What can I do for you?”

“We need to begin preparations for a skip,” Li replied taking the proffered seat. Tomlinson could see the agitation and the strain in Li’s voice and knew this was not a completely sanctioned mission. “Specific details to follow within seventy-two hours.”

“I take it that this mission will require an experienced team to ensure success?”

Master Li shook his head. “Not necessarily,” he leaned over the desk conspiratorially. “A rookie Assassin and experienced Cleaner Team should be sufficient.

“What we could really use is a way out of this.” Li gave his peer a quick synopsis of the Council meeting. “When can you have this set up?”

Tomlinson looked thoughtful, rubbing the two-day stubble on his chin for a few moments before taking a sip of his coffee. “Mission with these parameters,” he paused, deciding what he could reasonably get away with, “will take at least three days to assign an Assassin and Cleaner Team, and then another week to ten days to ensure proper preparation and specific mission training.”

“Two weeks,” Li smiled. “I'll inform the Council.”

* * * *

Reginald Mayweather stood before the Council, his coat and hat still on and covered with melting snow. He stood, casually, with a rather large smile on his face. He checked his watch and his smile widened. He had been out of the chamber for less than an hour when he got the call from the Secretary of Commerce.

He had made a dozen phone calls to various government agencies before he even left the Guild area. He ruined two politicians on the spot for not answering his call immediately. Photos and mistresses were still pouring from the shadows to talk about their tawdry affairs. He even bankrupted the country of Belgium just to prove he could. Mayweather considered all of that an appetizer for what he had planned for his rival.

"Have you reconsidered?" he asked.

The female Council member nodded her head. "You have given us no choice." She pointed a finger at the portly trillionaire. "But before we go ahead with this, you must know of the possible consequences of this action."

"We have not yet had time to explore the ramifications of killing the ancestors of your business associate," the graying Council member said, his voice weak and feeble. The man would have to retire soon and the Council would have to vote in a replacement. "There may be serious consequences to killing the entire family."

The female Council member nodded and continued. "We could alter history to an extent that your business never exists, or war erupts, or a host of other catastrophic possibilities."

Mayweather laughed. "This man's ancestors could lead to a war?" He laughed harder; a forced laugh that sounded hollow, too fake and too loud. "I've already done the research that you suggest. The family I have chosen is nothing—a teacher and an accountant. Not quite important enough to start a war over!"

"But important enough to send an assassin back to kill?" came the question.

Mayweather stopped laughing. "Yes, important enough to kill." His tone grew dark and his mood shifted to a dangerous degree. "I want Douglass Dent and his family killed. I want them wiped off the face of the planet, and I want it done, now."

* * * *

Apprentice 101 watched the motorcade leave from his classroom window. He continued to replay the morning's event in his head, when Apprentice 97 had her nose broken. Apprentice 101 blamed the trillionaire for the distraction that lead to his friend's injury. It was at that moment he realized she was more than a friend to him. He smiled and knew that he would have to find out if she felt the same way.

Girlfriend? That was the first time he had thought of her that way. His smile grew on his face. So engrossed in his thoughts, he missed Mr. Donovan's question.

"Apprentice? Apprentice! Mr. Lassiter!"

Apprentice 101 jumped, startled at hearing the name he had not heard in over a year. "Sir!"

Mr. Donovan studied the young man for a moment before continuing. "I don't know what is going on in that head of yours, but I can imagine after this morning's festivities." He walked around the room as he spoke. "Do not let your emotions cloud your judgment. As future assassins, you must be able to separate your feelings from your mission. And right now, Apprentice 101, your mission is to learn."

The instructor turned abruptly, placed his hands on the Apprentice's desk, leaned in close and looked him directly in the eye. "Put her injuries out of your mind," he whispered. "There is nothing you can do about them. She is going to live. Dwelling on it will only distract you, and that, dear boy, could cost you your life." He stood back up. "Put it out of your mind. You have a mission to continue."

Apprentice 101 straightened in his chair, neatened his robes, and nodded to the elder teacher. "Sir."

Mr. Donovan clapped his hands together and then rubbed them, washing his hands of the incident. "Now, your first year was spent learning about the Guild, hand to hand combat, physical endurance and some of the technology dealing with the Time Skip.

"Your second year continues that curriculum. However, one major component is added: Historical Studies.

"Yes, you studied some missions in the first year, but those were the milestone missions: the first skip, the farthest skip, etc.

"Now, you're going to delve deeply into *how* several of the more important missions were studied, developed and executed.

"You will each be given a different assignment. You will study, write a synopsis and give an oral presentation of your case. After your first case study, you will be given another. There is a catch." He smiled and paused, building the agony. "You will also study any and all previous reports submitted by your peers. You will find what your peers missed. By the end of the year, each event will have several reports and I should have a very complete case study on each assassination."

Mr. Donovan sat down at his desk, put his feet up and clasped his hands behind his head. "Let the games begin."

* * * *

"Here he is. The boy who couldn't stop his girlfriend from getting beat up."

Apprentice 101 was not in the mood. He was still upset about Apprentice 97 and her injuries. He had spent as much time as he could with her the night before, but she was angry and embarrassed by the incident and pushed him away. That only added fuel to his fire and as the morning arrived, Apprentice 101 found that he still wanted to beat Reginald Mayweather to death.

He had requested to miss the morning hand-to-hand session for fear he could not focus because of the previous day's events. A stern lecture about Assassins having to continue the mission no matter what was going on around them followed the denial of his request. He sighed, dressed in the proper gear, and stepped onto the mat. His first opponent was Apprentice 91. He groaned.

"What's the matter, boy?" came another taunt. "You don't wanna play today?"

Apprentice 101 looked around him, the students and instructors had stopped everything to watch his reaction to the verbal abuse. Although considered poor taste to try to anger, and therefore distract, your opponent, there were no rules against taunting. The guild wanted to teach technique and lethality, not cheap tricks. Since

Apprentice 91 did not need to distract his competitors to win, everyone within earshot knew he was simply picking on the smaller teen. Apprentice 101 did not care. He closed his eyes, calmed his mind and his heart rate, and assumed the proper defensive stance.

"Defense?" The larger man moved toward the teen, pushing the sleeves of his *gi* up on his arms as he moved. "Yeah, that about sums you up—"

Apprentice 101 attacked from the defensive stance, lashing out with a high front kick that connected on the larger man's left shoulder, spinning him around and knocking him back four steps. Apprentice 101 landed softly and assumed the same defensive stance as his opponent recovered.

Apprentice 91 rubbed his bruised shoulder, grimaced and felt his anger rise at the sudden attack. He paused to clear the anger but saw Apprentice 101 smile and move his fingers in a "come and get it" motion. Calm forgotten, Apprentice 91 charged.

Apprentice 91 executed a low leg sweep meant to put Apprentice 101 on the mat. The smaller Apprentice leapt over the sweeping right leg, brought his hands forward and slapped both of his attacker's ears. The concussion effect disoriented the larger man as Apprentice 101 landed, immediately leapt into a backwards somersault, and kicked Apprentice 91 in the nose. The larger Apprentice cried out in pain and stepped back again as Apprentice 101 completed his back flip and landed lightly on his feet.

The chief instructor of the day, Master Kwon, started to move forward to end the match when Apprentice 91 rushed his opponent and swept him into a bear hug. The attack was so quick Apprentice 101 barely managed to move an inch. Apprentice 91 squeezed until the smaller man could not breathe. With limited choices, Apprentice 101 went for the existing injury, he head-butted the already bloody nose.

Apprentice 91 did not drop his adversary. Instead, he screamed in pain and fell forward, pinning Apprentice 101 under him on the mat. Apprentice 101 gasped as he hit and then grabbed the larger man's robes and pulled him into an approximation of the Jujitsu guard position. Apprentice 101 lay on his back pulling the larger man down on him, effectively keeping his opponent close enough so that Apprentice 91's fists could not pound him.

Master Kwon saw the maneuver and tried to part the crowd but the students stood too tightly around the mat trying to view the match. He began pushing and pulling the students away from the mat, yelling. "Enough! Stop it! *Yame*! *Shichou*!"

Apprentice 101 felt his opponent pulled from him and breathed a sigh of relief. It was over. His relief turned to fear as Apprentice 101 felt his arms pinned and he looked to see his bloody opponent still on top of him—leveraged on his knees—and his two accomplices holding Apprentice 101's arms. The young Apprentice felt the first blows to his abdomen as he tried to wiggle his way out. Pinned by his three opponents, he could not move.

Half of the crowd cheered on the larger Apprentice while holding back the other half who attempted to free the smaller man. Master Kwon still yelled for everyone to stop. Apprentice 101 took in all of that information in a surreal, slowed-time perception before Apprentice 91 slid up onto his bruised abdomen and went for the face. With his legs free, Apprentice 101 fought back.

With a yell full of frustration, fear, anger and stress, Apprentice 101 raised his legs, locking his ankles under his opponent's throat, and brought his legs back toward the floor. Apprentice 91 ended the attack as his back arched, his pounding fists now reaching for the ankles that locked around his throat. His knees locked with his two accomplices legs as they held Apprentice 101 and Apprentice 91 had nowhere to go but backwards. His body bent and finally broke as Apprentice 101 slammed his legs down on the floor.

The crowd quieted as Apprentice 91 sprawled on the mat, his head tilted at an unnatural angle. The two men holding Apprentice 101's arms fell to the floor as a few of the other students finally broke through the crowd. Master Kwon arrived a moment later.

"*Shichou*!" he ordered and the crowd of students snapped to attention, unmoving. Apprentice 91's accomplices struggled slightly but two other students held them. They knew they had nowhere to go.

"You," Kwon pointed at one of the bystanders. "Go find the Doctor. You," he pointed to another Apprentice. "Go find Master Li."

Five minutes later, Master Li arrived. He took one look at the situation and ordered the Apprentices to their rooms, with the exception of Apprentice 101 and the two men that had held his arms. Dark Blue robed guards took the two students into custody and marched them out of the room.

"Explain!"

Apprentice 101 told his senior instructor the sequence of events, from asking to miss practice, to the taunts, to the inevitable conclusion. Master Kwon, nodded his confirmation of the details, received a nod of dismissal in return, and left the arena.

An Apprentice Cleaner Team arrived during the interrogation, removed the body and cleaned up the mess. By the end of the interrogation of Apprentice 101, the arena looked like nothing had happened.

"Come with me, Apprentice," Master Li said as two guards appeared in the doorway. "The Council wishes to see you."

Apprentice 101, like most everyone in the Guild, had never been to the Council Chambers. His heart sank with each step as he and his escorts made their way through the maze of corridors. Finally, head hung low, the corridor opened into a large antechamber. Apprentice 101 felt himself sinking even deeper into despair.

The young Apprentice, who felt his career over before it really started, began to feel that his life might be over as well. All of his dreams of travelling into history, seeing events as they unfolded, appeared to be over. Even as he sank deeper into depression, his imbedded training took over and he studied the antechamber in detail, including the darkened skylights. The double doors opened and Apprentice 101 found himself in a dark, round chamber. *Inside a fish bowl*, he thought.

The teenager saw five people, dressed in black robes, staring at him from a raised dais and he felt for sure that his life was about to end. He walked to the single beam of low light that flowed down from the ceiling and bowed slightly.

"Apprentice 101," the youngest Council member began. He was one of the few people the Apprentice had seen in the Guild who had hair. Jet-black hair, cut short, flowed from his head and ended in a shoulder length ponytail. "You killed a fellow Apprentice in unarmed combat."

Apprentice 101, unsure if it was a question or statement, simply nodded.

"The punishment for killing a member of the Guild is death," another Council member chimed in. He was bald, his left ear missing, and had a nose that had been broken more than once; it seemed to change direction three times, as it made its way down his face. "Explain your actions."

Once again, Apprentice 101 detailed the chain of events that led up to the death of Apprentice 91.

"Master Kwon verified those events?"

"Yes, Councilwoman," Master Li responded.

"Is this Apprentice worth saving?" asked Broken Nose.

"He has high marks in all classes and has showed acuity with every weapon he has trained on. His only detriment to date is his relationship with another Apprentice. It has not been a distraction, until now."

"How is Apprentice 97?" She addressed the question to the Apprentice.

"She is recovering, ma'am," he said, blushing slightly. He had not realized the entire Guild knew of his feelings toward the woman. "Her nose was broken." He noticed a bit of venom in his voice and corrected it instantly. "But she is expected to make a full recovery."

The female Council member nodded and sat back in her chair. She turned her head to the Chief of the Council and nodded, relinquishing her questions.

"Apprentice 101," the elder Councilman said as his fingers steepled in his lap. "We do not find you responsible for the death of Apprentice 91. It was a matter of self-defense in a three to one situation. This incident will be expunged from your files and this will not count on your official kill record.

"You are re-instated as Apprentice, second year, designate one-zero-one, but keep this in mind, Apprentice," the man concluded, "your re-instatement is on condition of your silence. Most of the Guild has no idea what the inside of this chamber even looks like, much less what goes on in here. You will never reveal what happened here today. Do you understand?"

Apprentice 101 nodded. "Yes, sir."

"Dismissed, Apprentice."

Chapter Three

APPRENTICE 101 STARED AT the books, memory crystals and photographs scattered over his desk. He rubbed his baldhead and gingerly touched the finally dissipating bruises on his face from the fight three days earlier. He looked up at the old-fashioned corkboard display over his desk at the course schedule, projects and due dates and uttered a low groan. The second year was not going to be easy.

He had discussed his first historical case study assignment from Mr. Donovan with Apprentice 97 the previous evening on their first 'date': a late meal alone in the cafeteria. Apprentice 101 asked the kitchen staff for the special service so Apprentice 97 could avoid the stares; the head chef had bought it. It was the first time he had been able to get together with Apprentice 97 since she had her nose broken and his meeting with the Council. Apprentice 97 felt better now that she was out of the infirmary, and said so.

She had heard about the fight and the account of Master Li escorting him away. Apprentice 101 stayed tight lipped about his meeting, despite the constant questions from his peers, including Apprentice 97. He knew, someday, he would tell her everything that happened, but, in the meantime, they both wanted to find Reginald Mayweather the Fourth and teach him a very bloody lesson.

"Arrogant bastard," she said nasally, her nose still swollen and bandaged. She grimaced slightly and cursed him again.

Apprentice 101 brought up the subject of his first case study and she laughed and gave him the advice to collect, review and report, the textbook answer from class. "But what did you do on your first assignment?" he asked.

She grinned. "I collected, I reviewed—"

"—and you reported," he finished, nodding his head as she laughed. "So you're not going to help?"

"Nope!" she replied, disarming him with her smile. It was a little lopsided under the bandage, but it still had the desired effect.

"Fine," he said, taking another bite of dinner. He decided to change the subject. "What about you? What are you working on?"

"I just finished my research on an assassination in the Middle East." Her voice rose with excitement as she began talking about it. "I actually interviewed the assassin that went on the mission!"

"What?"

"Yep, the mission was completed last week and there were apparently a few problems with it." She leaned forward conspiratorially. "I didn't get *all* the facts, but apparently one member of the Cleaner team still hasn't returned." Her smiled returned. "And now I am presenting the very first case study on the mission tomorrow!" Her smile grew as she talked and she began tapping the table, giddy with excitement.

"Don't you need to rehearse your presentation?" he hinted.

Her excitement swayed as she eyed her friend. "You really want to hear about this?"

"Yes, of course!" he smiled, genuinely happy that she was finally ready to open up, even if it was only about a case study. Normally tight lipped about her past, he knew he was slowly breaking down the barriers.

"You've done several case studies, so by listening to yours, I'll gain insight on how to do mine!"

She thought for a moment. Guild policy said she had to do the work, but it did not say anything about getting a critique from an audience.

"Okay," she said, gathering her notes. "I'll start like he did—at the end."

* * * *

"This is CNN..."

"Stay tuned to BBC America for more updates..."

"This is a Fox News Alert..."

Assassin 73, using the alias 'Donald Newberry,' flipped through the channels on the television and smiled humorlessly. All the channels reported the same story: Former Pakistani Prime Minister Benazir Bhutto had been assassinated in a suicide bombing.

Assassin 73 used the remote and raised the volume of the television in an effort to drown out the cacophony of noises from the bustling New York City Street outside the hotel window. Settling on a decent volume, the man listened intently to the report for another minute before he turned back to packing his meager belongings, the television blaring at his back.

It had been three days since the assassination and it was still front-page news. Today's update reported that a small controversy brewed over the actual cause of death. The Assassin smirked. Whether it was shrapnel from the human bomb or a traumatic head injury from the blast, it made no difference. The target was dead and Assassin 73's mission was complete.

As he continued to pack his small travel bag, he paused and took one more look around the dull-yellow painted hotel room, looking for anything he might have left. The Assassin ran his hand over the small bed, and then opened the doors on the single nightstand to verify the drawers were empty. The radio-alarm clock on the nightstand read 2:35pm. He walked to the window overlooking the filthy alley below and brushed against the television stand in the corner. He moved to the bathroom and checked the small shower, toilet and sink; there was nothing left to indicate his presence.

Assassin 73 had changed history. He did not know the extent of his actions yet, but he knew that things would be different when he returned home. He felt for the data disk suspended by a small titanium chain his neck; the disk contained all of the information on the timeline he had just altered—his timeline. He would be returning home to a brand new world, and the Council would want to know about the timeline he had changed.

The assassin usually did not ask a lot of questions before a mission, but for this one he had wanted as much information as possible; it was not every day that you're sent back two hundred years to send the Middle East back into the Stone Age. *It does not matter if you like the assignment or not, you go and do as you are told,* he thought.

Still, he wanted as much information about the mission as he could get. The Middle East in the early 21st Century was a hotbed of anger, radicalism, and hatred. Dropping a man of European descent into that was a recipe for disaster. He had studied the history of the timeline for days before skipping back. He spent hours without sleep in the archive library surrounded by books, history crystals and the few remaining ancient news reports.

His archive research had shown that in the original history, Benazir Bhutto had been the central figure in the Muslim Civil War of 2011. She had been one of the catalysts of the Arab Spring movement by changing Pakistan into the first true Arab democracy. Her calm presence and call for peaceful demonstrations had brought about the downfall of the strict regimes in Egypt, Libya, Syria and, eventually, Iran. The new governments embraced her peaceful message and eliminated the more radical elements of Islam—most notably the terrorist mentality that had dominated the world for over a decade—and provided human rights, maybe not equal, put definitely more humane, to the Middle East, especially for women. Subjugated for centuries, the women finally stood up and took the Muslim world by storm. The Prime Minister had brought women to the forefront of the Middle East conflict. Eventually she brought peace to the Middle East and then to the world. She had died of natural causes in 2038 at the height of her power.

Assassin 73, a.k.a. Donald Newberry, released the memory and watched the news report for another minute. *Not anymore*, he thought.

The Time-Skip had taken Assassin 73 back to September 2007, two weeks before the scheduled attempt. The advance team had set up the landing zone (LZ) in an abandoned warehouse and the assassin had quietly materialized in a transparent bubble in the East London building. The bubble dissolved with a barely audible pop, leaving him standing with his backpack in the middle of the empty chamber.

The skip always left him cold and shivering; traveling two-hundred years against the flow of time puts a lot of stress on the body and the mind. Some of his colleagues talked about being hot, some talked about tingling all over, it was the sensation of having been in wet snow that left Assassin 73 trembling from a time skip. He shivered, rubbed his arms to increase circulation, and then moved toward to a waiting car and the advance team.

Assassin 73 walked up to a tall, stocky man with long hair pulled back in a ponytail. The jeans, polo shirt and light windbreaker gave the man a relaxed appearance. Assassin 73 took Derrick Simmons' extended hand in a friendly shake. A second team member, an Arab man named Abdel Abdellah took his bag. He wore a traditional white *thobe*, a long sleeve one-piece dress that covered his entire body. The third team member, a woman named Monica Parker, sat behind the wheel of a nearby small van. After a brief flurry of pleasantries, the group exited the warehouse and left London behind.

Once in the van, the Cleaner Team Leader did a quick medical check of the Assassin. “Any problems?” Simmons asked. “You look terrible.”

“Some kid pushed me out of the way and threw himself in the time stream. They delayed my skip three hours.”

“A kid did what? What kid?” asked Simmons.

“I don’t know. Some Apprentice. He must have been suicidal.” Assassin 73 shrugged. “All I know is the Guild went nuts over the incident and I didn't think I was ever going to get out of there.”

“Everything checks out.” Simmons returned the shrug, trying to clear the air for the Assassin. “Welcome to the Twenty-First Century!”

An hour and a half later, they were in the Chunnel heading for France. The next three hours had them going over the information the advance team had been able to gather and analyze. The three men sat in the back of the bumpy van as Parker drove them through France. The Assassin analyzed what the Cleaner Team had already been able to establish.

Having worked with this team before, Assassin 73 knew that they were good, but they had never had an assignment this difficult. With all the different terrorist organizations and their hatred of anything “Western,” assassinations in the Middle East in the early Twenty-First Century were difficult to plan. Since Assassin 73 was not Middle Eastern, the setup had to be flawless.

"You did an excellent job, as always," the Assassin smiled. "How is Pakistan this time of year, anyway?"

"Hot, Boss," Abdel replied. He handed a dossier to Assassin 73. "This is the leader of the cell I've been in contact with. There are extremists, and then there is this nut. He almost had me shot, and I *am* a Muslim. When we meet him the day after tomorrow, we had better be ready for anything."

Abdel had voiced strong opposition about re-shaping the land of his birth. Finally, he relented on his objections after the Council had indicated the mission was going to happen with or without him. He realized that as a Middle Eastern man, he provided the best percentage for success, so he nodded and took the assignment. Abdel knew his co-workers and knew that if he did not do his job, they would probably end up dead.

"We approached the cell about three months ago," Abdel said as they sped through Germany. Night had fallen and Agent Parker swapped the driving duties with the Team Leader, Simmons. "We told them that the CIA wanted to intervene on behalf of the Middle East." Newberry gave him an inquisitive look in the fading light and Abdel continued. "We told them that the CIA thought Bhutto would shake up the Middle East and the oil might stop."

"And if it meant keeping the terrorists in power..." The Assassin shrugged, leaving the statement unfinished.

"The CIA wants to keep the status quo. Keep the oil flowing, as it were," Simmons said over his shoulder as he drove. "It looks like they bought it. At least they agreed to meet the CIA man." The van continued through the night.

Six hours later, the four-man team boarded a plane in Austria headed for Dubai and then on to Islamabad.

* * * *

The introductions in Islamabad did not go as expected. Assassin 73 found himself looking at the business end of an AK-47 while the team leader was strapped to a chair and a machete with red dried blood held to his throat. Parker, the lone female member of the team, stayed out of sight in an alley a few blocks away from the meeting in the warehouse. She listened to the meeting via a communicator, but did not move.

Abdel began to protest until a rifle butt slammed into his stomach and he hit the floor in a heap. He lay there gasping for air as the cell leader materialized from the shadows.

"Is this the infidel? The CIA man sent to kill our Muslim sister?" His teeth were stained black, almost to the color of his hair, and he spit a little as he said 'sister.' His dark complexion matched the dingy brown tunic he wore. The black cross-draw holster and pistol provided a subtle contrast to the outfit.

Recovering enough to speak, Abdel replied with a raspy "Yes" before gasping. He took another deep breath. Still on his knees, he hung his head as he gulped air again. He finally looked up, but did not make eye contact. "This is Donald Newberry."

The cell leader drew his pistol, a Russian Makarov 9mm, and placed the barrel between the assassin's eyes. "Why should I trust you, assassin?"

Assassin 73 had spent years in training and conducted countless assassinations throughout history, but this was the first time he had ever had a pistol pointed at his head. He found it a bit unnerving. Still, he relied on his training and he resisted the urge to disarm the terrorist.

He slowly crossed his arms and smiled instead. "Because if we wanted you dead, we would have dropped a JDAM on your house." He paused to let that sink in. In his peripheral vision, he saw one of the terrorists peek out of the window, looking skyward. "I'm here to keep the oil flowing to America. If that means Bhutto must die..." He shrugged slightly and left the sentence unfinished.

The terrorist's eyes rolled to the right for a moment as he contemplated the words and then holstered the pistol. He nodded to the man on his left and Abdel rose to his feet while the terrorist that had looked out of the window released Newberry's team leader.

The cell leader stepped toward the Time Assassin. "If you betray me, I will make your death painful and long. Allah will damn you to Hell," he said, looking the assassin straight in the eyes.

Assassin 73 simply smiled. He was in.

Mission planning began the next day, minus the woman team member who stayed out of sight. She continued to provide intelligence on what happened outside the safe house via tiny transmitters and receivers implanted just behind the ear. Her reports continued to be "all quiet."

Abdel and Simmons went over the information with five Pakistanis and three Saudis provided by the terrorist cell. The terrorists would provide the diversion and support during the assassination carried out by Assassin

73. Car bombs and AK-47s would make a spectacular diversion.

The eight terrorists and three men from the future stood around a shoddy mockup of the Islamabad Conference Center, which would host the debate in ten days. The table was the cleanest thing in the disheveled room. Broken chairs, a refrigerator with the door hanging by one hinge and dingy, curtain covered windows that let in dim streams of light surrounded the men.

"Okay, you men will park a series of cars in and around the Convention Center," Abdel explained, pointing toward the map with a broken ruler. "Mr. Newberry will set up here in this building,"—the ruler moved across a four-lane highway mockup— "facing the conference center entrance.

"At 1900 local, the first car will detonate. That should send the delegates to their cars. Depending on where the target's car is, we will detonate the rest of the cars in sequence, pushing the target to her vehicle." He looked at Assassin 73, standing on his right. "Mr. Newberry will be in a position to see all of the vehicles in the parking area and will take the shot as she enters her limousine.

"Shooting her as she gets in her car will hopefully make her death go unnoticed and make her bodyguards think she is safe. They will only be thinking of getting her out of there, instead of trying to find out who is attacking. Once the car door closes, you,"—he pointed to the terrorists—"will open fire at the limousine and give them a second reason to get moving.

"After the limousine is gone, everyone will withdraw and report back here in two days. It is very important that you do NOT come back here before then. Understood?"

The terrorists nodded and Newberry smiled, he knew he would be back in his own time sitting on a beach in two days.

"Good. Let's get to work on the explosives. You," Abdel pointed at the Pakistani directly across from him. "You're the bomb maker?" The man nodded, and the instructions began.

* * * *

One week later, Assassin 73 walked through a warehouse only six miles from the conference center. His stroll took him around a dozen stolen cars in various states of disrepair: hoods up, tires off and, in one case, the entire engine hung above the chassis. The assassin paused at the last car along his path, the only one that was complete. The Assassin did not trust his host, so he paused in his examination of the car to inspect his surroundings.

The warehouse was a flurry of activity. Members of the cell, along with Abdel and Simmons, stood among the cars, planting explosives. Sunlight streamed in from the high windows of the two-story building, providing plenty of light as the preparations continued. A huge roll up door dominated one side of the warehouse. Three of the nearly completed vehicles sat inside the door, which stood open about six feet. To the right of the door sat a small pyramid of 55-gallon containers. Empty or not, Assassin 73 did not know, but he filed the information away for later. Mechanic's tools lined the wall opposite the 55-gallon drums: tools and bomb making material.

Newberry turned his attention back the finished car in front of him and resumed his inspection. A series of gunshots outside the building interrupted the assassin's inspection of the finished car bomb. Mechanics and bomb makers dropped what they were working on and grabbed AK-47s and a host of other weapons as the warehouse erupted in chaos, and then became deathly quiet. Assassin 73 quickly finished tracing the detonator wire—he hated to leave anything unfinished—before he slipped quietly into a deep shadow nearby and waited.

A small door, to the right of the pyramid of 55-gallon drums, slid open and the terrorist cell leader walked in, his Makarov pistol in hand. He dragged a corpse by its blonde hair. He unceremoniously dropped the corpse and started yelling in Arabic. The warehouse workers put down their weapons and went back to working on the bombs and vehicles. Assassin 73 slipped from the shadows and took a closer look at the blonde corpse.

"Damn it!" Simmons yelled as he threw a wrench across the room. It clanged as it hit the wall and fell noisily to the concrete floor. Abdel was already leaning over the body. He looked up when Newberry got close. "It's Parker," was all he said before he turned and walked to a secluded corner, away from everyone, and began to pray.

Assassin 73 paused to look at the body for a moment, and then turned to the cell leader. "Why?"

"She was watching us, and she was armed. Women are not allowed to—"

"She was *my* spotter!" Newberry said, his voice rising with each word. He clenched his fists and stared eye to eye with the terrorist. "Why did you kill her?"

Simmons intervened and took the assassin off to the side before the terrorist could reply. The warehouse noise resumed as a few of the Pakistani men began to drag Parker's body outside. Abdel stopped them near the door and discreetly removed Parker's data crystal necklace and weapon.

He knelt, as if praying, and felt along her left arm, activating her skip beacon. He stood, nodded to the two men who picked up the body and continued outside. Simmons and Newberry watched as her body disappeared. The men returned to the warehouse moments later, laughing as if nothing had happened.

Abdel nodded to Assassin 73 as the men returned, raising his thumb and first two fingers. Newberry knew that in three minutes, the beacon would signal and Parker's body would skip back to its proper time. Abdel, head hung low, went back to the bomb maker. Assassin 73 took a deep breath to calm down and leaned toward Simmons. He gave a gentle nod toward the terrorist leader. "Before this is over, I'm going to kill that son of a bitch."

* * * *

Roving patrols, bomb sniffing dogs, seismic detectors, infrared sensors; the Islamabad Conference Center was a fortress. Abdel, from his perch south of the Conference Center, had a good view of the building and the security measures inside and out.

"Snipers on the roof," he breathed softly into the air, his hidden communicator transmitting every sound. "Three guards inside the main entrance, four more at the metal detectors." He milled around outside the security cordon with about twenty other onlookers.

Assassin 73 took a deep breath, breathing in the cool, clear, mid-October air as he listened to the report. He took another deep breath then settled in behind the scope of his modified Dragunov Sniper Rifle. The Russian Rifle was highly accurate up to eight hundred meters with a high velocity slug. This one was specially modified to shoot a more lethal and discreet projectile.

Team Leader Simmons had replaced the bolt assembly with a little gift from the Twenty-Third Century, a disintegrating crystal bullet that would penetrate the target and explode causing massive internal damage. The wound would then seal, sending any attending coroner into fits of confusion and rage.

Assassin 73 peered through the scope and scanned the conference center. The high power scope crossed the six hundred meters and brought the building complex, patrols and cars into sharp focus.

He watched the two two-man sniper teams—one to the north and one to the south on the roof of the Conference Center—and took careful notice of their mannerisms. They never looked up at his building, only scanning the crowd below. The assassin switched his visual scan to the parking area, focusing on each of his car bombs in turn. Satisfied, he followed a two-man and a dog patrol through their rounds. He briefly visualized pulling the trigger and, in his mind's eye, saw each man and the dog go down. He neither smiled nor frowned. He was too well trained and experienced to show pleasure or remorse for killing.

The crowd continued its ebb and flow in and out of the building; mainly small groups of dignitaries and bodyguards. It was almost hypnotizing to the assassin as he followed the people from their cars to the Conference Center; one after another. He studied the men, mostly in conservative dress but many in their colorful *thobes*, and the women in their *burkas* and *hijabs* and *khimars*, the traditional dress and head covering for women.

A slight smile lifted the corners of his lips, amused by the security guards attempts to verify the identity of the women in their coverings without violating their religious law. The momentary amusement allowed the Assassin to fight against the boredom that crept through his system.

At ten minutes until contact, the scene changed. Four white vans screeched to a halt in front of the conference center and dozens of armed men exited the vans. The men fanned out and formed a perimeter around the entrance to the Conference Center. Assassin 73 settled deeper behind his scope and watched the men as they created the barrier between the delegates and the onlookers.

He traced a group of six men as they darted across the four-lane road towards his general direction. He followed them with his scope until they disappeared beneath a crosswalk that connected his perch to the conference center complex.

"You have incoming," sounded Simmons' voice over his implanted communicator. "I count six. Another three vans have just pulled up to the rear of the building. The men are heading straight for the rigged cars."

"Straight toward them?" queried Assassin 73.

"Affirmative!"

He muttered an obscenity. "Abort! We've been compromised!" Assassin 73 ordered as he took a small can and began spraying the Dragunov. "Rally point Omega. I say again, Omega!"

Acknowledgements came from Simmons and Abdel, but the Assassin focused on spraying the rifle. The acid spray catalyzed with the air and began working immediately, breaking down the rifle at a molecular level. In minutes, there would not be anything left but gas vapor and a few particles of dust.

He removed the nozzle from the spray can and dropped it on the now exposed stem. The impact broke a small vial of oxygen inside the can, activating the acidic ingredients and the can dissolved itself next to the dust particles of the rifle.

Satisfied, Assassin 73 took a quick glance at the target area and immediately ducked down. The Security Force Snipers were now scanning his location and he had discovered on his last mission that he had an aversion to being shot at. He moved quietly toward the stairwell, keeping his profile below the lip of the rooftop. His escape route took him down to the fourteenth floor, to a room for which he had "acquired" a key and cached some appropriate clothing. From there, with more traditional attire, he planned simply to walk out, a foreign businessman on his way to dinner.

The sound of gunfire from the steps of the Conference Center stopped Assassin 73's escape. He involuntarily flinched, expecting the whine of bullets off the building around him. Hearing no ricochets, he continued his escape. More shots answered the gunfire. An intense battle erupted on the street below. Assassin 73 resisted the urge to walk over to the edge of the roof to look. He had to make it downstairs. He quickened his pace and spoke into his transmitter. “Report!”

“Those idiots panicked and opened fire on the police,” answered Abdel. “Simmons is pinned down and wounded.” Assassin 73 did not need clarification of who “those idiots” were. He could imagine the scenario playing out across the street.

“The delegates?”

“The police have everything locked down. No one is leaving the building.” A loud whine, like electrical interference, sounded through the communicator, then silence. “Simmons has skipped,” continued Abdel. “I’m bugging out. They are heading this way.”

The line went dead.

Assassin 73 continued his way down to his cache of clothing without incident. He did have to sedate the amorous couple that occupied the room, but they would awake in about an hour with no memory of the intrusion. Nodding to himself, he made his way into the hall, down the elevator, through the checkpoint in the hotel lobby and out into the night air.

Disappointed, he watched as escorted delegates were whisked away from the Conference Center to safety. He turned and disappeared into the desert night.

* * * *

“How bad is it?”

“Bad enough, boss.”

A security net locked down Islamabad; foreigners drew greater police attention, known terrorist cells found themselves attacked, and men on watch lists filled up jail cells. A massive sweep through the whole of Pakistan's capitol netted over three hundred arrests, but not Assassin 73 or Abdel. The National Police were on high alert and occasionally stopped people, especially foreigners, to ask for papers and their business in Islamabad. Abdel and the Assassin had an ironclad story.

Abdel read one of the local papers as the two sat in an outdoor café. He translated the ancient—at least to him—Arabic with ease. A sudden memory of his Grandmother teaching him as a little boy came to mind and he briefly wondered what she would think of his current mission. Abdel snapped the paper to align the folds and then folded it to highlight the article.

"'An anonymous tip led the National Police to the Convention Center where they discovered almost a dozen cars rigged to explode. A nearby hotel was searched for additional bombs or weapons but nothing was discovered.'" Abdel looked up from the paper. "Any bets on who tipped them off?"

Assassin 73 grimaced, but said nothing. Abdel continued. "'An official, under condition of anonymity, stated that although an assassination attempt had been foiled, the government did not know the actual target as there were over twenty-five delegates at the conference.'" Abdel paused to take a sip of tea and then continued. "'The delegates have met again, in secret, and elected their candidates.'

"'Former Prime Minister Benazir Bhutto will represent the Pakistan's People's Party (the PPP) during a series of debates and rallies over the next two months, before the election in January.'" He put the paper down and leaned in toward Assassin 73. "One of the debates?" he asked.

Assassin 73 watched the pedestrians on the street go about their business in their colorful clothes. He watched the women in their *burkas* and the children running down the sidewalk in peaceful bliss. He placed his elbows on the table and joined his fists together, deep in thought. "Yes, or a rally, closer to the election," he said slowly, almost in a whisper. "That will give us time to plan." He cut his eyes toward Abdel with a slight nod. "And time for you to heal."

Abdel nodded. His left shoulder was sore from the bullet he had taken during the escape. He flexed it as he folded the paper once more, wincing as he did so. The lone surviving advance team member checked the paper. "The last rally is scheduled for December the 27th, in Rawalpindi."

* * * *

Assassin 73 watched as the terrorist leader and a half dozen other men entered the safe house with a sense of grim satisfaction. It was mid-December and the assassin was tired of the game of cat and mouse he had been playing with the terrorist since the first failed attempt almost two months earlier. He had finally tracked the man back to the building where they had the initial meeting in September. It was now a simple matter to sit and wait.

It was the second time the Assassin had gone after the terrorist leader. The first attempt had been only a week after the aborted mission at the Conference Center. The terrorist, who was supposed to meet with a high placed Pakistani official, sent one of his lieutenants to the meeting instead. Assassin 73 shot the lieutenant, captured the official and, after some intense interrogation, confirmed the location of the cell leader.

That lead led to another location, which led to another and another. By the end of November, a month later, the Assassin had finally tracked down the terrorist leader.

"Get out, now!" Assassin 73 said into his implanted communicator. Five-hundred meters away, Abdel jumped from a second story rear window. He hit, rolled, and came up running with a slight limp.

"Damn," The Assassin muttered and scoped in the building in time to see rifle barrels poke out of a back window. Weapons fired on the fleeing man. He uttered another obscenity, rechecked his sights and pulled the trigger on his silenced Special Purpose Rifle.

Although he could not see the men firing, he could estimate their locations and sent round after round through the corrugated tin walls of the building. The firing abruptly stopped as the men inside realized they were being sniped. The barrels disappeared inside the building and Assassin 73 had no more targets. Out of sheer frustration, he unloaded the remainder of the magazine through the side of the building. The bolt clicked back empty and the assassin changed magazines.

"Abdel?"

"I'm out, boss," came the reply, Abdel's breath heavy and strained. "The fuse is set, just another minute."

The rolling door began to slide open and Assassin 73 put his sights on the man pulling on the chain. A slight adjustment and he pulled the trigger. The man went down just inside the building, falling away from the door into a dark shadow. Another terrorist grabbed the chain and the assassin shot him as well. He too disappeared into the gloomy interior of the warehouse.

"Four-Three-Two…"

A van crashed through the partially opened door, cutting off Abdel's countdown. Assassin 73 instantly sighted on the driver and pulled the trigger. The building exploded as the van turned the corner directly toward the assassin. A fireball engulfed the safe house as the assassin's bullets ripped through the windshield of the van, killing the driver and fatally wounding the front seat passenger. The driver's foot floored the accelerator and the van swerved into another car, tipped and rolled over on its side, the engine still revving. Debris rained down from the destroyed safe house.

Two men jumped from the back of the van and Assassin 73 took them out with one shot apiece. Nothing else moved for several seconds while the fires raged and sirens began to wail. Finally, the terrorist leader poked his head from the van. His AK-47 followed his head as he sprayed the surrounding area with bullets. He jumped from the van, still firing in every direction. Nothing came close to the assassin. Assassin 73 smiled grimly and simply waited until the terrorist's rifle went empty. The terrorist leader stopped waving the empty gun around after a moment and then stood silently. Assassin 73 had several seconds to sight in on the terrorist leader's head. He did not fire until the terrorist began to change his magazine.

The terrorist never heard the shot that killed him.

"Abdel?"

"Nice shot," came the reply. The sirens were getting closer. "But, I think it's time to get out of here." Assassin

73 heard a painful groan through the communicator. "I'm hit again, bad this time."

"I'm on my way."

* * * *

Abdel Abdellah knew he was going to die.

Three days after the assault on the terrorist compound and Assassin 73 still could not get the bleeding to stop. Short of going to a hospital, there was no way to stop the internal bleeding. The only thing keeping Abdel going was some Twenty-Third Century stim-tabs and his determination to finish the mission.

The hotel room in Rawalpindi was rank with the smell of blood, and littered with dozens of bloody bandages. Sunlight streamed in through the half closed curtains, creating a dim, gloomy atmosphere. It perfectly matched the mood of the two men.

"Abdel, let me send you home. You don't need to do this," Assassin 73 asked for the thousandth time.

Abdel simply shook his head, the same as he had for the last few days.

"I've never not finished a mission and I'm not going to start now!" He grimaced, coughed up a little blood into his kerchief, and smiled. "Besides, if this new plan is going to succeed, you're going to need assistance. There is no one else.

"My wounds are convincing, they will draw out the security around Bhutto and give you the opportunity for the shot." He coughed, his body heaving in pain. He dabbed a small of blood from his lips and smiled reassuringly. "We stick to the plan."

* * * *

Assassin 73 never felt the blow that knocked him unconscious. He stood over the kitchen sink in the rented flat, preparing a small meal for his wounded teammate, when the blow caught him. He dropped the colander of pasta, spilling noodles everywhere, as he collapsed on the floor.

Abdel dropped the remains of the lamp and checked the downed assassin. Out, but no permanent damage. Abdel checked his bandages. He had not pulled anything loose during the swing. He was as good as he was going to get. The lone Cleaner Agent dropped a note onto the Agent's chest, picked up a small bag, and left the hotel room.

Abdel made his way through the quiet streets of Rawalpindi; very few people were out at three in the morning. He paid little attention to the contrast between the modern skyscrapers in the distance and the mud adobe huts on the outskirts of the city. He had seen the city many times in his six months on the ground. His strained, and sometimes staggering, walk kept the few pedestrians away. He had made his way halfway across town by the time the sun dawned on the twenty-seventh day of December.

The sun rose behind the skyscrapers as the would-be assassin found a park less than a mile from the conference center. Abdel Abdellah sat down to take in the sights and sounds of his native homeland on the last day of his life.

* * * *

Groaning, Assassin 73 woke up. Opening his eyes, it took several moments to focus on the dimly lit kitchen. He partially sat up and felt something slide off his pasta-covered chest as a wave of nausea rolled through his body. He lay back down on the cold stone floor and closed his eyes as a throbbing headache overwhelmed him.

Blindly, he probed the floor with his left hand and found a piece of paper. Without trying to sit up again, he re-opened his eyes and moved the note in front of his face. He turned the paper a quarter turn and tried to focus on the Twenty-Third Century guild script. Not an easy task with a mind-numbing headache.

I'm sorry, Boss, but this is the best way. You and I both know that I'm a dead man. I'll never survive the trip back home.

I came up with a Plan B. It allows me to accomplish the mission and keeps you from getting your head chopped off on the internet. If a white man killed a Pakistani woman, there is no way to predict the consequences to the timeline. But I'm Middle Eastern. It'll be just another murder.

Get on a plane. Get an alibi. Go on home. Just stay away from the rally. - Abdel

"Damn it," he said under his breath and winced at the loudness of his own whisper. It took several minutes, but he finally got off the floor. He stood there for a moment, picking noodles off his shirt and wondering if the nausea would return. Noodles gone, he placed his hands on his hips and spent several minutes thinking of strategies, outcomes, and courses of action. He stood for several minutes; the only movement was his eyes as he followed each possible outcome to its conclusion. He grimaced, said another choice expletive or two, and started collecting his things.

* * * *

Throngs of people crowded around the rally of the Pakistan's Peoples Party in Rawalpindi. The crowd cheered as various chants, in support of Benazir Bhutto, filtered through the mass of people. Security was tight after the previous attempt, and roving patrols of officers streamed through the crowd constantly. Most of the security had arrived around mid-day to secure the area.

Abdel had been waiting there since dawn and was already inside the security perimeter. Several security officers had approached the Cleaner Agent, checked his credentials and marked him off as a homeless vagrant. His weakened body and demeanor helped sell his new persona. He had spent the last hour of the rally steadily moving toward the parking area.

Security would not permit him to get close the limousine, but Abdel did not need to. He wore enough C4 to kill everything within ten meters. He just needed to get close enough.

He continued to make his way through the cheering crowd toward the target. He was still fifty meters away when the rally ended and Benazir Bhutto made her way through the crowd toward the limo. Abdel cursed silently as she took a roundabout path away from him through the pulsing crowd. He had to get closer, but the crowd closed in around him, jostling him, and he felt something tear in the upper left quadrant of his abdomen.

Bhutto made it to her limo as the crowd encircled the vehicle, cheering wildly. She entered the left passenger door and within seconds appeared above the car out of the sunroof. The cheers grew louder as she waved to them. The crowd pressed toward the limo. He knew he would not be able to make it the last few meters. The crowd engulfed and jostled Abdel and he felt his wound tear open completely. A wave of pain made him double over and stumble. For the first time in his career, he tasted failure.

A loudspeaker screamed a Muslim prayer into the night, quieting the crowd momentarily as everyone turned to see where the call to prayer came from. The brief silence was replaced a moment later by screams of delight as the crowd began to chant along with the prayer thinking it was in honor of Bhutto. Abdel, without thinking, moved toward the limo and got within five meters before security stopped him.

Time seemed to stop. Abdel could see the security guard telling him to turn back. The crowds cheered wildly, almost hypnotically, along with the call to prayer. Benazir Bhutto, only a few feet away, with a look of embarrassment on her face. Out of the corner of Abdel's eye, a man stood on a balcony catwalk looking directly at him. Abdel recognized the man, nodded his thanks, and smiled as he touched the detonator.

Assassin 73 watched the explosion rip through the crowd and over the limo, causing the limo to sway back and forth on its shocks, but not overturning the vehicle. The driver, whether smart or panicked, stomped on the gas and the limo, charred and smoking, shot through the remains of the crowd and disappeared onto a side road. The assassin dropped the bullhorn off the balcony and disappeared into the crowd.

* * * *

His meager belongings packed, Assassin 73 sat down on the hotel bed and watched the news for another few minutes. The commercials were over and the pundits were once more discussing the assassination. He checked his watch and calculated that he had another few minutes before he had to leave. He knew he could leave anytime, but kept postponing the skip on purpose. This was his third trip to the early 21st Century and he had grown fond of the era. He really did not want to leave. He adjusted the television volume again to get the latest CNN report on the assassination.

"As we reported yesterday, the Interior Ministry of Pakistan has stated that the Former Prime Minister was killed when she tried to duck back into the vehicle, and the shock waves from the blast knocked her head into a lever attached to the sunroof, fracturing her skull," stated the announcer, a pretty redhead. "That is now being contradicted by new information from a hospital spokesman who stated earlier that she had suffered shrapnel wounds to the head and that this was the cause of her death. Benazir Bhutto's aides have also disputed the Interior Ministry's account."

Assassin 73 turned the volume down as the news once again went to commercial and he checked his watched. “Time to go,” he said to himself.

He dropped the remote onto the partially made bed and picked up his backpack. One last look at the room, then he took in the view out the window. He would never see this again. He threw his backpack over his shoulder, said a silent prayer for Abdel, Simmons and Parker, and then activated his skip beacon. A moment later, a glowing doorway materialized and formed his transport bubble.

He paused, stopping before the white, opaque door home. His home would be a different world. He knew that from the crystal archives from the other timelines. He knew that the Muslim Civil War would not happen now until 2246, almost a hundred and fifty years later than before. It was the same in almost every timeline. Time had a way of correcting itself. He took a step toward the time bubble and stopped again.

"My worst ‘success,’" he said as he remembered the last four months. He said another prayer for his three comrades.

Assassin 73, Donald Newberry, stepped into the transport bubble and disappeared. A moment later, the bubble collapsed onto itself with a barely audible pop.

* * * *

“That’s it. What do you think?”

Apprentice 101 sat pensively for a moment. “I think I have a lot of work to do before I do my presentation.” He stood and kissed her on the cheek. “That was a fantastic, by the way! You'll do great.”

"Wait, where are you going?"

"I've got to get started on mine. I only have a few weeks and haven't even started."

He made his way to his room where he had years of official data from the archives scattered over his desk: the assassin and cleaners' reports, the historical reviews of the time-lines pre-assassination (old timeline) and post-assassination (current history). Yes, it was confusing, but then, he was in the business of re-writing history. Well, almost in the business.

He took a deep breath, organized the data into categories, and began his study of the assassination of John Fitzgerald Kennedy.

Chapter Four

RICK BREWER THOUGHT OF himself as an oddity in the universe. He had the ability to *feel* when something changed in the timeline. That was one of the reasons he joined the Assassin's Guild as a teenager. He needed to come to grips with the intense déjà vu feelings he had when he read about historical events. He *knew* there had to be another side to the story.

As he stood before the gallows in 1789 France however, his gift of déjà vu was the farthest thing from his mind. He became reflective about his academy days, as he always did when he faced his own death, and he admitted silently, facing his own demise was becoming more and more frequent.

The man, once known as Apprentice 58, had braved the cold and the howling wind of initiation and had lost his left little toe to frostbite over the ordeal. Imagine his surprise a few days later when he woke up and it was back in place, good as new. He thought he was immortal! Six months later, in Mr. Donovan's history class, he discovered Assassin 22 had completed a mission in the ancient past that had involved one of his great ancestors, a man named Jacob that had moved his family from England to France. That resulted in a domino effect that had altered his life just enough so that he did not lose the toe.

There were other incidences, leading Mr. Donovan and many others at the Academy, to believe that Brewer had a rare gift for detecting temporal changes. The Council ordered him tested and Mr. Donovan chose him as his third 'Special Project.' That was the middle of his first year.

His second year saw him excel in history, weapons and tactics. His only real weakness was hand-to-hand combat. He completed his first case study: a study on President George Washington and a little known attempt by the British to assassinate the first President of the United States. It was in his third year where he would leave his mark on the Guild Academy.

The entire Guild thought that Apprentice 58 would have a brilliant career and eventually end up on the Council, but his career was cut short in his third year when he was caught copying the crystal history library. Of course, he was not copying the files, only researching Mr. Donovan's past because every time he looked at the Professor, he felt that the man was 'out of time.'

The accusation ended his career abruptly and the rumors began as to why he would copy the files: a group who wanted to end the Guild bribed him; he wanted to plagiarize his last studies; or, the more popular theory, that he wanted the history archives to conduct personal research to give him an edge in his career. His trial had been quick, the guilty verdict even faster, and his scheduled execution set for noon the next day.

The Guild Council did not take theft well, especially when they made up the charges.

On the way to his execution, in a moment of desperation, he attacked the guards, shoved an Assassin out of the way and hurled himself into the time vortex. The thought of the stun bolt hitting him in the back, to this day, made him flinch. He had fallen, semi-conscious, into the time stream.

Ravaged by the turbulence of traveling against the flow of time—he had not undergone the physical conditioning required by the Guild for a skip—he felt torn apart by the current. Electrical discharges arched across his body, a wave of nausea engulfed him from spinning through the current. Through all of the physical torment, nothing compared to the mental flashes of raw time on his 'gift'; it nearly destroyed his mind. He screamed the entire voyage to the past.

He landed in France in late 1782. The skip bubble released him some fifty feet in the air; he fell, still screaming, into a balloon that flew low across the French countryside. The balloon cushioned his fall, but Brewer and the balloon crashed into a pile of debris in the deep snow.

He lay among the broken balloon parts, gasping for air. His skin tingled with electricity and his throat was raw from the hour-long scream. He sat up and grabbed a handful of snow. He laid back again, letting the snow melt down his throat. He closed his eyes and listened to the quiet countryside.

He awoke a few minutes later, soaking wet and shivering from the snow. He stood, brushed himself off and knew he needed to find some thicker clothing. The robes he wore were a little too thin and he was freezing. He started walking to try to warm up and found a house nearby.

It was a typical one story French chateau: A frame roof, layered brick and stone and large chimney oozing smoke into the snowy sky. He found the door unlocked and quietly let himself in.

The home was tastefully, if moderately decorated. Brewer quietly sidestepped a table and chairs, an ornately decorated end table and made his way to a bedroom off the main room. He found the occupants asleep in the early morning. He took the man's set of clothes from the end of the bed and retraced his steps outside, grabbing a bottle of wine and hunk of bread as he did.

He dressed and then made his way back to the crash site as two men approached. Dressed in heavy coats and hats that covered their ears, the two men looked at the balloon, then the man with cuts and scrapes on his face, and made the connection. Immediately the two men began yelling at Brewer, pointing at the destroyed balloon. Brewer spoke several languages thanks to the Guild, but French was not one of them.

Brewer studied the wreckage only half-listening as the two men yelled at him. He picked up a few of the pieces, amazed at the artistry and engineering of the balloon. He snapped his fingers as he realized that he had just met the Montgolfier brothers on the cusp of their first successful flight of a hot-air balloon.

A couple emerged from the nearby home to investigate the noise. The man of the house recognized his favorite shirt and jacket on the stranger and immediately called Brewer a thief in French and then in broken English. The fact that Brewer still held the bottle of wine aggravated the mood. The man pointed an accusing finger at Brewer, threatening to beat the thief. Not wanting to interfere with history any further, or be arrested, or beaten, he politely made his exit and turned his back on the scene.

The Montgolfier Brothers picked up the pieces of their balloon as the Frenchman gave chase to Brewer. The man grabbed Brewer and spun him around. The renegade apprentice clapped the man on the ears. The man howled and staggered backwards. Brewer turned and ran, disappearing into the snowy morning.

* * * *

For ten days, Rick Brewer walked the snowy French countryside. He stole what he needed to survive—mainly clothing and food—and kept moving from those that prey on the weak. He found himself—cold, tired, and hungry—huddled in a small church, trying to stay warm. The small fire in the church foyer drew many citizens who were at the end of the line. Brewer joined them, thinking, *Death may have been the better alternative.* He took a small bit of watery stew from the nuns and shared it with a man named Pierre.

Pierre proclaimed himself a very good blacksmith. Brewer listened to the man's broken English as he explained how he had shod an Aristocrat's horse, how the horse had stumbled, throwing his rider, who had the unfortunate luck to be crushed by flailing hooves. Blamed for the man's death, Pierre left town two steps ahead of the lynch mob.

Brewer nodded repeatedly as the man told his story, but the renegade Apprentice found the story boring. He closed his eyes, about to try to sleep, when Pierre began talking about his true passion: magic.

"I have many tricks. I perfected them by performing for my friends." Pierre's voice grew distant. "When I had friends."

"Show me," Brewer spoke before thinking. Pierre spent the next six hours entertaining Brewer and the other patrons of the church to a magic show.

Pierre was gone the next morning, but he left Brewer with a plan on how to better his new lot in life. The would-be assassin stole new clothes and set out to the next town where he astounded a small crowd with a few of the tricks he had learned the night before. It was not a lot of money, but it was better than nothing, and Brewer set out again.

With each town, the crowds got a little larger and Brewer made a little more money. He combined his knowledge of science with the sleight of hand tricks of Pierre and then added his knowledge of history. He made objects disappear, predicted events and other supernatural feats. He began to make quite a decent wage and within months, he had hired two servants to carry his ever-growing bounty of personnel effects.

He arrived in the city of Annonnay in the heat of early June. He rode into town on a white stallion, dressed in a light blue suit and hat, and led his two servants who followed on a wagon filled with his possessions. Peasants from across the county appeared to witness the 'rich man' and his servants. Rick Brewer simply smiled and waved. *I could get use to this life*, he thought.

The town was packed with people who had come for the big event, something never before seen. The former Apprentice had chosen his arrival carefully. The Montgolfier Brothers planned to make their first public appearance in two days. Brewer wanted to see firsthand the first flight of a hot-air balloon, especially since he had destroyed their prototype.

Brewer and his servants performed a few shows for the peasants, increasing his personal wealth by only a fraction. Brewer's small show only added to the crowd. He set up a small booth on a corner surrounded by other street performers and musicians. The crowd seemed to swell on the 4th of June, when the event was to take place. The blue sky seemed to beckon the Earth to send something its way. The Montgolfier Brothers did not disappoint.

The brothers wheeled their contraption on a horse-drawn wagon, weaving their way through town to the market center, down the block from where Brewer had set up his magic booth. Jacques and Joseph demonstrated their idea for a floating balloon by holding flames under small paper bags. As more and more of the bags went skyward, the crowd's anticipation grew. The brothers soon turned their attention to their wagon and the main event.

Brewer stood with the crowd, watching the brothers unload and prepare for their first public flight. His thoughts drifted back to the events that led him here, to 1783 France. He smirked as the memories flooded back; like his life flashing before his eyes. Brewer realized that he was happy to be alive and living very well. Something lurked just beyond his consciousness however; something he had yet to find that hid in the recesses of his mind. Brewer let those thoughts die and turned his attention to the large blue balloon taking shape before him.

The brothers had constructed a large, mushroom shaped balloon, painted sky blue with gold accents. They poured over their creation for almost an hour, ensuring that everything was complete. Once they were satisfied that everything was in order, the Brothers released their balloon into the heavens.

A collective gasp escaped the crowd as the balloon floated out of the marketplace, above the city and finally into the sky. The people gathered in the city of Annonnay cheered wildly as the balloon sailed into the sky and moved with the wind out of the city. Many of the onlookers chased the balloon as is it flew across the countryside.

The rogue assassin filed the vision of the ascending balloon away as one of the most spectacular events he had ever witnessed. Brewer and his servants followed the Montgolfier Brothers for several months, watching all the test flights. In October, Brewer witnessed the first human flight in a Montgolfier Brother's Balloon. After the months of travel and watching history unfold before him, the rogue briefly wondered what else the future might hold for him.

Brewer amassed a fortune that landed him on the outskirts of the Aristocracy in 1787. He purchased a swath of land outside Paris and a title in the French Court. It was easy to get a title if you had the money, and Brewer had plenty of money. His fortune brought him luxury and favor. In 1789, it brought him to the gallows at the start of the French Revolution.

The people of France revolted in July of 1789 and attacked the Bastille Prison, a symbol of the French Aristocracy. With the King and Queen under arrest, Brewer abandoned his fortune and his servants to head for the coast to catch a vessel to Britain. He was caught just east of Calais trying to stow away onboard a freighter bound for England.

His abductors took him to Calais and sentenced him to death. No trial, no due process; Brewer reminisced he was in the Council Chambers again instead of standing in a long line of nobles, aristocrats, and other local politicians, awaiting their turn at the hangman's noose. Brewer watched as the first four men dropped through the door of the gallows' floor only to have the noose snap them to a halt. After those first few, Brewer closed his eyes and tried not to listen to the gallows drop.

Brewer became hypersensitive to his surroundings, keenly aware of even the slightest breeze. He heard the creak of the wooden platform, the friction of rope on cloth, and the gut-retching sound of the rope going taut. Although several feet away, Brewer swore he could hear every neck snap. *It's your imagination*, he told himself, but to no avail. He saw it all in his mind. Again, he thought that dying at the hands of the Guild might have been a better alternative.

The rogue assassin thought how much the scene resembled the old holo-movies he had watched in his youth. A masked man stood on the gallows platform, his hand on the lever to drop the platform. Two men stood off to the right side of the platform to reset the false floor after it fell, while throngs of dirty peasants' cheers became louder with each drop.

"Next!"

Another man, this one dressed in fancy Parisian clothing with long curly hair, walked proudly up the stairs, stuck his head in the noose and defiantly yelled, "Get on with it!" His face still held the smug, almost arrogant look a few seconds later as his body fell.

"Next!"

And so it went, the platform fell, the line moved forward and Brewer found himself on the bottom step of the gallows. He was now number five in line. The platform dropped again.

"That's all for today," called the gallows master, who had been standing behind the executioner out of sight. Wearing a finely tailored dark suit and sporting long blonde curls, he was obviously better off than the peasants who showed their disappointment by throwing rotten tomatoes and other vegetables. "We will resume at nine o'clock in the morning!"

That brought a cheer from the crowd as they began to disperse for their homes and dinner.

The gallows master made his way down the stairs of the gallows as Brewer and the others fell in line back to the jail. He watched for a moment, smiling, before he cried, "Halt!" and walked straight to the rogue assassin.

"I've seen you before," the man said, giving the dirty and ragged Brewer a long appraising look. He crossed his arms, his right hand on his chin thinking, as some of the crowd re-gathered to see if there would be one more execution before nightfall. The gallows master snapped his fingers and pointed. "You're the magician!"

This was not the reaction the crowd expected. Instead of cheering, they stood in a stunned silence.

“The magician, from Annonnay!” The man smiled and reached to shake Brewer's hand. “It's been years! My children still talk about you!” The man continued to babble for several minutes before finally asking, “How did you end up here?”

“An honest mistake, sir,” Brewer said, humbly. “It was reported that I am an Aristocrat instead of a traveling magician. I was captured trying to board a ship to take my show to England and well,” he shrugged, “now I'm here."

“Release this man!” ordered the gallows master. “I will vouch that he is no Aristocrat. Provide him food and drink and perhaps he will provide us an entertaining show this evening?”

The crowd cheered the Gallows Master and Brewer, who nodded his acceptance of the offer.

Brewer followed the Gallows Master to a nearby home where his shackles were removed and he was given clean clothes and fed. Clean and refreshed, Brewer weighed his options. He could stay, perform the show, and take his chances that his true wealth would not be discovered, or he could flee. It did not take long to conclude that flight was still his best course for survival. He did not intend to perform for a crowd that, an hour ago, cheered for his death. He became an Assassin that night on the outskirts of Calais as he killed the man who had clothed and fed him.

Rick Brewer boarded the next vessel leaving France. Ironically, the same one he had tried to stow away aboard the day before. He had narrowly escaped the noose and thoughts of immortality briefly surfaced. He soon realized it was more likely that dumb luck was his Fairy Godmother rather than immortality. He smiled at that thought as he settled into a small stateroom on the ship. He found out later that his servants were not as lucky. They had died in Paris at the hands of the rebels, as had the gallows master. It appeared that the crowd did not like it that he had favored an Aristocrat and set him free. It had cost him his life.

Brewer arrived in Colchester, England, well dressed and with a pocket full of francs, thanks to the Frenchman he had killed. He stayed in England briefly, long enough to earn enough money to move away from the persecution of anything French. He boarded another vessel and headed for the newly formed United States of America.

Brewer arrived in New York in 1792, destitute, wearing only the rags he had on. He began his traveling magic show that had been so popular in Paris only a few years earlier, but it failed to impress the sophisticated New Yorkers. Out of options in the big city, he headed west, to Pennsylvania, and took a job on a farm. He soon discovered that he did not like working on a farm. The work was too intense and, in many cases, back breaking. His way out arrived later that year with the Whiskey Rebellion.

In the late 1700s, the newly formed United States of America levied taxes on grain alcohol, known as the Whiskey Excise Tax. Farmers chose to distill their grain into alcohol for transport over the Appalachian Mountains so as not to pay the despised tax to settle the national debt. Those farmers, including the one that Brewer worked for, claimed the tax benefited the wealthier distilleries to the East. They refused to pay the tax.

Brewer rallied with the insurrectionists and even participated in a few of the more violent episodes of the rebellion. His Guild training gave him expertise that his fellow rebels did not have. He quickly gained favor with his comrades in arms. That approval took him to the inner circle.

Brewer stood with dozens of rebels on the outskirts of a small settlement in Pennsylvania as a lone rider approached. His horse near exhaustion, the rider jumped from the mount before the animal could stop fully.

“Washington leads the army,” the horseman reported.

None of the farmers wanted to fight Washington and the rebellion disbanded without further incident. Most of the farmers returned to their homes, but Brewer remained to see the end. Washington arrived to meet with the rebellion's leaders and Brewer witnessed it all.

Washington's stature and caring nature impressed the rogue Assassin. *The man cares more about the citizens and the country than himself*, Brewer thought. Brewer had never experienced that; the Guild came first and foremost in his former life. That gave him something new to think about and a new direction to take his life: politics

Brewer moved to Washington, DC, at the turn of the century, in time to see his first political event: the inauguration of Thomas Jefferson. The event, with all of its grandeur, pomp, and circumstance, brought back memories of the French Aristocracy. Brewer discovered that he missed the life of favor but resigned himself to live out his days peacefully. He took a job at the Department of State in 1802 and settled into a good, quiet life.

It was not until 1810 that he realized he was not aging.

The revelation hit him as he attended the birthday celebration of one of his co-workers—the third celebration for that man he had been invited to. The incident dredged up the forgotten thoughts of immortality, but those were soon replaced by more practical issues. How long could he stay in Washington while everyone grew older except for him?

The United States declared war against England in 1812. Brewer, saw this as an opportunity to avoid those impending questions about his age. He jumped at the option to leave Washington.

Rick Brewer tapped into his newfound patriotism and joined the Army of the Northwest. He travelled to Detroit and fought in the Battle of Thames. Wounded and out of ammunition, Brewer affixed his bayonet and charged the enemy. He killed the last six of the Redcoats by slashing, blocking, and stabbing his way through the lines. He awoke in a field hospital the next day where thoughts of immortality again surfaced. *Why am I alive when so many are dead?*

Lying in the field hospital, Rick Brewer realized that his life had taken a turn for the worse and once again wondered if execution may not have been the better prospect. He thought of the Guild, and how a small lie had led him to exile. He thought of the lies of the Government, Politicians and Generals that had brought him to the hospital bed. He thought, *Lies lead to death,* and wondered if there was any truth at all.

That line of thought led Brewer into a deep depression. He lay on his bed in a rented flat above a bar in New York, staring at the ceiling. Alone, lost in history, he started asking, *Why?* He began looking to assign blame for his depression. The political system that he had admired only a few years before came to mind first.

The Guild was a close second.

Rain fell, darkening his mood as he lay in bed. He began talking to himself, debating his next move.

"The political system and the Guild are institutions," he said. "I could fight forever and not bring them down.

"Then who?" he queried.

Donovan. Donovan was the one who lied to the Council. Donovan was the key. Brewer's dark mood increased slightly as the rain fell harder.

"But that's three hundred years from now. What if I don't live that long? There must be someone here. Now.

"A message," he muttered, getting up from the bed and staring out of the window. The rain stopped and he could see the clouds parting in the distance. His mood brightened with sky. "I'll send the Guild a message. I'll change history, but how?"

He glanced at a newspaper on the nightstand by his bed. The headline told of the presidential election soon. Brewer smiled as his dark thoughts congealed into a single, deadly conclusion. "I'll kill the President of the United States."

* * * *

Brewer spent the next twenty years studying the political structure of Washington. He learned the political parties, the influences and the give and take of politics. He became quite adept at manipulating people and situations. Determination replaced his depression as he progressed toward his revenge. He smiled as his first opportunity to influence history presented itself.

Henry Harrison, a Senator, a Governor, and a Former Major General, announced his bid for President for the election of 1840, challenging the incumbent Martin Van Buren. Rick Brewer had served with General Harrison in the Battle of the Thames and held the General responsible for not only his wounds, but the deaths of his friends as well. Brewer knew the political structure of Washington and the procedures employed by those who resided there. What he needed was a way to kill the President.

His history lessons showed Harrison served one rather uneventful term as President before retiring from public life. He died in 1853 from old age. The rogue assassin also recalled a trick used six hundred years earlier against King John. A few ingredients mixed together and Rick Brewer changed history. He introduced the newly elected President to a virulent strand of the common cold. President Harrison died in April of 1841 after one month in office. History would say he caught a cold after one of the longest inaugural speeches in history. That was fine with Rick Brewer.

Chapter Five

REGINALD MAYWEATHER STOOD IN front of Director Tomlinson's office within the Time Skip Control Room, watching the monitors and tapping his cane on the floor impatiently as the technicians scurried around in controlled chaos. The gentle tap-tap-tap of the cane joined the cacophony of noises in the control room.

Mayweather, and one other man, watched the screens on the far wall. Ten of the thirty monitors were active and displayed ten different events in history. The first moon launch displayed a rocket heading for orbit, one screen displayed Custer's final battle at Little Big Horn, and one displayed the Jupiter orbit disaster of 2219. Mayweather did not recognize the images on the other monitors.

There were thirty-two individual work stations in the control room, assembled as four rows of eight control stations arranged in a rough crescent all facing the wall of monitors. Each workstation was composed of a monitor, a control keyboard, and a highly trained technician monitoring one of a hundred variables for each mission:

reactor power, time coordinates, and medical status, skip retrieval, etc. Mayweather continued to tap his cane as he tried to absorb everything around him. He quickly discovered he could not fathom the information flooding through the room. It gave him a headache. He was accustomed to controlling every situation and he refused to display his ignorance. He simply looked thoughtful, distant and bored. The dull pain behind his eyes continued to sharpen.

"Can I get you anything, Mr. Mayweather?" asked the man standing beside him on the balcony.

Mayweather eyed the tall, balding man, with dark rimmed glasses. He wore a yellow smock that matched the walls and Mayweather hated yellow, the color of cowards. The color made his headache worse.

"Yes," Mayweather replied, frustration seeping into his voice. "You can get on with the show! I don't have all day and I want Dent's head on a platter before lunch!"

The liaison simply smiled, recalling the warning he had received about Mayweather's impatience and complete lack of civility.

"It won't be much longer, sir." He pointed at a control station on the left, near the solitary door in the room. "That station is the one to watch. When that station goes to green, the Assassin can depart."

"Mr. Tomlinson, I thought you had already sent men back to kill Dent! Now, you're telling me you're *about* to? What the hell kind of operation are you running here?" Mayweather's voice rose in volume with each sentence until he was yelling. "Do I have to buy this whole damn Guild just to get what I want?" The wealthy man lowered his voice and began mumbling to himself. “If I ran my organization like these clowns run this—”

"Mr. Mayweather," Tomlinson interjected nervously, adjusting his glasses, very unhappy to have to deal with the client. His control room was supposedly off limits to clients. The simple fact that the businessman was standing before him told Tomlinson a lot about the political clout of Mayweather. “We sent scouts back in time two weeks ago, after you first approached the Council. Because we did not have a specific date in mind for the assassination, the scouts went back to begin monitoring the family to determine schedules, weaknesses and patterns.

“Now that we have received a skip trace signal from the advance team, which means they have reconned the area and have a tentative plan, the Assassin will now go back and-pardon the pun-execute the plan.”

“I want to meet the assassin.” Mayweather leaned toward Tomlinson. “I want him to know that I'm paying a lot of money and I want Dent DEAD!”

That is not permitted, thought Tomlinson, but knew better than to say it. Every time someone had told Mayweather no, he went to a higher authority and got his way, and whoever told him no ended up out of a job.

The board turned green, sparing Tomlinson the anguish of the conversation. The head controller pointed as a man headed toward the door on the left.

The man sported a short, military style haircut on his tall, thin frame. He adjusted his dark leather jacket as he approached the door, reached up and slapped the top edge of the door-his version of a good luck charm-and stepped through the door. The Skip Room Director explained, in unclassified terms, what was happening as the Assassin stepped through the door on the left side of the room, and disappeared.

Mayweather watched as the room began to quiet. "That's it?"

"Yes, that's it. The Assassin is on his way to the year 2011."

"When will we know it's done?"

"You won't."

Mayweather's face began to flush red but Tomlinson held up his hand and continued quickly. "If the Assassin is successful, your life will change, everything around you will change, and you will never know that this timeline ever existed."

Mayweather's eyes brightened as he thought about that statement. "So, I won't even have to pay the Guild? This may just turn out to be a good day!" Mayweather smiled for the first time in weeks.

Mayweather's smiled faded quickly as the entrance to the Control Room opened and Mr. Donovan, with about half of the second-year class, entered. Mayweather's gaze immediately locked onto Apprentice 101 and Apprentice 97 and saw recognition and hatred from the two students. For some reason, the look of disgust in their eyes unnerved him. Mayweather was loathed around the world, why should these two kids bother him. Somewhere, deep inside, he felt something he had not felt since he was a young man: fear.

He looked away and tried to hide the emotion welling up deep inside, but could not. He took that as his cue and abruptly turned to leave the Control Room, gathering his entourage outside the room on his way. He paused at the door, flashed an arrogant smile in their direction, knowing that it was only a façade, and that the two Apprentices could see right through it. Without another word, he disappeared toward the main entrance of the Guild.

The two Apprentices watched him leave, staring at him until he was out of sight. Mr. Donovan waited until Mayweather was gone before he reclaimed the students' attention. “Now, this is the master control room for all Time Skips.” He motioned to the man standing before the office door wearing a dull yellow smock. “And this is Controller Tomlinson, the Time Skip Control Director.”

Mr. Donovan looked past the controller at the room. “Did we miss the skip?”

“Yes,” said Tomlinson, adjusting his smock and feeling relief that Mayweather was gone. “We just sent Assassin 46 back to the Twenty-First century to deal with Mr. Mayweather's problem.”

“What problem is that?” Apprentice 101 said, his voice not masking the disgust he felt. Mr. Donovan shot him a glance and Apprentice 101 knew he would be writing a paper later.

“Apprentice, we do not discuss ongoing missions with students.” Tomlinson smiled, then leaned in and whispered, “But between you and me, I feel the exact same way as you do about Mr. Mayweather.” That brought a laugh from the crowd and the tour began.

Halfway through the tour of the Control Room, a Skip Beacon trace signal activated and the room descended into controlled chaos. Technicians raced back to their workstations and began checking their computers. One man toward the front raised his hand “It's mine!”

"Are you expecting a return?" Donovan asked as he ushered the students against the far wall away from all of the action.

"Not today," Tomlinson said. "But that isn't unusual. We can't really predict when the mission will be over or when the Assassin's skip will deliver them back to us."

The Chief Controller pulled out his control pad and thumbed through the information received from the computer. His look changed from curiosity to worry. "This is an emergency signal." He looked up from his pad and stared at the door on the opposite end of the room.

The Skip Door opened, letting in the customary opaque light. A figure staggered through the door. The man's right hand was soaked in blood as it held his left shoulder. He took two steps into the room before falling to his knees.

"Medic to the Control Room!" someone yelled. Apprentice 101 saw it was a female technician, standing near the Skip Door, her hand on the comm button. He turned his eyes back to the man as he slowly slumped toward the floor.

"That's Simmons!" Tomlinson said as three technicians moved to catch the Cleaner before he collapsed further. The Controller's fingers flew over his status pad and within seconds he had pulled up the mission details.

Apprentice 97 turned to Apprentice 101 and whispered, "He was with Assassin 74 on the Bhutto Mission."

Apprentice 101 nodded and turned his attention to Mr. Tomlinson as he consulted his computer pad. "He is the second casualty. Parker's body was returned a few days ago." Tomlinson looked up at Donovan and shook his head. "What a disaster."

* * * *

Assassin 46 stepped from his transparent bubble into a shallow fountain on Boston Commons. The cool water surprised him and he fell forward, totally submerging himself in the pool. He stood up, standing knee deep in the water, laughed at himself, and started to splash around.

"Well, at least it's dark," he said aloud, thinking no one could see him.

"And you're making quite a spectacle of yourself," came a voice from the darkness.

Assassin 46 stopped splashing, his hand automatically going to his left hip, where his pistol sat. He stepped from the pool, not quite embarrassed but closer than he had been in a long time.

"There are many types of spectacles, my friend." He smiled and shook hands with the shadowy man. "My only saving grace is that no one would believe a scoundrel such as you, even if you could even find a friend to tell that I was dancing in a water fountain."

A hearty laugh came from the darkness. "If I were to call that dancing, they would know I was lying anyway!" Like the Cheshire cat, he emerged from the darkness smile first, and then his body materialized. Demetrius Faraday was a short, black man with close-cropped hair, piercing eyes and one gold tooth.

"Demetri, they would know you were lying anyway; you would be talking!"

Demetri nodded his agreement. “You have a point.”

Assassin 46 paused for a moment, allowing his body to cool down from the skip. The Assassin had a tendency to overheat.

Demetri watched the Assassin place his hands on his knees and bend over slightly. “How do you feel, boss?”

“Pretty good, actually,” he replied, straightening up. “I'm not burning up.” He moved his hands to his forehead and cheeks. “Maybe I should request a fountain to land in every skip. The water helped me cool off!”

“I saw you dance," came the reply with a sad shake of the head. "You were never hot to begin with!”

"Just lead me out of here! Where's the car?” the Assassin asked. He was accustomed to the verbal banter with his point man, and used to losing the battles.

Demetri smiled again, unmoving. “And what name are you going by this time? Let me see,” he began tapping his chin with his left forefinger in deep thought. “Dominic Durango? Richard Cranium? James Bond?”

The assassin frowned, a movement barely discernible in the dim light. “Let's go with Copper. Maxwell Copper.”

“This way, Mr. Copper, sir.” Demetri bowed and waved toward a distant parking lot with his right hand. The two men disappeared into the darkness.

* * * *

Maxwell Copper peered through the scope at his target, an accountant named Douglas Dent; a forty-something man with a balding head, a bad comb over, protruding belly, and a weakness for Jolly Rancher candy. Dent took another sour apple candy from the jar on his desk. The Assassin watched the target for several minutes, adjusting his scope. It would be an easy shot. The target was less than two hundred meters away, in the 32rd floor of an office building, sitting at his desk working on the computer. Assassin 46 silently moved his finger to the trigger.

"Bam!"

"Not exactly your historical figure, huh, boss?"

"Not exactly," the Assassin agreed. He removed the rifle from its perch and walked back toward the roof access door where Demetri held it open. He stopped at the door, began disassembling the rifle and then stowed it in the carrying case. "I've travelled back in time. I've taken out dictators, would be kings, even an ancient assassin with a bow and arrow in Medieval England." He waved toward the office building across the street. "But this is ridiculous!"

"It's a job, boss."

The assassin grumbled something under his breath and the two started down the stairs. The two men retrieved their car from a public parking garage and drove across town to set up—without the rifle this time—in a park with a good view of a private school where Melody Dent worked as a school administrator.

"Her office is on the far side of the school," Demetri said, consulting a miniature computer with a map of the area.

"Too public here anyway," the assassin replied. "It will have to be done at the house."

Demetri simply nodded. He had already provided the probable course of action to the assassin and that required a 'robbery gone bad' scenario at the Dent Residence.

The man known as Maxwell Copper, like all Guild-trained Assassins, insisted on seeing all of the target scenarios. Assassin 46 could decide on hitting each target separately, but Demetri would not have bet on it. Demetri had been a Cleaner a long time and knew what was going to happen.

"When, boss?"

"Tomorrow night. Thursday. They'll all be home," he turned to his partner. "They never go out on Thursday.

* * * *

Apprentice 101 sat in the middle of the history archives library, both of his hands rubbed his baldhead in frustration. The same rich mahogany that adorned the corridors covered the library walls, which were lined with shelves and bookcases. Memory crystals, ancient digital media and hard cover books lined the shelves and the desk that the young Apprentice occupied. The young Apprentice stared at the intricate clockwork diagram on the far wall and sighed.

He kept switching his attention from the JFK archives for his presentation and the family tree of one Douglas Dent. If he could find some way to disrupt the mission and cause Mayweather grief, he was all for it. It seemed no one liked the trillionaire, and he wanted to find *any* reason he could to call the mission off.

So he sat, surrounded by history crystals, and scanned the timelines for anything that might change in the event of Douglas Dent and his family's death. The family, and their history, was so boring it was driving him crazy. He stared again at the intricate clockwork on the wall and emitted a low growl in frustration.

"Enjoying your assignment?"

The apprentice flicked off the crystal reader and turned to see Mr. Donovan leaning in the doorway, watching him. "Just trying to get all the facts, sir," he answered with an embarrassed smile.

Mr. Donovan walked over and flipped the switch on the reader, the Dent Family archives popped in to view and the instructor frowned. "I thought I assigned you JFK?"

"You did," Apprentice 101 sighed. "But I thought I'd look into the Mayweather mission."

"The Mayweat–How did you find out about the Mayweather mission?" Mr. Donovan grabbed the archives and looked again. "And how the hell did you find out about the target?"

Apprentice 101 smiled slyly. "I overheard Mr. Tomlinson during the tour of the Control Room." He smiled shyly, and then, with a little more confidence, continued, "If I can disrupt Mayweather's life, I'm going to try."

"You are, are you?" Mr. Donovan laughed lightly. "There was another student some time ago that took it upon himself to delve into assignments he was not given." The instructor sat down and looked thoughtful for a moment. "He was caught copying the history archives instead of searching them as you are doing now."

"And?"

"And he was sentenced to death."

“I'm not copying anything,” Apprentice 101 protested as a fearful chill ran down his spine. “I'm only studying the—”

The professor raised his hand to stop the retort. “I'm not accusing you, Apprentice,” Donovan replied in a solemn and serious tone. He patted the young man on the back. “What have you discovered?"

“Not much on the Dent family, although I've only gone through about three generations.” He shook his head sadly. “None of them ever accomplished anything worthwhile.

“But I did find out one thing about the JFK assignment.”

“Oh?”

Apprentice 101 turned and looked him in the eye. “You were there.”

Donovan sat back in his chair and smirked. “I'm not an Assassin or a Cleaner, Apprentice. I couldn't have been there.”

Apprentice 101's grinned. “Don't worry. I'm not going to tell your secret, sir.” Apprentice 101 leaned forward. “Tell me more about this other Apprentice. The one killed for copying the archives.”

“I never said he was killed, only sentenced to death,” Donovan said. He sat quietly for a moment, and then edged closer, taking the young man into his confidence. “I always try to find one student who shows all of the qualities to not only make a good assassin, but who also shows the skills to one day be on the Council.”

“The Council? Right?”

“I'm serious. Do you know that only one in thirty students makes the link that I am, er was, part of the JFK mission? One in thirty!” He smiled as memories of past Apprentices flashed through his mind. “That one is who I focus on. I give extra assignments, additional studies, to mold and shape them into something other than just a killer.

“All of these things," Donovan waved his hands encompassing the whole room and beyond, “I do without the Council's knowledge. It is my gift to them for sparing my life twenty years ago.” Mr. Donovan laughed slightly. “Hell, for *giving* me a life twenty years ago!”

“So, I make a link that you have a past and now I get bogged down scanning through history files to 'mold and shape' me?” Apprentice 101's voice was sarcastic and disbelieving. “Thanks!”

“You will do it,” Donovan replied, followed by another pat on the Apprentice's back. “And you will find that you are a better man for it.”

Donovan got up to leave. “Continue to study the Mayweather case, Apprentice, but do it quietly. Do not let anyone, not even Apprentice 97, know what you're doing. Report any findings to me, immediately.

“You are not alone in your dislike of Mr. Mayweather, but learn to keep your feelings in check. An Assassin has to be able to control his emotions. Remember class two weeks ago.”

Mr. Donovan turned and left the room.

Absentmindedly, Apprentice 101 tapped a crystal on the desk and sat for almost fifteen minutes thinking about the conversation, and the plans set before him. He stared at the clockwork image on the wall and lost himself in the intricate cog and wheel system. Finally, he inserted the crystal into the reader and once again began scanning the Dent family history.

Apprentice 101 found himself actually *more* involved in his search. A by-product of the new motivation he felt as the conversation continued to play in the back of his mind. He traced the lineage of the family for one hundred years, each of the Dent family members, their offspring and so on. Suddenly, he stopped the scan, his eyes locked onto a specific branch of the Dent family tree. He grabbed the crystal from the reader and headed out of the library at a dead run.

* * * *

Professor Donovan bowed slightly. “Sir, Apprentice 101 has found something that could be detrimental to the Mayweather mission.”

Mr. Donovan and Apprentice 101 stood in the Council chamber, looking up at the five members of the Guild Council, their black robes as still as the air in the room.

“Apprentice 101 has found information?” The lone female paused. “Why was the Apprentice even looking into this matter?”

Apprentice 101 stepped forward and bowed slightly. “Council members, at the request of Mr. Donovan, I studied the family lineage of the Dent family.”

“At Mr. Donovan's request?” commented the Chief of the Council. “So, you've selected a new side project, have you?”

Donovan looked shocked. The Council was not supposed to know of his involvement in those matters.

The Chief motioned with his left hand by way of explanation. “Perhaps, you'll recognize our newest Council appointee?"

Donovan moved his eyes to follow the Chief's outstretched hand and found the very first Apprentice he had influenced, almost twenty years earlier. He was right. His gift to the Guild was a new Council member. His suddenly realized that the Council now knew of all of his extra-curricular activities and became apprehensive.

“And you, Apprentice,” the female continued, “standing before us yet again! If you continue to grace us with your presence, we may have to install a sixth chair for you.” The lighthearted jest was meant to put the lad at ease, and provide a warning at the same time. “We understand your disdain for Mr. Mayweather, Apprentice, but that does not give either of you license to conduct unilateral assignments.”

Apprentice 101 blushed, but he understood the thinly veiled threat. In an effort to steer the conversation anywhere but about him, he proceeded with his report. “As you are aware, the great-great-great-great-great grandson,” he counted on his fingers to ensure he had the accurate count of generations, “of Douglas Dent is a wealthy businessman today. He is the competitor of Reginald Mayweather.” Apprentice 101 tried to stop the nervousness in his voice and the tremble in his left leg. With a conscious effort, he forced the leg still and continued.

“A Cleaner team researched the lineage and found no catastrophic issues with the timeline, other than the normal instability. What the team didn't do was research the various marriages and divorces of the subsequent generations. There is a potential problem with the great-great grandson of Mr. Dent."

"The great-great grandson?" asked the man on the far left of the Council.

"Yes, sir," Apprentice 101 replied, feeling a little more confident now that he had the Council's attention. "The great, great grandson of Dent, one Desmond Flowers, married and divorced seven times producing some eight children along the way."

"Those eight children have not yet been vetted," added Mr. Donovan. "It is those children that pose a potential problem to the timeline."

The Council conferred quietly for several minutes, before the woman spoke again, looking directly at the Apprentice. "How long with it take you to completely research this new lineage?"

"Me?"

"You've taken it upon yourself to begin the research. It only makes sense that you continue it."

Another admonishment, Apprentice 101 began to realize just how much he had over-stepped his boundaries.

Mr. Donovan and Apprentice 101 looked at each other. Donovan shrugged.

"It could take weeks, ma'am," the Apprentice answered.

Another quick conversation between the Council members, followed by a summons, and a man dressed in brown robes entered the chamber through an unseen door on the right of the raised dais. A set of whispered orders and the man hurried back out through the door. The four men of the Council retreated out the Council door, leaving the woman alone with the professor and the student.

“We are recalling the assassin and his team until this research can be concluded,” she said. “How long before you can conduct the lineage research?”

Mr. Donovan pointed to himself with a questioning look on his face. Apprentice 101 stood unmoving.

“I'm talking to the both of you,” she continued. “You discovered the problem. How long will it take you to fix it?”

“I have my classes,” Mr. Donovan replied, as he pointed to the apprentice. “The boy has his studies, including preparation for his first case study.” The edge in his voice told Apprentice 101 that the JFK assignment should have been his priority all along. He rubbed his chin. “Again, it could take weeks, ma'am.”

“You have one month.” The woman allowed an edge into her voice. “And I expect you to use every bit of it.”

"Yes, ma'am."

“Apprentice, you are dismissed.”

Apprentice 101 bowed slightly and left the Council Chamber, making one last glance at the Professor as he left. Both men shared the same worried look. The massive doors clicked shut behind the Apprentice.

“Has your new protégé realized the danger you've put him in? I do not want a repeat of Apprentice 58.”

“I am watching him carefully.”

“Not carefully enough! He has already opened doors he shouldn't even have access to. This Council has had to cover up your messes too many times. We do not want to have to do it again! We will not sentence another

Apprentice to death to cover your mistakes, Professor. If it happens again, you will pay the price."

The Council member stood up and made her way to the unseen door, paused, and turned to face him. "Mr. Donovan, teach the boy the hazards of overstepping his bounds."

* * * *

"We have successfully intercepted Assassin 46 before he could kill the Dent family."

Apprentice 101 looked up from his crystal reader, nodded to Professor Donovan, and immediately went back to work. Data crystals formed an off-balance pyramid next to the reader while stacks of bound books lay across the table. Bookshelves extended into the darkness behind the Apprentice. Other books, pulled from those shelves appeared haphazardly replaced. Other than the Professor, Apprentice 101 sat alone in the library.

"Isn't that good news?" asked the Professor. He received a non-committal response. "Apprentice? Still, no response. "Apprentice, what are you working on?"

"I'm working on the Dent Family Lineage. I have almost finished vetting the fourth wife and kids."

Professor Donovan stepped over, turned off the viewer, and turned the Apprentice in his swivel chair. The determination on the Apprentice's face turned to anger as he turned. Acquiescence replaced the anger as the Professor admonished the Apprentice.

"Did you not hear the Council? Take at least a month?"

"But—"

"No buts, Apprentice," the reply was stern and sobering. The professor stood over him, teacher to student. "You will not research the lineage any further for at least two weeks. You will work on your case study and that case study only."

The Professor took in a deep breath. "I know you want to do a good job for the Council, but you have to learn to follow your instructions, even if they are counter to your nature." Mr. Donovan sat on the table beside the viewer and smiled at his student. "So, we will work on this in our spare time, and take the full month we have been allotted. I don't dare speak for the Council, but I imagine they are looking for ways to postpone or even drop this mission. And we are going to assist them in any way we can."

Apprentice 101 stood, facing the Professor. "But I may have already found a problem that could cause an abort."

"Then hold onto that information." Donovan smiled, nodding his head as he did. "Use it when it is needed."

The Assassin's Apprentice agreed reluctantly and then changed the subject. "I found something else of interest." He held up a handful of crystals. "I was combing through the files of Presidential assassinations, while researching JFK, and I found a few anomalies."

"Oh?" Donovan crossed his arms with a mix of anxiety and anticipation of a new revolution.

"As you know, we participated in the Kennedy assassination"—the Professor gave a quick nod—" and we researched, observed and catalogued the Lincoln assassination and several others." Another quick nod. "The correlation is in the After Action Reports." Apprentice 101 held up a pair of crystals. "Several of the reports state that someone in each team thought they recognized someone from the Guild."

Mr. Donovan learned toward the Apprentice, intrigue filling his voice. "Who? Who did they recognize?"

The Apprentice shook his head. "They didn't know for sure, but several team members had composite drawings made; drawings that were almost identical." He produced two rough sketches from the digital printer and handed them to the Professor, who gazed at the pictures for almost a minute before handing them back.

"Finish your case study, and then I want you to research Presidential Assassinations, all Presidential Assassinations. I want you to see if there are any other sightings of this man."

"There are only these two, and they are a hundred years apart. How can the same man be at two different assassinations that far apart?" He raised his arms, encompassing his surroundings. "Without the Guild to send him back, that is?"

"Good question." Donovan thought for a moment. "I want you to expand the research to include all political or high-profile deaths—assassinations or otherwise–in between those two Presidents."

"What am I looking for?"

Donovan gulped down his fear and astonishment at the news. "My former apprentice."

Chapter Six

APPRENTICE 101 STOOD AT the podium in history class. Nervous, he wiped the sweat from his hands on his robes repeatedly and his hand shook slightly as he took a sip of water. He hoped that he would calm down once he started the presentation.

Professor Donovan nodded to him from behind his desk. The Professor leaned back in his chair and waited. Apprentice 101 had never done well at public speaking and his first case study was one of the most involved and complex in history. He nodded his thanks, took a deep breath, and faced his audience.

"History reveals that President Kennedy was killed on November 22, 1963 in Dallas, Texas," Apprentice 101 began. "He was assassinated by Lee Harvey Oswald, who fired three shots from the sixth floor of the Texas School Book Depository Building.

"The Warren Commission, established by President Johnson to detail the assassination, determined that Oswald acted alone; shooting three rounds from a 6.5mm

Mannlicher-Carcano rifle and killing Kennedy, while wounding Governor Connelly.

"Lee Harvey Oswald was apprehended, interrogated and, while being transferred to a different holding facility was shot and killed by Jack Ruby on November 24th, 1963."

He had rehearsed that bit several times, but it had never sounded as dry and clinical as it did now. Apprentice 101 hoped the rest of the report was not going to be as mind-numbingly boring as his opening. He made a note to liven up his next report.

"These are the facts of history," Apprentice 101 stated, looking up from his notes and scanned the crowd before his eyes locked onto Apprentice 97, present as an assistant instructor. She smiled and nodded her reassurance.

He did feel a little better now that he was talking. "What I am about to reveal to you are the *actual* facts of that assassination: the Cleaners, the Assassin, and the emplacement of various myths and conspiracy theories to hide the Assassin's Guild involvement..."

* * * *

Dennis Lazenby never believed he would make anything of his life. He grew up a simple man in a small mid-western town, with a brother and a sister and in a happy childhood. His grades were mediocre and his athleticism was decent. He was of average height, a little on the skinny side, brown eyes, brown hair, with big teeth and big ears. Dennis thought himself an average man that would never do anything great in his life.

He had moved to Texas in his teens, attended the University of Texas at Arlington where he maintained his mediocre grades and met Anna. The woman who would eventually leave him at the altar, which was, unfortunately, the most exciting thing that had ever happened to Dennis Lazenby. He was happy in his mediocrity, but deep down, he longed for something to happen so he could leave his mark on the world.

The semi-transparent bubble that formed in front of him as he walked down the dark, deserted street was quite a surprise. The fact that the bubble produced a man with a small backpack was an even greater surprise.

Roberto Esteban was quite flabbergasted as well when he stepped from the bubble and stumbled into Lazenby. The bubble disappeared behind him with a barely audible pop.

"Pardon me, sir," Esteban said in slightly accented English as he pushed himself arms length away from Lazenby. He made an exaggeration of straightening the stranger's clothes, then his own. "Can you tell me where I am?" There was a pause. "And when?" He wiped the sweat from his brow and took a deep breath.

Thrilled, Lazenby thought he had suddenly become part of a magician's show or a game show. He glanced around but saw no one.

"Great trick, but no audience," he muttered, and then snapped his fingers. "Where is Allen Funt?" He glanced around again excitedly.

"I'm sorry, who?"

"Allen Funt!" Lazenby almost yelled. "You just appeared, here, in front of me, must be an act for *Candid Camera*!"

"I'm sorry, sir," came the chuckled reply, "but no." Estaban's study of the mid-twentieth century brought an instant memory to the forefront of his mind, recalling the long running television series. "Nothing quite that exciting."

Lazenby looked disappointed for a moment and then remembered the original question. "You are in Dallas, Texas and the date is October 23rd, 1963." He smiled, satisfied with himself for being helpful and he nodded to reassure himself. "There must be something going on if you are asking when and where you are," he said, waving an accusing finger at the newcomer. Lazenby's silly grin suddenly faded, replaced by a worried look. "Unless you're hurt and truly don't know where you are."

"Sir, I assure you that I am fine," Esteban said. He looked around, confirmed it was only the two of them that stood on the dingy, deserted street, and pushed a button on his tracker hidden under his jacket. "I am simply a traveler—" He stopped in mid-sentence and turned his head at the appearance of two more transparent bubbles shedding faint light on the dark street.

The bubbles appeared and disappeared quietly, depositing two more men onto the deserted street. The two new arrivals stepped from the Skip Bubble and stopped in mid-stride, startled by the stranger in their midst.

"Jacob Miller. Anthony Greene. This is...?"

"Dennis Lazenby," came the enthusiastic reply.

The men all shook hands. "And I am Roberto Esteban. Come, my new friend, there is much work to be done."

* * * *

Roberto Esteban was very happy to have found their new friend. One of the recommendations for any Cleaner Team on a skip was to find a local guide, if possible. Dennis Lazenby was turning out to be a fantastic guide.

In two days, the quartet had found a secluded place to stay, began their recon of the route the motorcade would take, and started on a very difficult plan. Of course, Lazenby had no idea what was going on, but he enthusiastically helped any way he could. Extremely happy to be a part of something for once, he planned to make the most of it. Involved in something big, exciting and mysterious made him the happiest he had ever been.

"Jacob, you and Anthony take a stroll over to the park," Roberto suggested with a wink. "Dennis and I are going to take a look at the Book Depository."

"The Book Depository?" Lazenby asked.

"Yes. I've always heard about it. Since I'm here I thought I'd check it out."

Lazenby looked confused. "Always heard?" he muttered and shrugged, but did not ask any questions. He had learned in the last two days that his new friends appeared strangely driven to a purpose. His father had always said that a man with a purpose is a good man. He nodded and waived briefly as the other two men left.

Jacob Miller and Anthony Greene left their tidy, light green painted apartment and made their way to Dealey Plaza. In order for the tentative plan to work, the two man team had to check out the soon to be infamous grassy knoll; a spot to the south of the Depository and motorcade route. The announcement of President Kennedy's visit had been released a few weeks earlier, but the details of the motorcade route had not been disclosed. Of course, the Cleaners had every detail of the event committed to memory.

The two men walked in the late October sunshine and spent the next few hours taking finely detailed pictures with a micro-camera they brought with them from the future. Miller, a tall, broad shouldered man, casually paced off distances and took video of the area. His shoulder length blonde hair constantly swayed in the breeze as his dark brown eyes surveyed everything in the area. Satisfied he had a good video view of the area, including the route, he went to find his partner.

Greene was a short, stocky black man. Well educated, he was well aware of the prejudices he was likely to encounter in the south in 1963. He was not disappointed. In the hour he spent taking still pictures with a 1960s era looking camera—actually a highly advanced 23rd Century holographic camera—he was accosted and ridiculed no less than a dozen times. Three young white men stood around Greene threatening to beat him to death as Miller rejoined his partner.

“Is there a problem here?” asked Miller.

“This ain't none of your concern, Mister,” said the leader of the trio.

“Actually it is,” Miller replied. “Mr. Greene is a friend of mine and you are harassing him.” He smiled politely. “Please leave him alone.” Several passers-by stopped to watch for a moment before they realized things were about to get out of hand, and quickly continued on their way.

“Oh, *please,* he said,” the leader replied, dragging out the word please. The three men sized up the large newcomer and mentally calculated the three to two odds of the fight. The ringleader nodded to his buddies and received nods in return. “Well, nigger lover, I guess we'll just have to beat your ass, too!” Three clicks followed that statement as all three men produced switchblade knives.

Greene turned away from the three men and gently placed the camera on the ground, well away from the inevitable battlefield. There was a chorus of 'coward' and 'nigger' as he turned away. The taunts abruptly ended as he turned back toward the three knife welders.

He took up position next to his partner and sighed. “Come on,” Greene said humorlessly as he waved them forward with his right hand.

The three men moved simultaneously and were met with a flurry of kicks and punches that left them lying unconscious on the ground, knives scattered about the knoll. Anthony Green suffered a small cut on the left arm, otherwise the two time travelers were unscathed.

Retrieving the camera, Greene smiled and nodded at the three men. “That felt pretty good! I could use *more* of a workout, though.”

“Let's get out of here before the police arrive,” Jacob Miller replied, also smiling. “We don't need you arrested for assault.”

“Me?” came the mock reply. “But they started it!” The argument lasted all the way back to their apartment.

* * * *

Dennis Lazenby had been to the Book Depository several times, had even applied for a job there once, but he had never scrutinized it as his new friend was doing.

Thinking he had missed something in his life by not looking at every floor and doorway, he began imitating Roberto Esteban as the two made their way through the building.

Roberto saw this out of the corner of his eye, and smiled.

The two men had entered the building through the north entrance, marked 'Employees Only.' A quick scan with an electronic lock-pick opened the door. The janitor's closet provided two sets of coveralls that loosely fit the men. Lazenby's coverall had 'Fred' sewn on the right breast while Esteban donned a set labeled, oddly enough, 'Bob'.

The scouts made their way floor by floor all the way to the top. Each floor they traversed was a maze of bookcases and boxes. The duo had to wind their way through several rows of boxes on the third floor to find the stairwell up to the fourth floor. More boxes lined their path on each floor and up the stairs. The two men finally made it up the stairs and found that the sixth floor was stacked even higher with boxes and books. Cobwebs linked the boxes into one giant octopus form that covered the entire floor.

Esteban made his way around the room and eventually to the window that overlooked the motorcade route. He stood there a moment and the clear, cool, sunny October day dissolved into the grainy film he had studied before skipping back. In his mind's eye, he saw the film and the ancient image of what was still to come: the car, the shot, the woman crying at the loss of her husband and everyone in the United States mourning the loss of the President. He allowed himself a few moments of calm reflection, before he brought himself back to October, 1963 and his own reflection in the window of the Book Depository.

"You okay, Roberto?" Lazenby asked after few moments. "You look like you've seen a ghost."

Esteban turned from the window and smiled. "You don't know how close you are, my friend. Come," he said, moving away from the window. "It's time to leave this place."

"Are we done here?"

Esteban looked at his new friend and knew that a pivotal decision was required. He slapped the man on the back and gave him a disarming smile. "We are done with our intel gathering. Now it's time to plan, and soon it will be time to act."

* * * *

Dennis Lazenby could hardly contain his excitement as the four men stood in a dark alley at two in the morning, waiting on the last member of their team. He hopped impatiently from one foot to the other as he constantly shifted his gaze up and down the alley watching for the transparent bubble they were expecting. 'Kid at Christmas' was a whispered comment at his back, but he barely heard it.

A streetlight flickered at the end of the alley and the four men paused to check their surroundings. The alley was similar to the one where the men had met weeks earlier. Garbage cans overflowed with refuse. Pieces of paper scampered along the ground in the light wind, and dark shadows could hide the men if the need arose.

In the two weeks since they had scouted out the Book Depository, the team had worked out a good plan on how to change their history to the timeline in the archives—the better timeline. Although Lazenby had no knowledge of the true implications of the mission, he was intelligent enough to understand that the men in the alley were not from 1963.

"Dennis," Esteban had told him before heading out for the alley. "If you stay with us, you are going to see things that you will not understand. But you must believe me," he looked into the brown eyes of Lazenby. "What we are doing, although strange to you, is for the best."

"You are going to kill someone," Lazenby replied, carefully choosing his words, watching the three men for reactions. "From the locations that were scouted, it will be someone in the President's motorcade."

Esteban nodded. "But, it's not quite that simple. Where we come from, this is all ancient history; something we studied in school. If we don't do what we were sent to do, then a lot of people will die that don't need to."

"You're going to kill the President to prevent a repeat of the Missile Crisis?"

Again, Esteban nodded. "Close. Our mission is to save Governor Connally and his wife.

"There are three possible outcomes of our mission here. One, we do nothing and the President, the Governor and his wife are all killed. If that happens, then the great-great granddaughter of Governor Connally—Elizabeth Denton—will not want to follow in her ancestor's footsteps and will not become the first female President of the United States. She will bring the US out of a terrible economic crisis about sixty years from now, so it is imperative that they live.

“Another possibility is that we take out the sniper and everyone lives. That path leads to the President using nuclear weapons against Cuba in 1965 and against Vietnam in 1967. That opens the door for a series of limited nuclear conflicts, 'the US is doing it, why can't I,' kind of thing.”

Lazenby nodded that he followed, and Esteban continued. “That leads to the eventual destruction of the Middle East and all of the oil.” Esteban used his hands to emphasis the story. “It takes over eighty years to overcome the setbacks of a world without gasoline.

“The last possibility—what we hope to do—is to save the Governor and his wife while allowing President Kennedy to perish. I know it sounds harsh, but to us, it's already happened.”

Dennis Lazenby looked thoughtful, rubbing his chin absent-mindedly. “What about your involvement? I mean, someone will figure out there were other shooters.”

“That, my friend, is where we drop clues leading everyone away from the truth. Besides, no one would believe time travelling assassins came back and killed anyone.” Esteban smiled disarmingly. “That's too fantastic to believe!”

“Yeah,” Lazenby replied, finally grasping he was in over his head. “Fantastic.”

Dennis Lazenby realized that the conspiracy junkies would talk about this for a hundred years. As he stood in the dark alley, Lazenby appreciated the plan would require perfect timing, a steady squeeze of the trigger, and a lot of luck.

A low hum, steadily growing louder, interrupted his thoughts. He stopped pacing and stood perfectly still as a faint glow and transparent bubble began to grow a dozen yards to his left. He turned and watched the bubble form. A man materialized in the middle of the soft glowing light. The newcomer stepped from the bubble, which began to fade almost immediately. The alley returned to its dim, quiet status as the bubble dissolved with a barely audible pop.

Assassin 22, a recent graduate of the Academy on his first mission, was young but ranked as one of the best in tactical assessment and marksmanship; two things abundantly needed for the assignment. He held onto his backpack with his left hand, up around his shoulder, and surveyed the alley. He recognized the three-man Cleaner team assigned to the mission with him. He did not know the forth man in the alley and hesitated, allowing his right hand to creep toward his hidden pistol.

Assassin 22 nodded his head at the unknown man. He seemed familiar, but he could not quite place how he knew him. He addressed his question to the Cleaner Team Leader.

"Roberto?"

"Dennis Lazenby," Esteban motioned for the Dallas native. "Meet Steven Newkirk, the leader of the mission."

Lazenby strode over to the man and held out his hand as his excitement flooded back through him. "A pleasure!" he said barely able to contain himself.

Assassin 22 gripped the proffered hand, smiled at the man, and shook firmly. "Nice to meet you, Mr. Lazenby."

Roberto Esteban stepped up. "How do you feel? Any affects of the skip?"

Steven Newkirk took a moment and performed a quick check of his body. He had no ill effects of the skip. He felt great, and he said so.

"Strange," Greene said stepping forward and checking the assassin's pulse. "Everyone experiences some kind of side effect of a skip." He checked the skin temperature, and breathing rate. "Except you, apparently." He smiled and shrugged.

Assassin 22 checked himself again and was satisfied that he was in good health. It was his second skip. The first being the ten minute skip that was a requirement for graduation from the Guild Academy. He thought briefly about that skip and realized he had felt great on that one too. He looked around the alley, confident he had made the right career decision.

"This way gentlemen," Esteban said, motioning back down the alley toward the lights of Dallas. "We have a plan to finalize and only a few days to act."

* * * *

Steven Newkirk and Roberto Esteban stood in the November wind watching as the Secret Service Jet taxied to the Dallas terminal. The jet carried the advance party for the President's visit and the two men watched as several agents left the plane and made their way to a waiting car.

Newkirk nodded toward the car as they made their way to a taxi. "Tag them."

Esteban bent over to tie his shoe and discreetly shot a tracking dart into the bumper of the Secret Service vehicle. Finishing with the shoe, he hailed a taxi, they boarded, and the car shot off.

Twenty minutes later, the taxi stopped in front of the Dallas FBI office building. The two time travelers watched as the Agents exited their car and headed for the doors. Newkirk paid the cab driver as Esteban opened his door, bent to tie the other shoe, and shot a transmitter dart onto the briefcase of the lead Agent. The small dart lodged itself discreetly into the faux leather. The time agents took a seat on a park bench opposite the building and fed the birds as they listened to the conversation inside the building.

"And you have no credible threats?" asked the lead Agent, identified as Winston Lawson by the archives.

"No, sir," came the reply.

"That is the same report from Washington," Lawson responded. There was some shuffling of papers. "What about the incident last month with the U.N. Ambassador, Adlai Stevenson?"

There was silence for several seconds, long enough that the assassin checked his reception with his ear implant. More shuffling, of feet this time, confirmed he was still receiving. "Sir, we don't have any informa—"

"I'm aware that you have no information," Lawson interrupted. "I had to read about it through civilian reports. Don't you think this might be important? A visiting U.N. Ambassador is protested one month before the President plans a visit and you do not think that is worth mentioning?"

The liaison with the Dallas Police Department chimed in and the conversation continued as they discussed some photographs of the protestors and other, somewhat limited, intelligence. The time travelers listened for another half hour, gathering very little that they did not already know from the historical files.

"What do you think, Roberto?" asked Assassin 22.

"We know the when and the where. We know the route and the security details. We even know the timing." Esteban nodded. "I think we are ready."

Assassin 22 nodded his agreement and the two men got up from the bench to head back toward their apartment. Ten days and counting.

* * * *

Air Force One touched down just after ten-thirty in the morning local time, amid smoking tires and roaring applause from the crowd gathered outside the airport. Anthony Greene joined the hundreds of Texans watching the jet as it rolled along the tarmac. Greene cheered along with the crowd, all the time watching the jet, the Secret Service and the Police that constantly scanned the crowd. He was not the only black man in the crowd, but there were only a handful and they continuously received more than their fair share of scrutiny.

Air Force One taxied up next to its sister jet, Air Force Two, and the receiving line formed, Vice President Johnson and his wife leading the procession. President John F. Kennedy, following by his wife, Jackie, Texas Governor and Mrs. Connally and Texas Senator Yarbrough, exited the jet, greeted the Vice President, and proceeded along a fence that separated the crowd from the politicians. The group waved and smiled as the crowd cheered.

Secret Service Agents formed a barrier between the politicians, the fence and the crowd. As the procession made its way along the fence, one plain-clothes officer stopped and stood next to Anthony Greene. For several minutes, the officer barely concealed his scrutiny and disdain of the black man. Finally, the officer moved on. Greene simply continued to cheer; he had nothing to hide.

The President and his entourage waved for a few minutes before making their way toward the 1961 Lincoln convertible—the Presidential Limousine. Agent Lawson moved ahead of the President and ensured the plastic bubble had been removed per his earlier instructions. The President and his entourage entered the limousine while the Secret Service verified everything was secure. Minutes later, sirens wailing, the motorcade left the airport.

Anthony Greene continued to wave as the motorcycles and cars headed toward Dallas. “Coming to you,” he said into the subcutaneous communicator implanted behind his ear. As the limousine faded from view, he walked away from the crowd toward a distant outbuilding.

“Acknowledged,” replied the voice of Jacob Miller in his ear.

Greene glanced behind him and noticed two men following: one uniformed policeman and the same plain-clothes officer that had studied him in the crowd. Greene ducked around the building.

“I'm being followed,” he said and activated his retrieval skip beacon. “I'm out! Good luck!” Ten seconds later a transparent bubble engulfed him.

The two police officers rounded the corner in time to hear fading laughter and a barely audible pop.

* * * *

Thousands of people lined the streets of Dallas, cheering and waving, as the motorcade slowly cruised through the streets. Four motorcycle officers led the procession, followed by Secret Service vehicles and, several cars back, the Presidential Limousine. President and Mrs. Kennedy sat in raised seats in the back of the limo with Governor and Mrs. Connally right in front of, and below, them. All four waved and smiled at the gathered crowd.

The motorcade turned right off of Main Street at Dealey Plaza. The slow moving turn provided an excellent view to Roberto Esteban and Dennis Lazenby who happened to be standing right at that turn. The two men, like everyone around them, waved at the passing vehicles. Both men cheered with the crowd.

“They’ve made the turn at Houston Street,” Roberto said aloud.

Lazenby nodded, he looked around anxiously, but said nothing.

One block away, Jacob Miller watched as the lead vehicles came into view. “I see them.” He had a good view of the motorcycles as they continued along the route. He turned his head and followed the motorcycles as they passed and stole a glance up and to his left at the Book Depository. He got a quick glimpse of something that moved in a sixth floor window. “He's there.”

Roberto nodded, wrapped his arm around Dennis and smiled. “Roger that.” His tone changed as he turned his attention to his nervous friend. “Relax; it will all be over soon.”

"I know," he said, looking at the ground. "But do you have to kill him? He is the President for God's sake!"

Several nearby onlookers overheard the comment and turned to look at Lazenby. They saw a Hispanic male supporting a pale white man who looked sick. One man muttered, "Damn drug addict," but no one made a move toward the two men.

"We've discussed this, Dennis. We've given you all the information we have on why this has to be done. Don't quit on me now."

"I know what you said," Lazenby replied, shrugging out from under the support of Esteban, "but I can't. I just can't let this happen!"

Lazenby turned away from the Cleaner and headed toward Main Street at a quick walk, pushing his way through the cheering crowd. The crowd seemed to split in some spots and close in on the Texan in others. Dennis Lazenby continued to push his way through.

"I won't help you kill him!" he yelled back over his shoulder as Esteban moved quickly to subdue his Texas guide. Lazenby's trailblazing made the task much simpler and the Cleaner closed the distance within a few yards. Esteban was within arm's reach before Lazenby took off running toward a nearby building screaming frantically about the President.

A half mile away, on the same grassy knoll where Greene and Miller had fought their brief battle, Steven Newkirk/Assassin 22 lay prone. Hiding under a specially designed blanket with 'intelligent' camouflage properties, he looked through the scope of his sniper rifle. The blanket bent light around him and changed colors, allowing him to blend into the knoll.

Newkirk followed the motorcade turn onto Houston Street with his rifle, spotted Esteban and Lazenby briefly, then panned the weapon over to the turn at Elm and spotted Miller. From his vantage point, he did not have a clear view of the School Book Depository.

"Lazenby is loose," he heard Esteban say in his ear and quickly panned the rifle back to his right, barely catching the two running before he lost them behind the freeway overpass supports. The assassin saw three men moving to follow Esteban.

"You've got three men following you. Deal with Lazenby. Now!" the Assassin ordered.

"I'm on it!" Esteban replied.

"They've made the turn onto Elm," Miller's voice interrupted. Newkirk panned the rifle back around and picked up the President's limo. "You've got less than thirty seconds."

"I have the target. Move to assist Roberto." The Assassin took several deep breaths to calm his heartbeat. "Get Lazenby under control," he said under his breath, his voice much steadier. He heard an acknowledgement from Miller but ignored it. He focused all of his attention on John F. Kennedy.

While researching the original Assassination, the team had to determine how to save Governor Connally without altering the fate of the President. The first bullet fired—according to the Warren Commission—killed Connally after passing through the President. The second shot killed Kennedy. The question was how to change the trajectory of the first shot without altering the second.

The team concluded that they needed to shoot Kennedy first, changing his body position enough to allow

Connally to live. The sniper, if he was good, would adjust his second shot to make the kill shot just like the history books told. Newkirk allowed himself a moment of reflection as the seconds ticked down. Would he miss? Was he really the man for the job-a rookie on his first mission? Was there another way to accomplish this mission? He shrugged all of the doubt away and cleared his mind. His timing had to be perfect. There could be no hesitation when the Assassin's watch alarm chimed.

Newkirk stared through the scope at the man riding high in the limo, waving. The assassin adjusted the rifle slightly, took a breath and held it. His watch beeped discreetly and Assassin 22 fired. The rubber bullet arched across the Plaza and bounced off Kennedy's left shoulder, turning him slightly, just as the first bullet fired from the School Book Depository.

The real assassin's bullet tore through Kennedy, hitting Connally in the ribcage and shattering several ribs before exiting and shattering his left wrist. Another shot, a head shot on Kennedy, followed by a third from the Book Depository Building echoed through the Plaza. The once cheering onlookers fled.

Newkirk watched the scene unfold in the Presidential Limo before moving his eyes from the sniper scope. He saw several people looking in his direction, including one nearby police officer. He decided it was time for his exit and he crawled back from the knoll out of sight, dragging his sniper blanket. Once he was clear, he took off running under the Stemmons Freeway, away from the Plaza. He heard shouts and knew that someone was coming up the slope to follow him.

He had only travelled a few hundred yards when he heard the high whining of engines as several vehicles accelerated behind him, entered the onramp above him and finally faded away down the highway. The motorcade was on its way to the hospital.

The Assassin stepped into a side alley away from the interstate, set the rifle's beacon on retrieval mode and wrapped the blanket and his brown jacket around the rifle. A few seconds later, the jacket, the blanket and the rifle within, entered the time stream and slipped back to the Twenty-Third Century. Steven Newkirk walked to a nearby bar and ordered a drink. He took a sip of the strong whiskey, calmed his nerves and briefly wondered if he would make it back to wear his lucky jacket again.

* * * *

Roberto Esteban caught Dennis Lazenby by thumping him on the back and making him crash into a pile of garbage along one side of the deserted alley. Lazenby collapsed in a heap, scraping his hands and his knees as he slid. Esteban overran his victim by a few feet, stopped and turned to face the Texan. Gunshots echoed in the distance.

"It's done!" the Cleaner said. "Now calm down before we both regret it."

"I can't be a part of this anymore!" Lazenby replied. His thoughts jumbled together: *I just killed the President! No, not me...them! I've been a witness. What are these men going to do with me? I need to tell the police.*

"I've got to tell them. Tell them you killed him!" He pointed a finger. "You killed the President!" He turned to flee back up the alley the way they came.

"Three men heading your way," came Miller's voice in his imbedded communicator. "Get out of the alley now!"

Roberto was faster and clipped him again. Once more, Lazenby ended up in the garbage, this time he curled into a fetal position, his panicked mind had shut down.

"I don't have time for this," Roberto said. He sighed as he pulled out a second skip beacon. He looked at the man curled up in the garbage. "Now I know why you said make sure to bring an extra beacon."

Esteban put the extra beacon on Lazenby and clicked the retrieval button. Nothing happened. A quick inspection revealed damage to the cover and the micro-circuitry inside. The Cleaner threw it against the brick wall and shattered it. "Damn!" he yelled. "This is Roberto, I've got Lazenby. Jacob, you have final watch!" Without waiting for acknowledgement, he activated his skip retrieval beacon.

It was risky for two people to travel in the same skip bubble. The system was not calibrated to move two people through at the same time. The Guild allowed it only in the direst of circumstances. It had only been successfully done twice before, a fact foremost in the mind of the Cleaner as the bubble engulfed them.

Esteban remembered his instructions from Professor Donovan and embraced Lazenby tightly. "I hope this works," he said as they disappeared.

* * * *

Two days later, Jack Ruby walked into an underground garage and shot the true assassin, Lee Harvey Oswald, twice in the chest. Jacob Miller and Steven Newkirk watched the drama unfold on the television as they sat in their little apartment. Both men were packed and waiting for the event to occur to ensure that history progressed on its new course.

"Right on time," Newkirk said, reading a summary of the events detailing how they should unfold in the new timeline. "Do you see any discrepancies?"

Miller read through three daily papers, reading all of the articles concerning the assassination, the capture of Oswald, the death of a local policeman at the hands of Oswald, the turmoil in Washington and now, the killing of Oswald by Ruby. "No, everything is on track."

"Then it's time for us to go home." The two men completed a final scrub of the apartment. The only things left were a few fingerprints that would lead nowhere, except to the Twenty-Third Century.

Both men activated their retrieval beacons and less than a minute later both men disappeared into transparent skip bubbles.

Less than fifteen minutes later, Jacob Miller stepped from his bubble sweating and dehydrated. He sat on the waiting gurney, surrounded by medical technicians who began a thorough exam of the returning Cleaner. He took an offered class of water, drained it as he looked around the pristine Control Room. "The Assassin?"

"Already arrived and taken to medical hold, "Esteban replied as he came into view, followed by Tomlinson and then Greene.

"Is he doing ok?"

“Assassin 22 is doing fine. He is one of those rare ones that show no after-effects of the skip,” one of the technicians replied. “We have him under observation and study. If we can determine why he has no adverse reaction to the skip, maybe we can develop some kind of drug that will aid the rest of you.”

Jacob Miller tuned out the technician as he droned on about the possibilities of a new drug. As the medics scurried around him, he laid his head back on the padded stretcher and smiled, he had survived another trip.

* * * *

“What happened to the man—Lazenby?"

Apprentice 101 looked up from his notes, held up one finger, grabbed his water, and gulped the cold liquid to sooth his parched throat. He finished the glass before he answered. “Well, his life was studied and the Council—the Council of some twenty years ago—determined that it was no loss for him to be taken out of his timeline.

“The Guild placed him in the academic facility as an advisor and he became one of the subject matter experts for the 1950s and 1960s era Cleaner Teams. He instructed Assassins and Cleaners for a few years and assisted in three other missions in that era, including actually skipping back to provide on-sight assistance to prevent an Assassination in England in 1953.

“After that skip, his records were sealed. I—I couldn't find out anything else about him.”

“What about the rest of the team?” Apprentice 95 asked. He had been one of the few students who had been completely engrossed by the discussion. Apprentice 95 had already given his presentation about an Indonesian Dictator in 2211 that had been saved by Assassin 88. With no other distractions, he had thoroughly enjoyed someone else in the hot seat.

"I didn't research their other missions, or the rest of their careers," Apprentice 101 replied. He turned to Mr. Donovan. "Sir, do you know what happened to the Cleaner Team?"

The look on his face told the instructor that he did know, but he wanted to ensure it was proper to discuss non-assigned missions. Mr. Donovan smiled, slapped his thighs as he rose from his chair, and nodded to the Apprentice. Apprentice 101 stepped aside and Mr. Donovan took the podium.

"Mr. Esteban, the team leader, was reprimanded and taken off active duty for bringing Mr. Lazenby back to the Twenty-Third Century. He was later re-instated and completed his career with honors.

"Mr. Greene retired last year, after thirty years of service to the Guild and over a dozen missions. He is currently a consultant to the Guild and a substitute instructor on Time-Skip Mechanics. Some of you may see him in your third year.

"Mr. Miller was killed on his very next mission. A very sad, very avoidable accident." Mr. Donovan noticed one of the other students—one of the borderline students—making a mocking face as he discussed the death of the Cleaner. "Apprentice 111, you will prepare a ten thousand word report, due tomorrow, on what happened on that mission and, in particular, Mr. Miller."

A groan sounded as acknowledgement of the assignment.

"Sir, what about Mr. Lazenby? Apprentice 101 said his records were sealed. Do you know what happened?" Apprentice 95 was persistent in his questioning.

Donovan sighed. "Due to his new status as consultant, he decided to change his name to avoid issues with students studying this case study. He actually took his mother's maiden name and became one of the instructors here in the academic wing. He has been teaching here for fifteen years." He then cracked a smile. "And the students love him!"

"Can you tell us who he is?"

"Guild law prohibits that information from being released, but I will say this, at some point in your academic career, you will be in one of his classes."

Chapter Seven

THE TRAIN PUFFED BLACK smoke into the clear blue sky. Its engines turned the wheels that carried the engine, the cargo and the passengers eastward. The engine, plus the nine cars, cruised away from the setting sun, heading toward the dark of night. Train stewards walked along the swaying corridors, lighting lamps to guide the passengers as they moved from car to car. Most of the passengers seemed to be making their way toward the dining car.

The rugged mountains of Colorado gradually gave way to the flat plains of Kansas. The wondrous beauty of infant America was lost on Rick Brewer. He had seen it before. The stranded time traveler sat, his tan Stetson pulled down, pretending to sleep. A fancy-dressed, pudgy, East Coast man, who shared his small cabin, continuously prattled on about nothing. He pulled the hat down a little further as the man rambled on about how his ancestors were part of the Boston Tea Party some hundred years earlier.

Brewer found his gloved hand resting on the butt of his pistol and his thoughts drifted to the idea of shooting the man. *At least it will be quieter in prison.* By shear will, he resisted the urge to draw the pistol and was rewarded by a moment of silence.

Another voice filled the air.

"Is this seat taken?"

Brewer raised his Stetson, allowing his dark hair to hang down and looked into the pale green eyes of a young, twenty-something blonde. His posture immediately straightened as he made room for the newcomer.

"No ma'am," he said in his best, and well-practiced, southern drawl.

"Thank you," came the reply as she moved to sit opposite the assassin.

The young woman wore a light green dress, adorned with small flowers along the hemline, with a white shawl and ruffled head cap. She smiled innocently as she sat. Her eyes darted to the window and the waning light. Brewer could see that she was far from home and mesmerized by the vastness of the world. The East Coast man sat in silence, also quietly eyeing the young lady. After a few minutes of awkward, yet blissful, silence, the older man started back into his family history and their involvement in the insurance industry since the mid-1700s. Brewer grunted, a little louder than he wanted, but the insurance salesman continued his family history. Brewer pulled his Stetson back down.

"How did you get your scar?" the young lady asked, interrupting the history lesson. The assassin sat back up, raised his Stetson and showed the discolored scar that led from his left ear halfway down his cheek. He opened his mouth to speak.

"Young miss," the insurance salesman began, "it is not polite to interrupt."

"It's quite alright," Brewer interrupted the man with a smile. He pointed to the left side of his face as he faced the young lady again. "This scar is compliments of a Japanese Katana —a short sword. The man wielding it did not like it that a *gaijin*—foreigner—was on Japanese soil."

The young woman's face lit up and her voice went shrill. "You've been to Japan? What was it like? Are they really savages? Do they really commit suicide for failure?"

The assassin held up a hand. "Slow down, Miss. There is plenty of time to tell you about Japan before we get to New York."

The young lady took a breath to calm her excitement and smiled, looking from the assassin to the salesman and back. Brewer took a moment and reassessed her age to eighteen or nineteen, instead of the twenty-something he had originally thought. The insurance salesman realized his audience was lost, gave out a grunt of his own, folded his arms and sat back beside the young lady with an angry look on his face.

The assassin took the young woman's hand and looked into her eyes. "It was ten years ago. I was assigned to Commodore Perry's expedition to open trade relations with Japan..."

* * * *

Smoke poured from the smokestacks and headed for the cloudy skies of July 1853. The fleet of four warships cut through the relatively calm waters of Edo as thousands of onlookers lined the shore to stare in awe at the giant dragons puffing smoke.

Commodore Perry, a graying sixty-year old veteran of the US Navy, stood on the bridge of the USS Powhatan and ordered the fleet to drop anchor. Rick Brewer, the political liaison assigned to the fleet from the Department of State, stood off to the left of the Commodore, well away from the Navy crew as they suddenly sprang into activity at the barked orders.

“Man those lines!” the Commodore yelled, pointing to the starboard side of the ship. “And get the anchor down, we are beginning to drift!”

The crew hastened to follow the Commodore's directions. The waters in the harbor began to calm as the vessels dropped anchor. The ships released massive steam vents that brought wails of fear from the Japanese who had lined the coast.

The Commodore could see that the Japanese were already reacting to the presence of the American Warships. A small flotilla of vessels rowed out to meet the fleet.

“Translator!” called the Commodore. “Looks like it's time for you to go to work.”

* * * *

The first men to come aboard wore traditional Japanese clothing, their heads shaved except for a tuft of hair held high on their head in a top knot. They approached the boat and the sailors with extreme caution, looking around nervously with their hands on the hilts of their swords. The two samurai's eyes constantly scanned the deck and the sailors. Their eyes immediately locked onto Rick Brewer, who was the only man not dressed like the others, as he descended the exterior stairs from the bridge.

Dressed in a conservative gray suit and black bowler hat, Brewer sported a slick handlebar mustache. He scanned the Japanese coastline as he descended the stairs, awestruck at what would become Tokyo. The beautiful, unpolluted coast stood in stark contrast to the Twenty-Third Century Japan that lay in ruins.

His eyes fell on the two Japanese men and the assassin bowed, as was the custom, and greeted them in Japanese. Their eyes widened in obvious surprise that the *gaijin* knew their language. After the initial shock wore off, they began a tirade of words and gestures. Brewer nodded then turned to the Commodore who had joined the men on the deck.

"Our guests are requesting we remove our ships from Edo, and go to Nagasaki."

The Commodore grunted a laugh and shook his head no. "Tell them we come on a peaceful mission and wish to meet with their Emperor. Tell them that we bring a message of friendship from the President of the United States."

Brewer translated and received a flurry of words in return. "They insist that we must move our ships. That's all they keep saying, over and over."

"Tell them we wish to meet with the Emperor or his representative and that we will not move our vessels until we do."

Another flurry of words.

Rick Brewer turned to the Commodore and shook his head.

“Please escort them from my deck.”

* * * *

“That's when one of the men pulled his sword and gave me a little reminder that we were on their soil, so to speak.”

“You poor man,” came the sympathetic reply from the young woman. “What happened then?”

“Well, they were escorted from the ship and I was sent down below to see the Doc. It took almost eight months, but we finally got the treaty that we were sent to get.” Brewer smiled at that. He had been a part of history, and had set Japan on its course to bring America into World War II, less than a hundred years later.

“Did you ever see the man who cut you again?” The young lady had moved closer to examine the scar. Brewer got a good whiff of her perfume and took a deep breath.

“Yes, actually,” he said, leaning back to clear his head of the intoxicating aroma. “We eventually became good friends. I taught him how to shoot and he taught me how to use a sword. We sparred quiet frequently up to the time I left in May of 1854.”

“That's an incredible story.”

“Yes,” came the disbelieving tone of the insurance salesman, who still sat with his arms crossed. “Incredible.” He lowered his hat, as Brewer had done, to show his dissatisfaction.

The green-eyed woman shot him a hostile look and then turned back to the assassin. “Are you still with the Department of State?”

Brewer looked out the window, partly at the young woman's reflection and partly at the darkening countryside. “No, I left that job shortly after my return to America. I wanted to explore the west again. A lot of territory has opened up since the last time I was out there.”

“You had been out west before you went to Japan?”

“I was in California in 1849; the Gold Rush,” he turned back from the window and winked at the salesman, who still observed the two under his lowered hat. “I was a Sherriff in the Colorado territory for a while, became bored with that and decided to have a little fun, so I robbed a bank.”

The salesman groaned and pulled his hat even lower as the young woman let her excitement take hold again. She squealed in delight. “A diplomat, a lawman, and a bank robber! How exciting!”

Brewer knew he had an audience, so he continued. “I even robbed a train! That was quite fun, so I did it again! But, I almost got caught that time and took a bullet to my right shoulder, so I decided being a bandit wasn't as much fun as I thought. I gave up my life of crime and headed back East to the Department of State translator position.

“But, enough about me, young lady,” the assassin eyed the girl with interest. “What about you? Why are you heading east all alone?”

“I'm heading to college at Columbia University,” she said proudly. “I'm going to be a lawyer!”

Another grunt by the salesman. “A woman lawyer? Indeed!”

Both Brewer and the young lady ignored him. “Your parents must be proud of you to be accepted to such a prestigious university!”

She nodded. “My father always wanted me to have an Ivy League education.”

Brewer nodded, but the salesman raised his hat and looked confused. “A what?”

“An Ivy Leag—” the young lady stopped in mid-sentence, looked thoughtful for a moment and a flush of panic crossed her face. “Will you excuse me, please?” she asked as she stood.

Brewer looked at her skeptically, “Of course, Miss...”

“Donovan,” she said and left the car heading toward the rear of the train.

“Donovan?”

Rick Brewer replayed the conversation in his mind. He was up and running after the girl a moment later. The rogue assassin ran all the way to the end of the train. He searched in every compartment and room but he could not find the girl.

Somewhere, in the back of his mind, while he searched, he was sure that he had heard a barely audible pop.

* * * *

“I screwed up.”

Apprentice 97 stood in the skip control room, out of breath, disheveled and sweaty, hugging Apprentice 101. She was nearly in tears. Professor Donovan, Master Li and

Mr. Tomlinson stood nearby, waiting for the embrace to end while the technicians shut down the retrieval system. The five-person group moved to a nearby conference table, out of earshot of everyone in the skip room.

"Apprentice, your report, please," Donovan finally said, after the embrace went on for nearly a minute. Master Li made a comment under his breath about forbidding romance between the students that earned him an elbow from Tomlinson.

"I made contact with the man that Apprentice 101 had researched and determined could be your lost apprentice," she said, regaining her self-control and the confidence she always had on display. "After talking with him, I believe that he is your apprentice, Richard Brewer," she ended, nodding her head.

That statement raised a few eyebrows and Apprentice 101 received several nods and even a pat on the back from Donovan. The young Apprentice nodded and remembered weeks of mind-numbing research-hints of a man matching Brewer's description all over the world-to find any evidence of the rogue assassin. The only solid leads were of the State Department Mission to Japan and a verified sighting in Washington, DC in 1864. It was guesswork and a series of quick skips to determine which route Brewer had taken across country.

"What did you discuss?" asked the gruff Master Li.

"I asked him about a scar he had. He told me that he got it while on an expedition in Japan in 1853. There was a little more small talk about his travels before Japan, but nothing significant. He did some small time criminal activity and spent some time in law enforcement."

“Apprentice 101,” Mr. Donovan intervened and turned toward the Apprentice. “Research lawmen in the 1840s and 1850s, see what you can find.” The professor turned back to Apprentice 97. “Please continue.”

The woman nodded. “He asked what I was doing on the train, and we talked briefly about my going to college. I said I was on my way to Columbia, an Ivy League School—”

Mr. Donovan held up his hand, interrupting the report. “You said 'Ivy League'?”

She nodded.

“Damn, that tipped him off, didn't it?”

She looked a little confused. “I don't think so.” She shook her head. “What made me think there was something wrong was the other man in the compartment. The other man asked what the 'Ivy League' was, and he was from the East Coast.

“After he did that, I thought I might have made a mistake, so I got up to leave, and that's when he asked me my name.” She shivered visibly. “I told him Donovan. That's when he got up to chase me. I knew I was in trouble so I hid, activated my beacon, and escaped.”

Mr. Donovan looked thoughtful. “Did you discuss his future plans?”

“No, sir.”

Apprentice 101 spoke up for the first time. “What was so significant about 'Ivy League'?”

He turned to look at the Apprentice. “The Ivy League phrase was not coined until the 1930s, Apprentice,” Mr. Donovan said in a tired and frustrated tone. “My apprentice—”

“Former apprentice.”

"Yes, thank you, Master Li. My former Apprentice may not have known that fact, but a man from 1860 would not have recognized the phrase. When he voiced his puzzlement, it raised Brewer's suspicion.

"You did the right thing, Apprentice," the Professor said, turning back to Apprentice 97. "Now, go and rest. Understand that you are not to discuss this mission or the skip with anyone outside of this group."

"Yes, sir. Sorry, sir."

"There is nothing to apologize for," came the nurturing reply. "You accomplished your mission," Professor Donovan smiled. "You positively identified the mark and lived to report back. That is a success!" He spread his arms as he spoke, a reassuring gesture that did not quite work.

Apprentice 97 nodded, turned and slowly walked away. Apprentice 101 stood unmoving, not sure if he was also dismissed. "Continue your research; find out what else Richard has done. Find out how much he has tampered with the timeline, if any. But do it tomorrow," Donovan said, motioning toward the young woman walking away. "Go to her. She needs you."

Apprentice 101 nodded, half bowed to Master Li and hurried down the hall. The trio of men watched them disappear around a far corner.

"He has been good for her. She has really opened up since he was admitted into the Guild. Without his friendship, I feel she would never be a truly effective assassin."

Master Li grunted his agreement as Donovan spoke. "We thought she might have problems, coming from the environment she grew up in. She had the psyche of an assassin, but I wasn't sure if she had the ability to overcome her inner-demons. Apprentice 101 seems to have removed some of the bitterness from her."

"I hope sending her on this expedition doesn't make her regress. She is taking this as a failure when she really did quite well," Tomlinson replied as he poured himself a drink. He offered the bottle to his companions. Donovan nodded while Master Li held up his hand and shook his head.

"I still think we should forbid student romances," the martial arts instructor opined. "This will end in tragedy for someone." There was no response and the room quieted.

Tomlinson was the one to break the silence. "Is this renegade going to be a problem?"

"I'm not sure, yet, Mr. Tomlinson," the Professor replied. "But we need to watch this situation carefully. If he is just living his life, so be it. But if he starts interfering with the timeline, we will have to deal with him."

Master Li gave another grunt. "He was banished from the Guild and sentenced to death." He turned to leave the control room with an accusing stare at Donovan. "He should be dealt with anyway."

* * * *

"Are you okay?"

Apprentice 101 knew it was a stupid thing to ask, but he had no other way to get Apprentice 97 to open up. They continued through the maze of corridors toward the living quarter's wing of the Academy.

"I will be," she said, smiling at the boy that held her hand. "I have never been so scared." She shook her head. "I just need a little time."

"What did Professor Donovan say to you?"

Apprentice 101 let her change the subject. "He told me to keep tracking Brewer...and to take care of you." He smiled.

She returned the smile, squeezed his hand, but said nothing. After walking the corridors for several minutes, they arrived at her door. He took her hands into his and stood there looking at her. She needed the quiet support.

Apprentice 97 had never had anyone truly care for her before. She grew up in a series of orphanages and foster homes, with uncaring people more interested in slave labor than caring for the children in their care. Her last foster father had beaten one of her siblings into a coma and threatened to do the same with her. She had beaten him nearly to death while he slept.

The Guild, through its Government contacts, had spared the girl a prison sentence and indoctrinated her into the fold, hoping to harness the rage and instill a sense of purpose; two of the aspects of a good assassin. No one told her the price of failure if she did not meet the standards of the Guild. She had figured that part out on her own right before she had met the man standing before her, holding her hands and watching her intently.

She had finally found that piece that she had always been missing: compassion.

She kissed him. "Thank you," she said, turned toward her door and stopped. She turned back to him and kissed him again. "I love you."

It was the first time she had ever spoken those words to anyone.

Chapter Eight

RICK BREWER SAT AND stared out of the window of his hotel room in Washington, DC, watching the rain turn the dirt streets into a giant mud puddle. He could see the construction of the Washington Monument in the distance; the scaffolding and materials soaked in the downpour. He stared at his reflection in the window and thought about the last two weeks. He could not get the encounter with the green-eyed woman out of his mind.

He had spent the better part of an hour exploring every nook and corner of the train before giving up. The assassin had returned to the compartment, and to the salesman who had immediately started back telling his family history. Brewer killed him with a single punch to the throat and then threw his body out of the window without so much as a second thought. It was only after the train had reached New York that he realized what he had done. He found it did not bother him in the least.

The assassin had scoured the train station looking for anyone who resembled the young lady, but finally let it go.

His mind kept telling him that he had heard the closure of a time skip bubble, but he refused to accept that the Guild would send someone back in time just to make small talk. Either he had mistakenly thought he had heard a transport bubble, or the Guild was trying to carry out his sentence.

In either case, he had more important things to do than worry about a Guild three hundred years in the future.

From New York, he had taken a stagecoach to Washington where he now sat, watching the rain. He absentmindedly toyed with a piece of paper in his hand as he stared out the window. The piece of paper was hard to come by in Washington. It was a ticket for the play *Our American Cousin* on April 14. Rick Brewer was in DC to watch Abraham Lincoln die.

* * * *

Ford's Theater was filled with the well dressed and affluent. The rich and the want-to-be rich were out en mass. The formally attired patrons were loud and boisterous, not because of the impending show, but more for the fact that the President and Mrs. Lincoln would be attending the evening's performance. All of Washington, DC, had heard of the Presidential presence. The cast and crew of *Our American Cousin* were nervous and anxious.

Rick Brewer sat in the floor seats on the left side of the concert hall, opposite the balcony where President Lincoln would sit—if he would ever get there. Dressed in a black suit, like most of the other men in the theater, with his black bowler in his lap, he had shaved his big mustache after the incident on the train. He had even gotten his long, rugged, Western look haircut to a more traditional, East Coast look; short and well trimmed.

Set to the front, the stage had a deep orchestra pit separating it from the audience. The seats were arranged in rows of twelve in an amphitheater style, with a set of six balconies, three on either side of the auditorium. Brewer could only see four exits: one door on either side of the stage and the main doors in the rear of the theater and one set on either side at the rear of the theater.

Brewer took all of that information in with a glance; a moment of scouting the theater as he and the crowd waited for the President to arrive. There had been a persistent rumor all day that Lincoln would cancel his appearance, but the banished assassin knew that would not happen.

The crowd erupted in applause as the President arrived, flanked by his three-man security detail. Brewer took a moment to look for other security, saw only one other man—in the back of the theater—that watched the crowd instead of the President. *That makes four*, Brewer thought as he continued to clap with the rest of the audience. He desperately tried to recall his history lessons on how many security guards where actually there. Not that it mattered. He was only there to watch, this time.

The President took his time waving and greeting the patrons on the ground floor before he finally ascended the stairs and made his way to his private balcony. A few minutes later, the play began. Rick Brewer checked his watch, an old-fashioned, silver pocket watch with a long chain attached to his vest. He tried once again to recall his history lessons on exactly when the assassination was to take place. The details escaped him, so he continued to watch the balcony across the hall.

Midway through the first act, Brewer took in the scene with another quick look around the theater. Most of the crowd watched the play, with a few stealing glances at the Presidential balcony. The rogue spied the bodyguard in the rear of the theater and realized that the man had focused his attention on the assassin, staring at him intently. Brewer decided to pay a little more attention to the play.

At the end of the first act, Brewer took a moment to stretch and stole a glance toward the bodyguard in the rear of the auditorium. The man stared directly at the renegade assassin. Unnerved at the undue attention, Brewer turned his attention to the balcony where the President sat. Lincoln stood, stretched, and waved at the mass of people in the theater below. The crowd again cheered and applauded.

As the second act began, Brewer stole another quick peek at the security guard in the back of the theater and confirmed that he had the man's undivided attention. Brewer once again verified there were only four routes out of the theater, and realized the bodyguard sat right in between two of them. Brewer sighed and turned back to the stage. He would have to take his leave when the shooting started.

The second act came and went with little fanfare, other than the normal applause. The Time Assassin continued his occasional glimpses behind him and across the theater. Nothing had changed. He checked his watch again; it was just before ten pm.

* * * *

Assassin 46 sat quietly in the back of the theater. It had taken the Assassin almost the entire first act to identify the man on the left side of the theater as the rogue, Richard Brewer. Assassin 46 had spent the entire second act doing a visual recon of the theater and felt confident that he could stop Richard Brewer from interfering with the assassination.

Dressed in a formal black suit circa 1865, Assassin 46 had blended into the crowd, mingled for a while, then made his way to his current vantage point; a place where he could see the entire theater with the exception of the balcony seats. As he continued to watch his target, he felt that Brewer knew he was there due to the increasing frequency of glances in his direction. At the start of the third act, Assassin 46 decided to move closer to the man he identified as Brewer. He wanted to have a better angle of attack if the rogue interjected himself in the assassination.

Assassin 46 knew there was a Cleaner Team in the theater, here to document the assassination for the archives, but he did not know who they were. The assassin let an evil grin creep onto his face. *They won't see this coming*, he thought as he proceeded quietly down the outside aisle to a point less than fifteen feet behind where Brewer sat.

His watch read 10:10.

Not long now.

* * * *

A few minutes into the third act, Brewer again glanced toward the back of the theater to check on the security guard. The security man was not there. The renegade jumped out of his seat and looked around in a near panic. It took two double takes before he recognized the man only a few rows back. Brewer saw the man rise from his seat. The gunman's right hand was on his holstered six-shooter. Brewer instinctively dashed away from the man and toward the stage. As he ran, he heard a shot ring out from the Presidential Balcony and then a woman screamed. Brewer cursed silently, he had missed it.

The rogue assassin made it to the orchestra pit as the crowd stood and headed for the exits. He pushed a trombone player out of his way, shoved a tuba player into a trumpet player and was halfway through the musicians when John Wilkes Booth dropped from the balcony, smoking Derringer still in his hand.

Booth landed hard, tangling in a US Treasury Flag that hung on the outside of the Presidential balcony. Lincoln's assassin screamed in pain over his broken leg. Brewer thought he heard the snap of the leg, but the panicked screams of the crowd drowned out just about everything around him. He lowered himself and duck walked the rest of his way through the orchestra pit.

Booth stood and unwrapped himself from the flag, looked at the panicked crowd, and yelled, "*Sic Semper Tyrannis*!" before he jumped from the stage and limped from the theater out one of the rear exits.

The audience was up and moving toward the exits in a near panic, jostling, pushing, and shoving in an effort to get away from the man who had killed Lincoln. In the chaos, no one went after Booth. Assassin 46 lost his target when Booth jumped to the stage, startling him as his attention was squarely on Brewer. Assassin 46 drew his pistol and thought about shooting Booth, but dismissed the idea and re-holstered the weapon. Brewer had done enough to the timeline for one night, and Assassin 46 did not want to risk changing things any further.

Rick Brewer faintly heard the yell from behind him and knew that Booth had yelled *'Thus always to Tyrants*!" in Latin. He had no time to ponder the history he had almost witnessed. However, he had to get out of the theater and away from the security guard. Brewer allowed the crowd to carry him out of the theater. Once outside, he dislodged himself from the masses and ran down a nearby alley, disappearing into the night.

Assassin 46 joined the crowd and made his way out of the theater. Once outside, the Assassin began a systematic study of every face outside the theater, but did not find his target.

"Damn it!" he said aloud. Several nearby theater patrons expressed the same sentiment, but for a very different reasons. President Lincoln was dead.

A man approached from the crowd and Assassin 46 recognized him as one of the Cleaners. He did not know his name, but he had seen the man in the Guild before. The Assassin waved off the Cleaner, he did not want to get into a conversation about the night's events. The Assassin turned away from the man without a word and continued his search. After searching for another half hour, Assassin 46 made his way to the back of a nearby building, away from the crowd.

He stood and gazed at the stars in the sky for a moment. He could not see any stars back home because of interference from city lights, so he took it all in. It was a tradition that Assassin 46 always cherished. It gave him closure after a mission. The Assassin then activated his Skip Beacon and disappeared into his transport bubble.

Rick Brewer, hiding less than two hundred feet away, watched the man disappear and knew that he had narrowly escaped his death sentence. He also knew that the Guild, from three hundred years in the future, was indeed watching. Two visits in less than a month. The rogue assassin made a mental note to pay a little more attention to the people who entered his life from now on.

He stood in the field and stared up at the night sky. Just as the stars provided closure for Assassin 46, the stars created a fire in Rick Brewer that grew with each passing moment. He clenched and unclenched his fists for a full minute before shaking his right fist at the sky.

"Fine!" he said to the stars. "You wanna watch me! Fine! Watch what happens now!"

* * * *

"Brewer escaped the theater," Professor Donovan said. "Have you been able to pick up his trail again?"

The professor stood at the end of an oblong conference table addressing the small group gathered there. Apprentice 101 sat to the left, with Apprentice 97 by his side. Mr. Tomlinson and Master Li sat on the right, and Assassin 46 sat at the opposite end of the table from Donovan.

The six-person team assembled in secret, in an attempt to locate the banished assassin and, if feasible, eliminate him. Professor Donovan wanted to keep it from the Council as long as possible. Master Li had protested, saying the Council should be informed of any potential threat to timeline stability, but the Professor insisted, knowing that the Council already frowned upon his sideline activities. Master Li had reluctantly agreed.

"I think so, sir," Apprentice 101 replied, inserting a memory crystal into the reader. "In conjunction with the report from Assassin 46, I researched the Cleaner team report. They are pretty much identical except for one detail. The Cleaner team reports that a man, matching the description of Brewer, was seen in a field a few hundred yards from the theater, yelling up at the night sky. None of the team were close enough to hear what was said," he paused, "and they didn't know he was a person of interest so they didn't pursue.

"The Cleaner Team is quite displeased about not knowing that Assassin 46 was in there on a separate mission and have filed an official protest which, luckily, had to go through Mr. Tomlinson's office."

"Continue, Apprentice." Donovan motioned with his right hand.

"His name, or description, pops up occasionally in the public archives from 1865 until 1881. He disappeared after President Garfield was assassinated."

"Is there a connection?" asked Tomlinson.

"Nothing direct, sir," the apprentice reported, scratching his head as he looked over his hand-written notes. "The assassin—Charles Guiteau—was a disgruntled man who had been refused a federal job by the President. However, from what I have gathered from Garfield's staff archives, Brewer did work in the White House and may have told Garfield not to hire the man, knowing that the man was unstable and might kill the President."

"So Brewer is killing by proxy?"

"In some cases, yes," the apprentice replied. "In some cases, as with President Harrison in 1840, he carried it out himself."

"You have confirmed that President Harrison died by Brewer's hand?"

The apprentice nodded. "I went back to the medical archives. President Harrison died of flu-induced pneumonia. That particular strain of the flu didn't develop until the 1980s."

"Okay, so how, or why, did Brewer pick Guiteau? I mean, our timeline indicates that Garfield died in September of 1881 anyway!" stated Donovan.

"How did he die originally?" Tomlinson asked.

"He was thrown from a horse and died from a head injury," Assassin 46 answered.

"Guiteau was delusional, so he was a prime candidate to maneuver into position and plant the right suggestion." Apprentice 97 answered the professor's question.

"The more I research Brewer, the more I think he is trying to make a statement," Apprentice 101 said with a touch of envy and respect in his voice. He quickly blocked the tone, looked back at his notes and continued. "He disappeared from 1883 until 1898; no record of him anywhere. I think he might have changed his name for a while. I've asked Apprentice 97 to assist with that research.

"In 1900 he reappears, almost as if he wanted us to find him. I cannot, as of yet, find a link between him and President McKinley who was assassinated in 1901, but we are continuing to research that possibility. McKinley's Assassination was part of our own timeline so I believe Brewer was there just to show us that, like Lincoln, he could be there. The pattern continues after that. Brewer drops from sight for at least a decade and then reappears right before any Presidential death."

"How long does this pattern last?" asked Tomlinson, who had a look of fear and disbelief on his face.

"I've researched as far as the 1960s. The initial report I read from Mr. Greene indicates that he might have seen Brewer in the crowd. In fact, Greene now thinks that Brewer was one of the three men that followed you and Cleaner Esteban into the alley."

Professor Donovan visibly gulped, knowing that he had barely escaped that crowd and, if Brewer was one of those men, he probably escaped being beaten to death. The room dropped into an uneasy silence.

"If he had killed me in 1963, we would have never met here in the Guild. He may have never been caught with the archives and never banished, which means he would not have been in 1963 to kill me." Donovan shook his head. "What a twist to the timeline that would be!"

"How is he not aging?" asked Apprentice 97. "That's over one hundred and twenty years, and when I saw him in 1865 he was still a young man."

"He had not yet undergone any conditioning when he threw himself into the time-stream," Mr. Tomlinson replied, staring at the young woman. "Like the injections that you received before your skip several weeks ago." Apprentice 97 nodded and the Skip Supervisor continued.

"Since his body was not prepared, he now ages slowly, if at all. I suspect if he were to catch up to the Twenty-Third Century he would resume his normal aging."

"You're saying he doesn't age because he is not in his correct time?" asked Apprentice 97.

"It's one theory," nodded Tomlinson. He snapped his fingers. "There is one other possibility. We've seen it before, mmm, twice, I believe." He stared at a spot over Apprentice 97's head, deep in thought.

"What have you seen twice before?" Master Li asked.

"Some people have a 'sixth' sense when it comes to time. They can sense when something changes in the timeline. It's a kind of déjà vu.

"Assassins 33 and 69 had that ability. They also did not age while on mission. Assassin 69 spent 17 months tracking down a Columbian General in the 2170s. When he returned he had literally not aged a day. His hair did not even grow while deployed. The Cleaner team that was with him, by contrast, had aged normally."

Silence again gripped the room as everyone pondered the information. Professor Donovan broke the quiet. "Whether he is aging or not, we need to track him. Since we know that he had nothing to do with Kennedy's death, skip ahead to 1980. Find out if he was there when the Guild killed the 40th President."

Chapter Nine

RICK BREWER WAS BORED.

Again.

It happened every twenty to thirty years. The banished assassin would grow bored with his life and feel the urge to intervene in history. On occasion, he would dabble in Presidential politics—such as killing Harrison. Other times he would simply find a pivotal moment in history and, as he liked to say, 'tweak it.'

The last time he had intervened was 1922, when he had guided a team of archeologists to the tomb of King Tut. Brewer owed Lord Carnarvon, the leader of the expedition, because he had lost a bet over the outcome of a battle in World War One. Brewer had to pay with something big. The renegade assassin had forgotten that the battle in question was won by the Allied forces. Ironically, it was a battle in which he had fought.

Without Brewer's guidance, the expedition would have missed the antechamber and King Tut would not have been discovered for another thirty years. Brewer had felt a touch of déjà vu over the whole ordeal and wondered if the Guild had also decided to tweak a little history.

Before that, it was 1896 when he helped Henry Ford finish the first gas-powered automobile. That allowed Ford to have the first successful engine instead of Milton Longfellow, who was working on the same type of engine.

Longfellow owed the assassin money from a poker game and would not pay, so Brewer had once again 'tweaked' history. Brewer's intervention in history ensured Ford's fame and Longfellow's obscurity, and eventual death: drunk, broke and alone.

In the early summer of 1944, with war waging throughout Europe and the Pacific, Brewer once again found himself bored. Even though he was working as a double agent for both the Allied and the Axis Forces, he felt the old impulse to help history along its path. The rogue continually provided both sides with accurate, but old and therefore worthless, information. He made quite a fortune providing secrets that he knew from his studies in history, but even with all of that, it was not quite enough to occupy his mind. He wanted to do something big to leave his mark on history.

On June 6th, 1944, Brewer leaked to the German High Command that a massive invasion force was on its way; but failed to tell the German's exactly when it would arrive. The Allied invasion was already well underway before the Germans could even begin to mass a counter-attack. Brewer's timing was perfect. He gained favor with the Axis powers without actually changing history. He did not want the Nazi's to take over, that would put his own life in jeopardy, but he did like to walk that fine line. The rogue assassin felt exhilarated by his success.

Sometimes, almost changing history was enough, he thought.

It was the catalyst he was looking for. Within days, he was summoned to Berlin.

He arrived in Poland, via Zeppelin, on the 26th of June, 1944, as the Allied Forces continued to advance across France. A Gestapo Major and two Sergeants met him at the foot of the Airship's ramp. Pleasantries exchanged, the men entered a nearby open air car and left the airfield. Brewer turned to get a better look at the airfield and its half dozen Zeppelins.

If memory serves, an Allied air raid will destroy all this the day after tomorrow, he thought. He made a mental note to be on the other side of the city at that time.

The four men rode in silence through the outskirts of the city and finally out into the pristine countryside. Other than the humming of the engine and the whistling of the wind through the open car, the only other sound was the consistent buzz of Messerschmitt BF 109s on patrol.

The Major broke the beautiful, serene day as they neared *Wolfsscharize*. "Tell me again, Herr Brewer, why you should have an audience with the Fuhrer?"

Brewer smiled as yet another 109 roared overhead. He knew the Gestapo Officer attempted to get the assassin to change his story. "I've already told you, Major." He sat and folded his arms, staring absently at the blue sky. "I have information on a plot to kill the Fuhrer."

The car stopped at the first of three security checkpoints. A dozen guards, both on the ground and in towers, razor wire topped eight-foot high fences and two machine gun nests marked the outer defense of the Wolf's

Lair. After a brief inspection of IDs and crisp salutes, the car was allowed through.

The Major picked up the conversation. “I receive information on a plot to kill him daily. Why is yours so important as to gain you a private audience?”

“I can provide a date and time for the next attempt,” Brewer smiled, “and how to prevent it.”

The conversation came to a halt by a second checkpoint; a brief stop with more guards and machine guns. A few minutes later, the driver stopped the car outside of the bunker complex that served as Adolf Hitler's Eastern Front Military Headquarters. The complex, located in Northern Poland, was in a heavily wooded area and held a number of bunkers fortified with six-foot thick steel reinforced concrete along with a dozen other less fortified buildings. The Wolf's Lair spread out over two and a half square miles with fences, guard towers and roving patrols. It was Hitler's home away from Berlin.

The Gestapo Major, one of the Sergeants, and Brewer were escorted from the car down a long winding tunnel into the bowels of the Wolf's Lair, to the inner sanctum, and the final checkpoint. Another check of IDs, under the watchful eye of two soldiers armed with submachine guns, and the trio was finally allowed inside.

The Major picked up the conversation yet again. “Provide the information to me, Herr Brewer,” he said in English with a heavy accent, “and you won't have to waste any more of your time.”

“It's not a waste, Herr Major,” Brewer replied in German. He wore a polite smile as he took a seat in the antechamber of Hitler's stateroom. The Sergeant took up a position near the door, his hand on his holstered sidearm, his eyes watching the two men. The Major grabbed a cup of coffee from a nearby carafe before sitting opposite the rogue assassin. The Major sipped his coffee and simply stared at the man across the table. Brewer matched the glare and the room grew silent.

The uncomfortable silence grew for over five minutes before the stateroom door opened and Adolf Hitler entered the room, with his head of the SS, Heinrich Himmler, the Nazi Press Chief, Otto Dietrich, and several other top German officials in tow. The Major and Brewer jumped to their feet while the Sergeant at the door almost broke his back standing even straighter. The Fuhrer looked at each man in turn and then motioned for the Gestapo Major and Brewer to follow him into the private conference chamber.

Brewer allowed them to lead him into the conference room where, unless he changed history, Hitler would die in a little over three weeks.

“I'm told you have information as to yet another attempt on my life,” Hitler began as the group sat down in his conference room. Dressed in his customary brown uniform, his black hair cut short and his mustache trimmed just so, Brewer thought he was even more comical in person that in the history books. He fought back a laugh.

“Ja, mien Fuhrer,” he said. He made a show of producing a small leather briefcase and shuffled through a stack of papers before finding the one he wanted. Of course, he had known exactly where the page was, but he wanted to be theatrical.

He skimmed the paper with his finger before stopping halfway down the page. He thumped the page with the finger to demonstrate he found what he was looking for. "My sources indicate that an attempt will be made to kill you on the 11th of July." He looked up."You and Herr Himmler."

"Why both?" asked the Gestapo Major.

"The resistance is concerned that if the Fuhrer is killed, the Chief of the SS will step in to continue his work."

"A reasonable assumption," replied Dietrich, writing everything down. He looked up at the silence that gripped the room, saw the dangerous look from Hitler, smiled weakly and lowered his head to keep writing. He folded another page in his notebook, touched his lead pencil to his tongue, and then continued to scribble on the paper.

"If you are correct, how do we stop the attempt?" asked the Major.

"Simple, you separate the Fuhrer and the SS Chief for a few days leading up to the eleventh and a few days after. My sources said the resistance wants them together. They don't feel they could pull off two separate attempts."

"Who are your sources, Herr Brewer?" Himmler chimed in casually, removing his glasses and blowing on them as if to clean them. "I think we should talk to them personally." The SS chief smiled humorlessly at the remark, making his short mustache arch menacingly.

"My sources wish to remain anonymous."

"And I wish to meet them," Himmler said coldly.

The Fuhrer stood and interrupted the conversation. "You two can discuss this later. We will assume the information is correct and develop a plan to disrupt the attempt and find the conspirators.

“Major, you will work with Herr Brewer to develop this plan.

“Herr Brewer, you will arrange a meeting with your sources and Herr Himmler. I want these conspirators found and this nonsense ended!”

Everyone in the room rose from their seats, raised their right arms and saluted. “*Heil Hitler*!”

* * * *

“The Fuhrer has sent Herr Himmler on an inspection sweep of the Gestapo Headquarters,” the Gestapo Major said as he came up behind Brewer. The rogue assassin did not even bother looking up from the Wolf's Lair's blueprints he studied.

“Good. That should slow down the attempts, at least for a little while.”

“You know, you have presented the perfect plan to kill the Fuhrer,” the Major said, taking a seat across from the assassin. “You tell us the resistance will attempt to kill the Fuhrer and Himmler, and we send Himmler away. What happens when they abandon their plans on the 11th?”

“There will be no assassination attempt,” came the reply and a knowing smile. Brewer knew where this was heading.

“Exactly. And we will not know if our precautions were the reason,” the Major leaned over the table, “or if there was never really a plan to kill Hitler on the 11th.”

“You could always put them in the same room and see what happens,” Brewer shrugged with a smirk. “The important thing is, the Fuhrer is safe and we need to look ahead at any future attempts.”

"Which brings up my next point," the Major said, sitting back and crossing his arms. His glare spoke volumes to the Assassin. "Your contacts in the resistance seem very well informed. I want to meet them."

Brewer looked back at the blueprints, studying them. "As I told Herr Himmler, they wish to remain anonymous," he said in a low, distant voice.

"And as he said, we wish to meet them."

The men sat in silence. Brewer studied the blueprints, occasionally tracing a load-bearing wall with his finger while the Major studied the Assassin.

"What are you looking for?" the Major asked.

"Ways to improve security, or to improve the fortifications."

"Mr. Brewer, there are three levels of security here. Two battalions, including the Fuhrer's own Security Battalion, are stationed here. The resistance would never survive a direct attack on the Wolf's Lair."

"I don't disagree," Brewer responded, still studying the layout of the base. "But the resistance would never outright attack the Lair. It would be suicide. So, you are correct, Herr Major. They would never launch a full out attack. Rather, I believe, they would infiltrate the base and inflict damage from within."

"Again, there are three levels of security here. The resistance would never gain entry," the Major's voice betrayed his weariness of the conversation. "You're wasting your time studying those blueprints."

"And if the resistance uses German Officers to infiltrate the base? Men with the credentials to get past security? What then?" Brewer looked up, locking eyes with the Major.

It only took a few moments for those words to sink in and the Gestapo Major realized that Brewer had hinted as to the identities of some of the conspirators. He leaned over the blueprints. “Tell me what you have in mind.”

* * * *

“We need to reinforce the conference room,” the Gestapo Major briefed the Fuhrer's staff.

The assembled men sat in the conference room in question; a rectangular room with a ten-foot vaulted ceiling and an alcove that led to the corridor outside. A long, triple pedestal table, with a dozen chairs around it, filled the room. The only chair that was empty was the Fuhrer's, at the end of the table. “Intelligence, from both Gestapo and independent sources, site a future plot to bomb the Wolf's Lair. The most likely point of attack is this conference room when the Fuhrer and all of his staff are present.

“Last week's aborted plot by the resistance shows that we are getting close to finding them, and the closer we get, the more desperate they will become.”

"Do we have confirmation of any sympathizers within our own ranks?" asked a one-eyed Colonel in the back of the room.

“We have a few names, sir,” the Major replied, his voice ice cold. “We are questioning those now.”

That brought a chuckle from a couple of Colonels who were familiar with the questioning techniques of the Gestapo. One of the Colonels, his left arm missing at the elbow from an air raid in North Africa, made a slash across his throat with his right hand and silently laughed.

“Stay on it, Major,” ordered a Colonel in the back, his baldhead and his medals gleaming in the light. “The Fuhrer has called for a meeting in three days. Have your enhancements in place by then.”

* * * *

The modifications to the structure and the furniture took the entire three days: reinforced windows, another tier of concrete/steel mesh on the exterior of the building, and a double layer of wood and steel lattice on the furniture in the room. Everything that Brewer recommended was done, no questions asked.

The Major stood beside Brewer overseeing all of the modifications. The Gestapo Officer knew that Brewer had more information than he was divulging but could not drag the information from the agent. On the second day of the modifications, the Major even toyed with the idea of interrogating the agent. That was before a Colonel, the same Colonel that was missing his left arm, told the Major to stand down and leave Brewer alone. The Gestapo Major knew then that Brewer had high connections.

“What do your spies tell you, Herr Brewer?” he asked as the workers finished the modifications just a few hours before the scheduled meeting. “Is today the day?”

“I guess we'll find out, Major,” Brewer replied, his face and voice emotionless. “The briefing is in a few hours?”

“Yes,” the Major replied, and smiled. “But you will not be attending.”

Brewer looked hurt for a moment and opened his mouth to protest.

The Major continued. “I do not trust you, Herr Brewer. You are not German. You sell information to both sides.” Brewer's face blanched. “Yes, I know exactly what you are. Do you think you are the only one who deals in information?” He pointed his finger at the rogue assassin. “You will not sit at a meeting where you could glean information to sell to our enemies.”

Brewer did half bow-half nod to the German Officer and abruptly left the room. He wanted to be nowhere near the explosion that would occur in that conference room, but he did not want the Gestapo Officer to know that. He continued out of the bunker, into the same open air car that had brought him to the complex, and drove back to the airfield he had arrived at a weeks before.

The airfield had been destroyed, right on schedule. Construction crews were rebuilding the control buildings and hangers while other crews tried to remove the debris from buildings and Zeppelins. A lone surviving Zeppelin stood waiting. Brewer boarded the vessel and left Poland. Whatever happened now, only history would know.

* * * *

Rick Brewer sat at a cafe in France, reading the paper and sipping some very strong coffee. Word had spread across Europe that Hitler had survived and the resistance was paying a heavy price for the attempted assassination.

The newspaper had a detailed, yet inaccurate, account of what happened in the conference room. Hitler and Dietrich had dreamed up a grand tale of the attempt, but had conveniently left out that the conspirators were actually officers of the German Army—a fact that the history books would one day correct.

Brewer folded the newspaper and thought back to his own history books and his research into the mid-Twentieth Century. His details were sketchy, but he knew that his memories were more accurate than the propaganda he read.

Colonel Claus Von Stauffenberg was a tall, highly decorated combat veteran with a stump for a right arm, two missing fingers on his left hand and a black eye-patch over his left eye. He was the Chief of Staff for the Commander, and the lead conspirator in the plot to kill Adolf Hitler.

He had been waiting for the right moment to kill Hitler and his top advisors for a month, but the Colonel had never found the time when all of the targets were present. With the Gestapo closing in, Von Stauffenberg decided to move forward with the plan no matter who was present.

The Colonel moved through the corridors of the Wolf's Lair with several other high-ranking officials; all carrying briefcases with notes, maps and orders. Von Stauffenberg's also carried a bomb that ticked down. The men made their way to the recently refurbished conference room and settled in for the meeting.

Generals, Colonels, and Gestapo agents packed the conference room, filling every seat in the cramped room: over twenty officers, from every branch and division, crowded around the wooden table. Von Stauffenberg noticed the windows were open to let air into the oppressively hot afternoon and wondered if he had enough explosives.

Too late now, he thought as the clock struck 12:30.

Hitler entered the room to a chorus of salutes. He took his seat and the meeting began.

The Colonel placed his briefcase on the floor next to the Fuhrer and sat down to wait. He studied the brief on the African Campaign that had caused his injuries and grimaced.

The campaign was not going well and that simply made the man more determined to carry out his mission. Hitler must die if he was to save his beloved Germany. The Officer listened quietly for several minutes before excusing himself to take an urgent phone call from Berlin. The Colonel mentally calculated he had three or four minutes before the bomb exploded.

With only a minute to go, one of the other attendees inadvertently moved the briefcase behind one of the oak table legs as he got up to get a better view of the war map. The re-enforced table leg shielded Hitler and most of the staff from the bomb as it exploded moments later. Burned and battered, Adolf Hitler suffered punctured eardrums and received numerous cuts and scrapes, but he survived. Miraculously, thanks to Brewer's modifications to the room, only four people died, even though the blast injured everyone in the conference room.

The Gestapo Major that had been in charge of the fortifications had been one of the four killed. He later received the highest German medal for heroism, posthumously, of course.

Captured with a host of other conspirators in Berlin several hours later, Colonel Claus Von Stauffenberg stood trial, found guilty and his sentence to be put to death occurred before midnight.

Brewer read the paper and smiled, he had once again changed history.

Only time would tell how much.

Chapter Ten

REGINALD MAYWEATHER WAS LIVID.

"Six weeks ago, you told me that you needed time to do your research." His crimson face matched the garish red suit he wore. The same red suit he wore two months earlier when he first approached the Council. Mayweather spat a little as he yelled. "Now you're telling me you that you need *another* month?

"You *will* kill Dent's ancestors today, or you will find your charter revoked!"

He took a moment to catch his breath as he glared at the Council seated above him. That was something else he would address to his friends in the Government. His staff had already built his own meeting room based partially on this design. He had discovered his business associates felt intimidated by his towering presence. Business dealings were quicker and more profitable now that people were uncomfortable standing, staring up at him. That reaffirmed to Mayweather that these people should be looking up at him, too!

"Mr. Mayweather, we are not yet convinced that there is no danger in killing the entire family," responded the female Council Member. She started to continue, but Mayweather turned to leave, stopping the conversation.

He paused at the door. "I'll own your charter before the end of the day!" He left the Council chamber, his entourage falling into step with him as he exited the door.

The lone female Council Member sighed and touched a button on her chair. An acolyte in gray appeared immediately.

"Find Professor Donovan and Apprentice 101 and bring them to me immediately!"

* * * *

Professor Donovan and Apprentice 101 silently stood in the Council chamber. Only the female Council Member, in her black robes and red face, sat in her chair on the dais. Her silver blue hair seemed grayer today as she stared down at the two. Apprentice 101 felt beads of sweat on his baldhead and his robes stuck to him in the heat and humidity in the room. He stole a quick glance at Professor Donovan, his hair plastered to his skull. The two men were extremely uncomfortable. *By design*, thought the Apprentice. *This isn't good.*

Professor Donovan gulped as the Councilwoman got up from her seat, made her way down a hidden stairwell, and appeared to their left, seemingly from thin air.

"You two were given an assignment six weeks ago; one that you did not complete." Icy steel filled her voice. "Now I find out that you two have been working on a project without Council authority and have put this Guild and its operations in jeopardy." She never raised her voice. Her level tone set Apprentice 101 trembling in fear and he found he wished she would scream at him. That he could handle.

Professor Donovan opened his mouth to speak, but the Councilwoman continued, so he closed his mouth and stood perfectly still.

"In the ten minutes it took you two to get here, I have received three vid-calls from high ranking government officials ordering this Guild to do anything Mr. Mayweather wants—*anything*!" She walked a little loop around the two men, reminiscent of when Master Li circled Jason Lassiter during initiation. Apprentice 101 found the diminutive woman even more imposing than Master Li had been.

"This Guild is not inclined to do whatever Mr. Mayweather wants," she continued, stopping in front of the apprentice. "So, I hope that you have found something that I can give to those officials to hold them at bay." She let the sentence hang, giving the young Apprentice a chance.

Apprentice 101 took a breath to calm his frayed nerves. Thoughts of Donovan's former apprentice and his death sentence filled his mind. His anxiety rose.

"Ma'am, although I did not finish researching all of the children of the great-grandson of Dent, I did find that one of the children was directly involved in the Mars colonization of the Twenty-Second Century," Apprentice 101 reported. Her demeanor changed, less intimidating, and he relaxed as well; however slightly. "I didn't get all of the details, but in my initial research she was instrumental in the success of the colonization. Without her, the mission would fail."

"You confirmed this?"

"Yes, ma'am," he said. "If we kill all of Dent's family in the Twentieth Century, Mars will not be colonized in the Twenty-Second, at least not by Major Amelia McIntyre."

The Councilwoman seemed to calm and resumed her circular pacing. "I need proof of this to provide to the government," she said to the two men. She paused looked directly into Mr. Donovan's eyes. "And I want a detailed report of what has distracted you to the point that the Guild's charter is in jeopardy."

* * * *

Reginald Mayweather was having a very bad day. Someone else told him 'No.' Not accustomed to being told no, he did not like it and was completely frustrated by it. Mayweather leaned back in his plush leather chair and stared at the man on the vid-phone, a man he used to call his friend. He prepared to level another verbal barrage at him.

"Reg—" the man began, but Mayweather cut him off.

"Malcolm, I want this man *and his family* dead! You control the Guild charter. Make the Guild do it!"

"Reginald," the Government man began again. Mayweather could see him in the vid leaning back in his chair; arms wide in a pseudo-stretch then placed his hands behind his head. "The Guild has sent information that proves that killing the entire family is just too dangerous. Timeline instability could—"

"I DON'T CARE!" Mayweather yelled. "I chose Dent because he was nothing, a nobody. Now, tell the Guild to send someone to kill him, or I swear that I'll buy another politician that will!"

Malcolm the Government Politician leaned forward in defiance. Yes, Mayweather had contributed a lot of money to his campaign and yes, he owed the businessman, but he was the Government Official and he did not need to be talked to like a teenager. He studied the office on the vid: a Rembrandt, leather chair, fine oak desk, expensive carpets and a view that was better than any in the Capitol. He sighed, and knew he could not fight it. "Fine, Reginald. Fine!" he succumbed. "I'll give the order. Maybe I won't live to see the consequences."

Mayweather smiled. "Or maybe, just maybe, you'll be better off in the new world." He signed off the vid and continued. "Especially when I own it!"

* * * *

Professor Donovan stood in the conference room with Mr. Tomlinson, Master Li and the two Apprentices. They were all in disbelief that the Council had ordered the assassination of Dent and his family. No one spoke their thoughts, but they were all thinking the same thing.

Apprentice 101 finally broke the silence. "Professor, what about Brewer? The Council wants to know what we've been working on."

The Professor nodded. "I will prepare a report for the Council explaining everything. That is not your concern."

"But—"

Donovan held up his hand, stopping the protest. "What is your concern is your schoolwork." He sat down heavily in the chair at the head of the conference table. The others sat as well. "I've had you so engrossed in tracking Brewer that you are now at least a month behind. From this point on, your only mission is to finish your Second Year curriculum."

Professor Donovan nodded at the young woman midway down the table. "Apprentice 97 is far enough ahead in her preparations for her finals that she can assist me if needed." He received a nod from her in response.

"In the meantime, Mr. Tomlinson has a skip to prep for and Master Li has a new Apprentice standing outside in the cold."

"Two, actually," Master Li responded, rising from the table. He flashed a rare smile. "One of them has scores even higher than Apprentice 101."

That raised a few eyebrows and Apprentice 97 smiled as she snuggled up to her boyfriend. "Good." she said affectionately. "If this one doesn't work out, there is another candidate!"

A round of nervous laughter echoed through the group. They all wondered if there would even be a Guild before this was over.

* * * *

Assassin 46 stepped from the skip bubble into the middle of Boston Commons, right next to the fountain that he had splashed into two months earlier. He looked at his watch and thought, *Two months my time, but across town, I just skipped home.*

He was alone this time, no Cleaner crew, but he did not think he needed them; the planning had already been done. It was going to be a simple smash and grab with a family murdered, a robbery gone bad.

Simple.

Something that had been done a hundred times throughout history.

He could not quite figure out why he felt like it was about to blow up in his face.

* * * *

Apprentice 97 stood before her classmates, prepared for her final presentation. She was not nervous, this was not her first time to stand there, but she did feel anxious. If everything went well this would be the last time she would give a presentation to her peers.

In the back of her mind, her thoughts kept returning to the series of events over the last two weeks, including her first skip. That was not something any of her peers had done, nor did they know she had done it. Professor Donovan and the others would get in trouble if anyone else knew. Apprentices were not authorized to skip.

Her blue robes swayed lightly as she did her final check on her notes. Professor Patton, her evaluator, ordered the class to silence. The room quieted and Apprentice 97 began.

“The Assassin's Guild was established before recorded history, dwelling in the shadows for thousands of years. In all of that time, only a handful of events in history threatened to expose the Guild, most of those dismissed as rumor and lore.

"However, there are two events that truly provided proof to the Guild's existence. The most recent was the development of time travel in 2248, when the Guild actually did emerge from the shadows and into the mainstream world.

"The other event occurred in 2076, during the final years of the Russian Consortium. A Russian Operative developed a plan to save the Consortium by destroying all of the enemies of his country. He was directly responsible for the deaths of more people than Hitler, Mao and Pol Pot combined.

"For seventeen months, an Assassin and Cleaner Team pursued the man across the globe; from the jungles of Columbia, to Britain, to South Africa, to Russia. The Assassin and Cleaner team eliminated rogue elements in every country they visited.

"When the Assassin finally caught up to the Russian, it was not a sniper's bullet or a simple dose of poison that killed the man." She shook her head to emphasize the point. "It was a firefight in front of the Kremlin that lasted for over two hours.

"I am not going to bore you with details of the seventeen month trek across the planet. Instead, I'm going to focus this study on the final days. To show you that in our profession, secrecy is paramount to our safety, and our success."

* * * *

Rick Brewer stood atop a windy hill in Washington D.C., staring intently at the Marine Corps Drill Team practicing for their upcoming Veteran's Day performance.

One unfortunate Marine dropped his rifle and received a verbal onslaught from his superior. Brewer simply smiled in the cold late October air, happy the days of answering to higher authority were over.

Footsteps turned him to see a fat man in a heavy brown trench coat, hands thrust deep in his pockets and a scarf draped around his neck, approaching from a parked limousine. The man made it to the top of the hill, his breath visible with each rasping gasp. It took him several seconds before he could finally speak.

"Mr. Brewer. You understand that this meeting never took place, and we never met today." The man used the end of the scarf to wipe a bead of sweat from his forehead.

He's going to die just walking up here, thought the tall, lean man. Dressed in slacks, a gray turtle-neck sweater and deep brown leather jacket; his dark tanned skin was only a few shades lighter than the jacket. The tanned skin highlighted the faded scar on the left side of his face. His brown eyes, several shades darker than the jacket, studied the man for a few seconds before responding. "I understand. What is it you want done?"

"My employers do not like the path this country is taking." A smooth, politically persuasive voice replaced the raspy breathing. "They seek a regime change, if the election next week does not go in their favor."

Rick Brewer turned back to watch the Marine Drill Team, now performing flawlessly as the unfortunate youth was out of the formation, doing push-ups in his dress uniform. "Regime change," he gave a slight grunt, "fancy way of saying 'Assassination.'"

"Perhaps, Mr. Brewer, but it has a more polite ring to it." He took a large manila envelope from his jacket and took one-step toward the Assassins' back. "If the election does not go our way, and you agree to accept the assignment, then your pay will be considerable."

Turning back to face the fat man, Brewer took the offered envelope. "It will have to be. No one assassinates a President and simply walks away."

* * * *

"That was an excellent report, Apprentice," Professor Patton said as the class dismissed. "It was informative, thought provoking and extremely well researched and presented." The professor waited until she was alone with Apprentice 97 before continuing.

"However, it did not meet the criteria of the presentation, which was a study of the techniques and tactics of an actual assassination." Apprentice 97 started to protest, but the professor intervened. "This particular case study is very difficult, as it resulted in an armed incursion, not a quiet assassination." She smiled. "This is why Professor Donovan insisted you get the assignment."

"Professor Donovan?"

"This case study is reserved for those with the most promise in each class. It is quite an honor to receive the assignment," Professor Patton steepled her fingers and looked over her hands at the apprentice standing before her.

"It is always interesting to see how a student will approach the assignment." The Professor smiled. "And I can honestly say that I've never had a student simply skip to the end.

“I have every confidence that you will do great things for the Guild.”

Apprentice 97 left the classroom in a rush. She had to find Apprentice 101. After months of accelerated study, her days at the Academy were ending.

* * * *

She found Apprentice 101 in his room preparing for his own presentation and an end to his second year at the Guild Academy. His roommate saw Apprentice 97 and silently gathered his books and disappeared down the corridor. Apprentice 101 never looked up.

She stood behind him for several minutes, quietly controlling her urge to hug him. He finally smiled without looking up. “Just how long are you going to stand there?” He turned to her and she kissed him.

“I passed!” she said breathlessly.

“I never doubted,” he said, and meant it. They kissed again. He suddenly turned very serious. “Can I ask you something?”

She closed the door, locked it, and thought, *This is one great day!* She sat in his lap, arms around his neck. “Yes?”

“What is your name?”

That was not the question she was expecting, and she fell out of his lap, stunned. She scrambled to pick herself up and paused as she stood. It had been three years since she had even thought of her name. She stammered, “Rachel...Rachel Sullivan.”

He stood and extended his hand. “I'm Jason Lassiter.”

Apprentice 97 uncomfortably shook his hand. Apprentice 101 gripped it firmly, smiled mischievously, and pulled her, laughing, onto the bed.

A great day indeed.

* * * *

Professor Donovan caught Apprentice 101 in the hallway before class. "I just gave my report to the Council. They are not at all happy with us." He looked frightened and relieved at the same time. "During the break, they want you to continue to track Brewer. No down time. That is your punishment for keeping this from them. Sorry.

"I'd say we got off easy," he continued in a whisper. Apprentice 101 nodded and wiped the sweat from his forehead. Then Donovan straightened, teacher to student. "Are you prepared, Apprentice?"

"Yes, sir!"

Professor Donovan opened the door and Apprentice 101 found himself at the podium, preparing to give his final report in his second year curriculum. He cleared his throat.

"One year ago, I stood before you and told you a story. A story about four men sent back in time to change history. The two timelines in that story were nearly identical. The only real change involved two lives and a political career. You have all done similar reports." He watched as several of his peers nodded.

"Now I am about to tell you another story. This story involves two radically different timelines, and the death of millions.

"It starts, as most political stories do, with an election..."

Chapter Eleven

THE BANQUET HALL WAS one of the largest that Atlanta, GA had to offer. Decorated with red, white, and blue banners, American Flags, and a well-stocked bar, hundreds of people, including uniformed officers, strained to see three televisions. The man of the hour had yet to make an appearance, but word filtered around that the President-Elect, the not yet official title, was in the building and making his way to the hall.

Each television broadcasted one of the major news channels: ABC, NBC and CBS. All three predicted the same thing, a major sweep. Another state, Colorado, went to the challenger and the crowd let out a roar of approval and began clapping madly. That put them over the top! With their applause at its zenith, their candidate made his entrance.

He was black man in his early fifties, with close-cropped graying-black hair, well-trimmed mustache and large nose, dressed in a conservative black suit with a blue tie. The crowd, somehow, got even louder. His small group of bodyguards made a way for him through the crowd and he proceeded to the podium as his supporters continued to applaud. Finally, ABC made the prediction first, and gave the election to the first black President of the United States.

Dr. Martin Luther King Jr stood at the podium and let the audience continue their applause, not because of vanity or narcissism, but because he knew what they wanted. They had worked hard for all of this, and he wanted to give them their moment. Finally, he raised his hands and the crowd quieted.

"Seventeen years ago," he spoke softly. "I stood before a crowd much like this one. A crowd that wanted equality. A crowd that wanted to be heard. A crowd that wanted to be understood.

"I told that crowd in 1963 that I had a dream! I had a dream that one day this nation would rise up and live out the true meaning of its creed: 'We hold these truths to be self-evident: that *all* men are created equal.'"

The applause thundered.

"Today," he said. The crowd noise and applause subsided. "Today is not that day." He shook his head and the crowd, anticipating his uplifting words, abruptly quieted as they heard something else, something unexpected. Dr. King waved his right hand in the air and smiled. "The world has heard you. Your voices are loud and clear. But we are not equal. Not yet.

"Equality will only come when we can all work together, for a common purpose and the common good; all Americans, regardless of the color of their skin. It will be hard work and it will be a long, hard road.

"Tonight is the first step down that long road. It is a road that we must travel together. A road that will have many hardships and trials. A road, that leads to freedom!"

* * * *

The election results scrolled across the screen as the news anchors and pundits talked endless about the Presidential Race. Dr. Martin Luther King, Jr. held the lead by one of the largest margins in history, collecting state after state of electoral votes. After only a few hours, the news anchors on all three networks called the race.

Rick Brewer watched the news with little real interest. He focused on the envelope that the fat man had given him a week earlier. Feet propped up on the coffee table in the sparse apartment, the table, a couch and the television were the only items in the living room. The other rooms in the apartment were as austere. Brewer opened the envelope. It was a typical dossier of a political candidate; nothing to help plan an assassination. The phone rang and interrupted his page turning.

"Mr. Brewer?"

A smile pursed his lips. "I was expecting your call."

"I'm sure," came the not too happy sounding reply. "Are you watching the election results?"

"What happened to the other guy?" Rick asked, changing the subject. "The fat man?" he clarified.

"Mr. Smith passed away last week after your meeting." The tone was simple and matter-of-fact; there was no compassion or sense of loss. "Heart attack." There was a pause. "Are you watching the election results?" he asked again.

"Yes."

"This is the turn of events that we were concerned about. Our organization would like you to initiate the changes that were discussed. We would like you to do this quickly and publicly."

"It will take time," Rick commented, and smirked. *Time*, he thought, *I have time*. "This isn't something I can do overnight. You do realize that other people will take his place?"

"You do not need to concern yourself with other people or their political affiliation." The voice showed a hint of strain as if the speaker did not like the path the conversation was taking. "We have that under control. Your task is to initiate a change. Quickly and publicly, Mr. Brewer. Those are your criteria for this assignment."

"And if that doesn't fit into my plan?"

"Then we will terminate your employ and find someone who is more flexible."

The phone went dead and Rick Brewer gave another smirk and exhaled, forcing his head backward. "Terminate?" he said aloud. The threat did not go unnoticed.

* * * *

The history contained within the Oval Office instilled a since of awe and humbled the group of men that inspected the room. Historical pictures adorned the walls, busts of dignitaries from around the world sat on pedestals, and the Presidential Desk stood, as if on watch, in front of the bay window. King ran his hand along the desk that, in 1964, the Civil Rights Act had been signed on. He had stood behind President Johnson as the President signed the bill. He smiled briefly at the memory of that day; which had ultimately led him back to this room as the President elect. The American people had come a very long way since the 1960s.

President-elect King and his top advisors were escorted from his future office down a corridor and eventually down to a sub-basement briefing room. Thrilled to be in the presence of the first "man of color" elected President, the young blonde woman escorted them, chatting incessantly about the history of the White House and the Oval Office.

President-elect King and the others ignored her.

They finally settled into a sub-basement briefing room with a large oblong wooden table, a stage with a podium, a projector and a screen. Ashtrays doted along the table and a thin layer of smoke already hung in the air. A single door near the back of the room was labeled 'Restroom'. The four new arrivals sat opposite President Ford, who was finishing his second term of office, and two of his key advisors: Treasury Secretary William Simon and Defense Secretary Donald Rumsfeld. Introductions made their way around the conference table and then everyone turned their attention to a Navy Commander who was to brief them on International Affairs.

“Gentlemen,” the Commander began, somewhat nervously. He was in his mid-forties with thinning, black hair, a slight paunch, and an out of regulation mustache. He had chided himself before the briefing that he had forgotten to trim the unruly mob of mustache hair. He stood before the assembled men in his Dress Whites and grasped the podium firmly with his left hand while he pointed to the screen behind him with the right.

"This is a classified briefing detailing current events around the world that may affect your policies both here and abroad. The briefing is not designed to detail every aspect of the world's political climate, but instead, it is designed to provide you an overview of the political landscape so that you will be informed when you create your own policies. This information is simply meant as a rapid-fire introduction to the world arena that most American's are not privy to. A more detailed series of briefings will be given to your advisors and cabinet appointees over the next few months leading up to the inauguration.

"Are there any questions before I begin?" The assembly remained silent. The President-elect shook his head. The Commander continued.

"First, the Middle East:

"As you know, Iranian Revolutionaries stormed and took over our Embassy in Tehran in November 1979. They continue to hold over fifty hostages despite our best diplomatic efforts and the threat of military intervention. Ruhollah Khomeini, the revolution leader, still holds the hostages. However, he is losing his support from the Iranian people over the whole ordeal. Intelligence summaries show that the citizens fear an American reprisal, although they do not know when.

"G2 estimates that the hostages will go free within six months."

"G2?"

The Navy Commander looked up from his notes and stared for a moment at the speaker. Clarence Jones looked back with an inquisitive look. Selected to be the Attorney General, Jones was an older black man with a balding head. "G2; Intelligence. Sorry, sir, I'm not used to briefing civilians."

Mr. Jones nodded, and the Commander continued. "Continuing in the Middle East, we have the Soviet incursion into Afghanistan." The screen behind the Navy Commander changed from the highlighted country of Iran to its eastern neighbor. "In December of 1979, Russian troops entered Afghanistan at the request of then Prime Minister Hazifullah Amin. In less than a month, the Russians had shot Amin, installed Babrak Kamal as the new Prime Minister, and deployed over eighty-five thousand troops to the country.

"The Afghan resistance, called the Mujahedeen, has been fighting the Soviets for almost a year now. They have begun to inflict some heavy losses on the Soviets with our assistance. We are working through intermediaries to provide some intelligence, training and arms.

"The Mujahedeen do not trust the US any more than they do the Soviets, so working through third parties is slow, but necessary.

"The United Nations is expected to vote on several resolutions early next year to condemn the quote-unquote invasion." The Commander raised his hands and exaggerated the quotation symbols as he spoke. "But those resolutions are likely to be voted down by the Soviet Union and its Communist allies.

"Next, still within the Middle East, are the border disputes between Iran and Iraq." The screen changed again, leaving Afghanistan and highlighted the two counties to the west. "Diplomatic talks between Iran and

Iraq, moderated by Egypt, seem to have stabilized the region...for now. Our intelligence in that area is limited." The Commander took a drink of water then continued. "But we believe that the borders will hold for the foreseeable future.

"The tenuous peace between Israel and Egypt, brokered by the United States two years ago, seems to be holding as well. However, our intelligence bureaus are indicating that the calm in the Middle East is still erratic and if it does not stabilize, that peace may fracture.

"Turning to Europe, Margaret Thatcher appears to be handling the British Parliament with ease. She has reversed several policies of her predecessor, especially fiscal related policy, and appears to be on track to becoming a powerful Prime Minister. She has vowed to continue the good relations with the United States and the new President.

"Also in Europe, the USSR is gearing up for their annual military drills throughout the Soviet Block. As the weather improves with spring we can expect to see Russian Divisions deploy all along the border." The screen behind him changed again, showing groups of military symbols massing along the Cold War borders.

The Commander took a few minutes to answer questions about what each symbol meant and the capabilities of each symbol. Once he had answered all of the questions to the satisfaction of his audience, he continued.

"Next, we turn to Central and South America." Again, the map on the screen changed. "The Sandinista Rebels have solidified their government in Nicaragua after seizing power last year. The Marxist government now controls all media and business enterprises in that country.

"And finally, gentlemen, we have Southwest Asia. Two years ago, Vietnam invaded Cambodia in an effort to remove the Khmer Rouge from power. That incident escalated into a regional conflict with the People's Republic of China launching a counter attack on Vietnam on behalf of Cambodia. Although that particular campaign has been over for almost ten months, the significance is that the Soviet Union encouraged the Vietnamese to invade Cambodia. Russia is tremendously over-extending itself by getting involved in Asia, Europe and the Middle East.

"Pending your questions gentlemen," the Commander finished as the screen went dark, "that concludes this portion of the briefing."

President Ford looked across the oblong table at his successor, who nodded. Clearly, he knew about much of the world's turmoil. Ford nodded in return, and turned his attention back to the Naval Officer. "Thank you, Commander Mackenzie."

The Navy man exited the stage and made his way toward the door, passing an Army Colonel dressed in his Dress Greens entering the room. The nametag read 'Abbott.'

"Reverend King, this is Colonel Abbott," President Ford said, introducing the man. "He is going to brief you on domestic affairs including the current state of the economy."

"A military man is going to brief us on economic issues?" The question, from the youngest of the President-

Elect's advisors, came across as unfriendly and uncooperative.

"Colonel Abbott has a Master's Degree in Economics from Harvard and is one of the top analysts and financial managers at the Pentagon," responded Treasury Secretary Simon. The graying man held his pipe in his left hand and smiled. "I have worked with him extensively and if he'd ever retire, I'd hire him on my personal staff immediately." He lit his pipe, puffed a few times and sat back in his chair, nodding.

President Ford smiled. *America is changing*, he thought. *For everyone.* Then aloud, "Colonel, please proceed."

Colonel Abbott stepped up to the stage and, once behind the podium, cleared his throat. "President Ford, President-elect King." He nodded to each man in turn. "Cabinet members and advisors, I am Colonel Abbott, US Army, and I am here to provide you a short briefing on the financial situation of the United States.

"Currently, the US is recovering from a mild recession. Inflation is currently at 13.58%, interest rates have dropped to 18.75%—that is down from 21.5% last quarter—and the unemployment rate is currently at 7.1%.

"What this means, gentlemen, is that the United States is recovering, albeit slowly. Now, if you'll turn to page three of the packet in front of you..."

Thirty-seven minutes later, the President-elect had a new respect for Colonel Abbott and his understanding of economics. Dr. King had taken the hint from Secretary Simon and offered the Colonel the job of Treasury Secretary. The Colonel accepted and tendered his resignation to Secretary of Defense Rumsfeld on the spot.

"Thank you for the briefings, Mr. President," the President-elect said as they shook hands inside the door of the conference room. "You've given me a lot to think about over the next few months." He flashed a sincere smile. "And a Treasury Secretary!"

"You're welcome, Reverend," replied the President. "I wish you nothing but success."

With that, the President-elect and his advisors left the sub-basement, politely declined the rest of the White House tour and left Pennsylvania Avenue.

* * * *

It was a relatively warm day in January as Dr. Martin Luther King, Jr. placed his hand on a worn Bible and made history.

The Chief Justice of the Supreme Court asked the President elect to raise his right hand. The first black man elected President complied. The oath was taken as America watched, waited, and cheered.

When the applause died down, the new President shook hands with the Former President, who waved briefly and left the stage. President King stepped up to the microphone, took a deep breath, and stared out at one of the largest crowds ever assembled for a Presidential Inauguration. He checked his notes, smiled, and began.

Rick Brewer stared through the sniper scope and watched as the new President gave a long, rambling speech that many journalists and historians would label his best. It was destined to go down in history as one of the ten best speeches ever written. Brewer scanned the crowd through his scope, watching the men in their suits, the women in their dresses and the Secret Service watching everyone. It always amazed the assassin how people could flock to someone, how people seemed to worship politicians. He had been around politicians for almost two hundred years and he had learned to hate them. The Assassin listened to the speech for a full two minutes before he moved his finger to the trigger, took a deep breath, and steadily pulled the trigger.

Of course, nothing happened. The rogue assassin was over a mile away listening to the speech on a personal radio. The bolt clicked on the empty chamber and Brewer visualized the bullet arching across the distance, bypassing the melting snow puddles and impacting his target.

"Soon," he mumbled and moved from his vantage point. He saw a Secret Service team check a nearby building and knew it was time to make his exit.

Staying low, below the roof ledge, he moved to the stairwell door and his hidden weapon case. He moved his head around, checking the area as he absent-mindedly disassembled the Russian rifle, stored it, and then carefully hid it in the brick structure.

He stood up, moved back five feet, and could barely make the outline of the case. He knew that in a month, or two, or six, the President would hold a function in the courtyard only four hundred meters from the building and that would be his time to fulfill the contract.

They want it quickly and publicly, he thought as he left the roof and made his way down the stairwell. *It may not happen on their timetable, but it will happen and it will be public.*

Outside the building, the assassin hailed a cab, and vanished into the traffic of Washington.

* * * *

Spring brought warmer weather, a waning interest in US politics, and Russian War Games all along the European border.

Satellite imagery showed the Russian divisions as they began their pre-planned run across Eastern Europe, much as they had done for the last decade. Tanks, infantry and paratroopers advanced from the Western borders of Mother Russia all the way to Berlin. The war games were in full swing. The difference this time was they were not playing a game.

The tanks did not stop in Berlin, Warsaw and Budapest as they had in the past. The tanks continued westward. The Russian Divisions devoured all of Germany, Belgium, and the Netherlands. The attack was so quick, so unexpected, that the world simply sat and watched as the Russians took one third of Europe in ten days. Then, they stopped.

The United Nations Security Council called an emergency session, condemned the invasion and called for sanctions against the Soviet Union. The Russians simply laughed, disapproved the sanctions against them, and continued their preparations for the invasion of the rest of Europe.

France, Spain, and Portugal, fearing they were next on the list, called on the US to intervene. President King assured all of Europe he would talk to the Russians, and did as he promised.

The Russians laughed again and continued westward, to the ocean. Their lightning fast attack was met with heavy resistance this time as the European community fought back. Thousands died as the European countries fell one by one.

The situation room in the White House was full as the President received the latest briefing: the Russians had all of Europe except for the United Kingdom, who was equipping and preparing for an invasion.

“When do we expect them to invade England?” he asked. He had been in office only three months and was facing one of those scenarios that he really did not want to consider.

Growing up a black man in the South, he was accustomed to name calling, prejudice and even a few death threats, so the almost weekly threats he was receiving since taking the oath was unsettling, but ignorable. The Secret Service was doing its job. But he, and the free world, was now being threatened by an enemy that would, and could, destroy him and all he had worked for.

“Actually, Mr. President, we think they'll head for Africa,” replied an Army General from the end of the table.

President King looked at the General with a puzzled look. “What?”

“The Russians have all of Europe. They have England surrounded, and the British and the Scottish are preparing for an invasion,” the General continued.

“We actually think the Scotts are looking forward to the fight," came a murmur from the side. A quick glance from the General silenced any other remarks.”

The General continued. “Satellite imagery shows many of the Soviet tank divisions and at least three Airborne Brigades are moving south, staging in Spain and Portugal for a dash across the Mediterranean into Egypt, Morocco, or Libya. They may be planning to let the British sit for awhile and then attack them later.”

“Or, they could launch an attack from Spain across the channel,” came the input from Clarence Jones. “Isn't that a possibility?”

“Yes, sir, it is,” replied the General. “Or they could launch a two pronged attack at both. We really do not know, but, Britain is prepared for an invasion where the African Continent is not. The way the Russians have moved so far indicates they prefer soft targets. That is why we think it will be Africa.”

Attorney General Jones held up a hand and nodded, deferring to the military man and his expertise.

“What can we do to assist our allies,” the President asked, “and our potential allies in Africa?”

“Sir,” Joint Chief of Staff Ronald Tutwieller began. He was a short, light-skinned man with a pug nose and ever-present cigarette. He took a long drag on the cigarette in his hand. “We recommend deploying the Atlantic fleet along the coast of Europe, through the Med, and along the coast of Africa. That would put us in a position to effectively intercept the Russians wherever they go.

“We further recommend to plus up our Marines in Lebanon and bolster our support—our public support—in Afghanistan. We need to show the Russians that we will not allow further aggression and we are prepared to go to war to protect our allies.

"Our troops that were stationed throughout Europe, some three hundred thousand troops, were scattered during the invasion. Some were captured and are still being held by the Russians. Others were killed. Some managed to cross the channel, joining our forces in England to prepare the defense of the UK. We estimate that we lost some twenty thousand, we have sixty thousand captured and the other two hundred or so have joined the resistance and are currently fighting the Russians."

"Do we have any contact with our forces still in Europe?" ask President King.

"Sporadic at best, and with only a few units." The General crushed out his cigarette and lit another. "The Russians have some sophisticated jamming technology we didn't know about."

The President was quiet for a few minutes, contemplating the information given. He rubbed hands through his short cut hair. "Deploy our forces as you see fit, General," he ordered. "But make it clear to all of our forces, even those still in Europe: do not engage the Russians without my approval, no matter what the situation is. If we go to war, I'll be the one to give the order. But we will do everything we can do avoid that order."

* * * *

'Everything' was not popular with the American People, or the Europeans, or the Africans. Country by country, the Russians attacked the African Continent.

They invaded and conquered Libya, Tunisia and Egypt, and the US did nothing.

At least, not openly.

President King used the forces at his disposal in clandestine missions that hampered the Russian advance: the Seals destroyed a frigate in the Med, Marine Force Recon intercepted a resupply convoy that left a Russian Battalion without food and fuel, and the Special Forces dropped into countries like Mali and Senegal and began training the Africans to fight.

In three months, the Russians had taken over all of Europe, five countries in Northern Africa and were massing their forces to enter the Middle East. The US forces scattered through Europe were fighting, albeit with little affect. The world waited for the US to stop the Russians.

The Russians waited until October when the weather cooled and their battle weary troops could rotate, rest and reconstitute, to begin their Middle Eastern campaign. Then, in late October of 1981, the Russians invaded Turkey and Greece.

* * * *

Rick Brewer lay prone on the roof of the same building he had watched the inauguration from in January. By some twist of historical irony, it was the same hotel he had stayed in before Lincoln's death in 1865. His Russian Dragunov rifle lay cradled in his arms as he sighted in the scope at the Washington Monument some six hundred meters away. The Monument looked very different from his first view of it over one hundred years earlier. It was now complete.

A cold and windy day enveloped the Assassin as he adjusted the scope. He clicked the adjustment knob twice, allowing for the wind, and focused the scope on the podium where his target would be in just under ten minutes.

The news had reported that the President would be making an address concerning an improvement in the economy, but most people were more worried about the Russian domination over half the planet. The American populace and the world wondered when—not if, but when—the US would become involved.

Brewer lay still, a camouflage net covered him, making him nearly invisible from the air or from nearby rooftops. The Secret Service would have to come up to this building to see him, and that was unlikely because they already had a two-man team on the roof. They did not know the two men were already dead.

Brewer waited patiently for the President, the cool air relaxing him. His mind began to drift back to the recent encounter with the third assassin sent back to kill him. It was a woman this time, and she was, by all accounts, much better than the previous threats. She had gotten close, very close. She had even climbed into bed with him. She had made her move too soon, however. He shook his head. If she had been willing to bed him, she would have succeeded. Lucky for him, she brought the syringe to bed and, well, it cost her.

He had found her retrieval beacon, written his customary 'Better Luck Next Time' message, and sent her body back to the Guild. He figured that one day, maybe soon, they would send someone back with better luck.

"Condor is enroute," called the Secret Service over the headset he borrowed from the now dead agents. He turned his attention back to the podium.

The announcer started his dribble about why they were there, where the bathrooms were, and to please pick up after themselves, blah, blah, blah. Brewer thought about shooting him just to shut him up. He smiled, a moment of inward reflection. *I guess I'm not as patient as I thought!* He resisted the urge and let another three minutes tick by. The President took the stage and readied his speech.

* * * *

President King began talking about the Russian incursion into Mali when the sniper's bullet missed his left ear by less than an inch. He heard a grunt behind him before he heard the rifle's report echo across the courtyard. The Secret Service swarmed in, covering the President and his advisors, as a second bullet slammed into the wounded man behind King. Treasury Secretary Abbott died as the second bullet tore through his throat.

"Out! OUT! Move the President!" one of the Secret Service Officers yelled as he stood between the Reverend and the direction of the shots. He spotted movement and raised his walkie-talkie. "Building three," he yelled, "sniper on—"

He died as Rick Brewer released the trigger on his third shot. He scanned the scene again, saw the President was covered, two men were down and a whole squad of

Secret Service was running across the six-hundred meters towards his perch.

The banished assassin dropped the rifle, placed his prepared manifesto on top of it, and then moved from the rooftop, staying low to avoid counter-sniper fire.

One bullet whined past him and ricocheted into the overcast sky.

Brewer quickly travelled down three flights of stairs, pulled out his pistol, and waited until the agents were only one floor below before he began ascending the stairs again. The Secret Service caught up to him as he approached the roof door. His timing was perfect.

"Freeze!"

Brewer halted and raised his hands. "Federal Agent," he whispered.

Slowly he produced a badge and handed it to one of the agents around him. The assassin had paid a small fortune for those credentials. The agent handed the identification back to Brewer and ordered him out of the way. Brewer complied, made his way down the stairs and left the building while the Secret Service searched the building for the man they had let get away.

* * * *

"The assassin escaped, Mr. President."

President King sat in the back of the limo as it sped through Washington. A convoy of police and Secret Service surrounded the Presidential Lincoln and provided escort to the vehicle. The President looked visibly shaken as the driver continued to swerve in and out of traffic. "How?"

“We don't know, sir,” the Agent replied, handing the President a glass of water. “The only person that they found was a Federal Agent who left the building and disappeared.” The President gave a sour look, as if to say find him, and the Agent continued. “We are already trying to locate him.

“They found two dead Secret Service Agents on the roof of the building, and the rifle—a Russian Dragunov Sniper Rifle. There was also a note from the assassin saying that he killed you for Mother Russia.”

“But he missed me. Who was it that he did kill?” President King drained the glass in one nervous gulp, spilling a little on his suit and the plush upholstery. His hands shook from the adrenaline of the near death experience.

“Treasury Secretary Abbott died from multiple gunshot wounds.” The Agent stopped for a moment and regained his composure. “Agent Thomas Walker died from a single shot to the head.”

“You knew him?”

The Agent stared out the window for a moment, watching the scenery fly by. “Yes, sir. I knew all three, but Walker was my partner for sixteen years.”

The Reverend nodded as the limo slid onto Pennsylvania Avenue. He grabbed hold of the door handle to keep from being tossed across the speeding car. “I'm very sorry. Let's find this man and ensure that your friend didn't die in vain.”

Agent Ronald "Tuck" Tucker nodded to his boss and gave a weak smile. “He didn't die in vain.” His voice cracked and tears welled in his eyes. He checked his emotions and steadied his voice. “You're still alive, and I plan on keeping it that way.”

* * * *

“I want to assure the American People that the killer of Secretary Abbott, Agents Walker, Franklin and Campbell will be found, and brought to justice.”

The President sat in the Oval Office, behind the desk that countless Presidents had sat behind, and looked into the camera. He had his prepared notes in front of him, but had abandoned them as soon as he had said, “Good Evening, America,” preferring to speak from the heart. The American People deserved a heartfelt speech, not a cold and emotionless one.

“I also want to assure America and the world that I am unscathed and unharmed.

“I have spoken with the Kremlin and condemned their attempted assassination. They assured me they were not behind the incident. The Russian government says they do not want to bring the US into their conquest of Europe, Africa and the Middle East." He paused for a moment, looking somewhat older and grayer than he had hours earlier at the Washington Monument. “I tend to believe that they were not behind yesterday's events.

“However, I also believe that the US can no longer sit idly by, while the rest of the world suffers under the advancement of Russian forces.

“So, here, tonight...” He took in a deep breath and kept his hands clasped together on the desk, “I am asking the Russians to return to their borders, to return those countries which they have invaded, to the citizens of that country.

"I am giving them forty-eight hours to withdraw their forces or I will send US forces to intervene on behalf of the world."

* * * *

Rick Brewer smiled as he watched the President give his ultimatum to the Russians. It was exactly what Brewer had wanted when he had planned the mock assassination. He sat back on the worn couch and smiled with satisfaction.

He had spent weeks working on the details to kill President King, but when the Russians had continued their advancements and King did nothing...well, he could not resist the urge to interject into history-again.

His history told of the US staying out of world events until all of Europe, Africa and Asia were under Communist rule. It was when the Russians began a South American campaign that the US got involved, but that ended very badly for the US and Russia. That was when the Chinese took over.

Instead of shooting King, he had decided to kill whoever was standing behind him. It just happened to be that former Army Colonel, what's-his-name, and then frame the Russians. The Secret Service Agents were an unexpected bonus. Their deaths really fired up the population and worked to sway public opinion and, ultimately, the President's plan.

However, the people who had hired him to kill King would not be pleased and he would have to relocate. He insured his pistol was stuck in his waistband holster; he checked his extra magazines and then began packing his meager belongings in his DC apartment. He did not know when company would come, but he knew they would.

As if on cue, his phone rang.

"Mr. Brewer," came the voice he had dubbed as Scarred Throat; it was deep, raspy and, the more he thought about it, foreign. "Your actions are causing some great concern in my organization. My superiors are beginning to think you are not the man for the job."

"You hired me to do a job," the assassin interrupted, "and I'll do it. You wanted it quick and public; well, it will be public. This was just the appetizer."

"We do not want an appetizer, Mr. Brewer," the voice trailed off momentarily. Mumbled talking in the background filled the earpiece as the assassin finished packing his one small bag. The handset cord on the phone became a tangled mess from stretching all over the room. Finally, the foreign voice returned.

"Mr. Brewer, we are terminating your contract," the voice stated matter-of-factly. "Your actions have jeopardized our organization and our plans. You are now a liability. Good day, Mr. Brewer."

"If that's how you feel about it, fine," Brewer said as he pulled his pistol, checked the safety and got behind the overturned kitchenette table. "But understand this. I was hired to do a job and I'm going to do it. Partially because of the payment promised; partially because it fits into my plans." Brewer let that sink in for a moment. He heard floorboards creaking in the hall.

"First, a little advice." Brewer let his voice grow cold as he aimed the pistol at his apartment door. "If I were you,

I'd tell your men good-bye before you send them to kill me."

The door crashed open and the shooting began.

Chapter Twelve

THE NEIGHBORHOOD SAT DARK and quiet. A light rain fell, adding more water to the already saturated ground. It had been a steady rain for almost two days and everything was wet. Nothing was immune to Mother Nature.

Assassin 46 skulked through the quiet streets. The rain masked his footfalls, easily concealing any noise he made. Virtually silent, he slowly made his way from shadow to shadow. Two blocks away, a dog barked once, whimpered, and went silent.

The Dent home was a standard two story Victorian, built in the early 1900s, with a wraparound porch and a rose covered latticework trellis opposite the garage. The red brick combined with the rain to create a dark, imposing presence set back from the street in the Boston suburb.

Assassin 46 took his time, insuring that everyone in the neighborhood was asleep as he continued his advance. He paused occasionally, listening for anyone or anything that might discover him. He heard nothing. At two-thirty in the morning, the assassin stepped past the lattice and froze, waiting.

He stayed there, crouched, for over five minutes. Nothing stirred. He finally made his way over to the back door, pulled out his lock-pick set, and began his work. The deadbolt went first, then the handle lock. The door opened silently, until the security chain caught. He cursed silently. There was no way to quickly, or quietly, undo the chain. He began looking around for something to snap the lock with, when he saw an open window on his left.

The window carried the dark shadow of a man into the laundry room. His feet left muddy imprints on the dryer and the floor as he landed quietly. Again, he waited, heard nothing. He left the laundry room and began scouting the house.

Nice furniture decorated the family room; a china cabinet occupied one whole wall of the dining room, a downstairs office contained a computer and oversize monitor. Satisfied he had mapped out the downstairs, he quietly headed upstairs.

He checked four rooms and found them all occupied. He stood in the doorway to the master bedroom for several minutes, contemplating the best way to finish the mission. He decided on his course of action and headed back downstairs. He silently stashed a few items in his backpack and then made his way to a table at the bottom of the stairs. He grabbed a plant-filled vase and dropped it on the floor.

Douglass Dent awoke with a start and sat up. His wife, Melody, rolled over sleepily. “What was that?” she asked.

Dent struggled with the covers for a moment. He had not had a good night's sleep in over a week and now this. “I’m going to kill that damn cat!”

He grabbed a bat that he kept in the closet and proceeded down the stairs. “Here kitty, kitty.”

He turned the corner toward the kitchen, saw the vase, and saw a shadow move. His eyes said 'cat' before his mind realized that the shadow was too large to be the cat. Dent's eyes and brain caught up as the shadow moved toward him and stabbed him with one of the knives from the kitchen.

Dent tried to yell, but the assassin had rendered him silent with the first stroke. Dent fell to the floor and died less than a minute later.

“Doug?” came the female voice from upstairs. “Everything okay?”

Assassin 46 rounded the corner, aimed his pistol and fired up the stairs. The shot echoed through the house as Melody Dent fell. The Assassin followed the shot and went back to the second floor. He continued through the house until everyone, even the cat, was dead.

As sirens wailed in the distance, Assassin 46 broke out a window in the master bedroom, away from all of the neighbors now crowding the lawn, and then activated his retrieval beacon. A minute later, he stepped into the bubble and the world closed in around him.

The first thirty seconds of the trip was the usual serene opaque nothingness that marked a time skip. That abruptly changed. In the last three minutes of the trip back to the Twenty-Third century, Assassin 46 experienced gut-wrenching spins, electrical surges that left his fingers tingling and, something he had never experienced in over a dozen skips, the sound of someone screaming in agony. He thought that especially odd since there was usually no sound at all in the time stream. He finally realized that he was the one screaming as the electrical currents and time eddies buffeted his body.

He spotted a black dot in the turbulence and tried to concentrate it on it to give his mind something to think about other than the agony he was experiencing. The dot began to grow as it slowly filled the white opaque time vortex. The dot turned into a roughly door shaped aperture. The door approached rapidly and opened as it engulfed the Assassin.

The skip was over.

He stepped through the open door, breathing heavily. He flailed his arms, patting himself, as he tried to get the electrical surges off his body. He fell to the floor of the Time Skip Control Room and lay there for a minute or so, still slapping at his legs and abdomen as the pain subsided. The worst over, he slowly stood and was greeted by Mr. Tomlinson, who, somehow, looked much older than he did yesterday. Behind Mr. Tomlinson was a man in scarlet robes that he had never seen before and Mr. Mayweather.

"Assassin," Tomlinson said. "Welcome." His voice had an edge he had never heard before. Assassin 46 took it as a warning that things were not the norm.

"Mr. Tomlinson," he nodded in greeting. He intentionally paused, taking in the whole control room before speaking again. Most of the technicians were monitoring their consoles, but a few were staring at him intently. He noticed that the control room had changed. There were no giant monitors covering one wall. It was filled with what he would call antiquated equipment. Not the state of the art set up he had left yesterday.

He decided he had no idea what was going on, so he looked at the man in scarlet and voiced his opinion. "Okay, what the hell is going on?"

"We need a debriefing immediately," came the gruff response and three more men, all dressed in scarlet, materialized at the Assassin's side. "Come with us."

The group left the Control Room and proceeded down the corridor toward the Council Chambers. Assassin 46 was concerned. No one was taken before the Council unless there was a severe failure. Those usually ended with the death of whoever screwed up. He forced himself not to jump to conclusions and followed the crowd, but in the back of his mind, he began to run through scenarios to ensure his survival. He silently admitted it looked bleak.

The seven men arrived at a set of metal doors, one of which was already open. Tomlinson entered first, followed by the scarlet leader, the Assassin, two guards, Mayweather and then the last guard. Assassin 46 took note of the order and wondered if Mayweather was in as much trouble as he was. *Did the mission go badly?* thought the assassin, preparing to fight his way out of the Guild, if necessary.

As he entered the room, his attitude changed from fight and flight to utter confusion. This was not the Council Chambers. The chamber appeared to serve as the administrative office of the Guild. Assassin 46 was flooded with memories of his Guild history and the offices in the late Twenty-Second Century, when the Guild began working with the concept of time travel.

The group stopped in front of a short, balding man with a large belly and tobacco stained teeth. He looked up from his paper-strewn desk, eyed the newcomers and stopped his gaze on the assassin. He sat back in his chair, which creaked from the weight shift, placed his elbows on the armrests, and steepled his fingers under his chin. "And who do we have here?"

"We haven't asked," the scarlet leader replied. "Once he came through the time door, we brought him straight here."

The administrator nodded and turned to look at the assassin. "Who are you?"

"Assassin 46."

"Your name?"

"We don't use names in the Guild," the assassin replied. "I haven't used my name in almost twenty years."

The administrator nodded absently, half dismissing the statement. "How did you arrive in our Control Room?"

The Assassin watched the scarlet robed men from the corner of his eyes for a moment, and then turned his attention to the Administrator. Assassin 46 wanted to study his reaction. "I completed my assigned mission and my skip retrieval beacon brought me here." He paused. "As it always does."

To his credit, the administrator did not flinch. Tomlinson, however, clapped his hands and danced around for a moment. "It works! It works!"

"Tomlinson!" yelled the Administrator. The Control Room Director stopped instantly and looked at the floor, his excitement barely in check. The Administrator turned back to the Assassin. "How many missions have you completed for the Guild?"

“I've completed nine assassination missions, and four Cleaner Skips.”

“Cleaner Skips?” asked Mayweather.

The assassin looked at him and he could not help the odd look that he knew was plastered on his face. “I went back to either assist a Cleaner Team in evaluating an assassination, or to evaluate the team for a future mission.”

“What is a Cleaner Team?” asked Tomlinson.

“It's a new concept we've been toying with,” answered the Administrator. He had a look of worry, frustration, and disbelieve on his face. He sat even further back in the chair until it almost tipped over. “It's a team that will deploy to set up an Assassination, or evaluate a particular moment in history.”

“So you can set up a comprehensive archive of not only this timeline, but alternatives,” finished Assassin 46. He looked from the Administrator, to Tomlinson and back to the Administrator. “You've never completed a successful Time Skip, have you?”

Tomlinson looked to the Administrator before he answered, receiving a shrug for his efforts. “Not yet. We were just about to complete our finals tests when the system switched on to receive, and you appeared.

“You are our first successful Skip!” he stated with a nod.

“I'm just returning from a mission, that's all. I would say that I stepped out of the skip too soon, but that wouldn't explain Mr. Tomlinson—"

“What was your mission?” interrupted Mayweather.

Assassin 46 looked at him for a moment. “Before I answer that, I'd like to know, what is your function around here, Mr. Mayweather.”

Mayweather looked slightly taken aback. “I am the lead programmer and computer technician for the Time Skip.”

“Mr. Mayweather has been instrumental in the theories, calculations and innovative mechanics of the Time Skip.”

The Assassin looked at Mayweather. “You blew it.”

Mayweather looked confused.

“I was sent back to the year 2011 to kill Douglas Dent and his entire family.”

“Why would anyone want to kill an ent—” began Tomlinson.

The Administrator interrupted, he turned his head to the Assassin. “Ordered by whom?”

“By the Council, who was hired by you,” he turned to the computer programmer, “Mr. Mayweather.”

Everyone turned their attention to Mayweather at that point, giving Assassin 46 a moment out of the spotlight. The moment was short lived. “Would you explain that, Assassin?”

Assassin 46 spent the next ten minutes explaining how Mayweather was one of the richest men on the planet and had hired the Guild to make him even richer. He described the plan, and the assassination of the Dent family. The only part he left out was the wild and unsettling retrieval skip.

“I'm rich?” Mayweather muttered. The technician focused inwardly as he absentmindedly stepped away from the group.

The Administrator waved a dismissal hand at Mayweather knowing he was out of the conversation for at least a couple of minutes. "And you apparently altered the timeline with the death of this family."

"Apparently," the assassin agreed. "You appear to be about a hundred years behind my timeline, but running pretty much parallel in the development of the technology."

"What do we do now?" asked Tomlinson. "If we could undo the death of the Dent family, this timeline would reverse itself into the line that the assassin came from." He looked hopeful. "We could have avoided the death of billions in the Nuclear War of 2032."

Assassin 46's face paled. "Nuclear W—" His voice caught and he struggled with the thought that he could have caused the deaths of billions. "There wasn't a war," he denied.

Tomlinson saw the look on the Assassin's face and explained. "There was a war in this timeline," he paused, "and it nearly destroyed the entire world. It set us back at least a hundred years."

"You have to send me back to fix this," the Assassin implored.

"This timeline is progressing normally for us," the Administrator replied. "We don't know what further tampering would do. It may correct what you know of history, or it could further damage the current timeline." The Administrator stood up and came around the desk. He cleared off a corner space and sat on the corner. "We need to research this more before I will authorize another attempt at a Skip."

"I can undo this," Assassin 46 protested. "Send me back and I'll reverse all of this."

"That is not possible," Tomlinson replied, shaking his head. "We will have to send someone else back to intercept you. We cannot risk having two of you in the same place at the same time."

The Assassin nodded. "Alright, then who is your most promising Apprentice?"

The Administrator rubbed his chin. "Find Dorian Gabriel and bring him here."

The three scarlet robed guards turned to carry out the order.

"No!" cried Assassin 46. "You can't use him!"

Everyone paused and looked at the assassin.

"That's my real name!"

* * * *

Three days later, the Administrator sent for Assassin 46, Tomlinson and Mayweather. The group convened in a conference room down the hall from the open-air office the Administrator favored. The blinds were open and the four men sat in the bright light in quiet reflection for several minutes.

"Gentlemen, I have discussed this situation with the other Administrators and we agree with the Assassin. We must go back and undo this. If we can avoid the War of 2032, then we can save billions of lives."

"Who are we sending?" asked Tomlinson.

"An Apprentice named Lassiter," replied the Administrator, checking a dossier packet lying on the table. "Following the new protocol introduced by our new friend here, Lassiter has been dubbed 'Assassin 39' and he will be sent back to intercept Assassin 46 and stop the Dent assassination." Assassin 46 picked up the file on Lassiter and began thumbing through it. The Administrator looked at the Assassin. "Do you know him in your timeline?"

"I've heard of him. He is supposed to be one of the brightest in his class." He laughed slightly as he thumbed through the file. "I can see that holds true across several timelines. Funny how time parallels..." His voice trailed off for a moment and then he refocused on the dossier in his hands. "At least he is someone I've heard of before. Shouldn't be a problem."

A knock at the door drew everyone's attention and in walked a young man, around twenty, with a head full of hair and a confident air about him. "You sent for me, Administrator?"

"Mr. Lassiter." The Administrator rose and shook the young man's hand. "We have a special assignment for you." The young man remained silent and watched everyone intently. "We need you to perform a Skip to stop an assassination."

"Stop one, sir?"

"Yes." The Administrator motioned toward Assassin 46. "This is Assassin 46. He arrived a few days ago from an alternate timeline. We need you to go back and stop him from changing history. Stop him from completing his mission."

"How do I do this?" He turned to the Assassin. "No offense, sir, but I doubt if you met me on the street you'd listen if I said, 'hey, don't kill that guy.'"

"I was ordered to stand down once already, being told twice is unusual, but believable. Besides, I know Apprentice—I mean, you, Mr. Lassiter. We were working on a project for the Guild Council in my timeline. There won't be any issues."

"We were working on a project together? An Apprentice was working with an Assassin?" The young man's voice seemed to gain even more confidence.

"You tell me the mission is cancelled, I'll return to my time before killing the Dents and everything returns to normal."

"Excellent!" the Administrator smiled. "Prepare yourself Assassin 39. Tomorrow you will be the first Assassin, from this timeline, to skip back in time!"

* * * *

Assassin 39 stepped from the time bubble feeling electric tingles all over his body. Shaking his hand to remove the weird sensation, he gritted his teeth until the pins and needles stopped. He worked the sensation from his legs before he checked his surroundings and immediately wished he were somewhere else.

He stood in the middle of a ballet class dance floor surrounded by ten-year-old ballerinas in training and two thirty-something female teachers. The two women stood there in shock while the students began to giggle at the young man who had suddenly appeared with twitching limbs.

One little girl mumbled, "Do the hokey pokey."

"My apologies, ladies," he smiled politely as he moved toward the studio exit, his face flushed red with embarrassment. “The magic show is one block over. I think I'll use the door this time.”

Outside, Jason Lassiter breathed a sigh of relief and broke into laughter as his mind recalled the looks on the poor women's faces. Once the laughter subsided, he took a deep breath and began his trek toward the Commons where he would, hopefully, meet up with Apprentice 46.

The rain ended but the sky was overcast, cool and dreary. Lassiter made his way across the city of Boston. He had never been here before. The city had been destroyed by the war. The young Assassin had always heard of the beautiful city, one of the oldest in what had once been the United States. He checked his watch, decided he had time to spare, and took a little time to see the sights.

He had lunch at a corner café, ordering something he had never even heard of before and enjoyed it thoroughly. After lunch, he found his way to a local shopping plaza and was amazed and intrigued at the people and the shops. In the end, he concluded that today was one of the best afternoons he had ever spent.

After spending the day in the city, he began asking directions to the Commons. He made his way through Boston and began observing and cataloguing the Twenty-First Century. The first in his timeline to travel back in time, Lassiter wanted to provide a good report to his superiors when he returned. He had thought about the two timelines and concluded that Assassin 46 would return to the other timeline, and Assassin 39—he could not get use to the new name—would return to what he considered the 'correct' timeline.

That made him pause for a moment. He stopped so suddenly that the woman walking behind him almost ran into him. He apologized, and then started again, wondering if every Time Traveler thought of his timeline as the 'correct' timeline. That was something he would have to discuss with Mr. Tomlinson and the Administrator.

About two hours before sunset, the young traveler made it to the Commons. Disheartened, he had no idea that the Commons could be so big. He found a map of the Commons on a billboard, planted a look of determination on his face, and began a systematic search of park.

Three hours later, Lassiter was hot, tired and completely discouraged. He had checked the date on a discarded newspaper. It was the right place and time. After searching the entire Commons, he had found no trace of Assassin 46.

He stopped at the park fountain, waited until he was sure no one was around, took off his shoes and socks, and then dipped his feet in the cascading water. He sighed as the cool water soothed his aching feet.

He heard footfalls and turned to face a group of six teens approaching him in the dim light. Assassin 39 identified the newcomers as gang members by the colored clothes they wore. The men, all late teens early twenties, quickly encircled the fountain and the young assassin. Lassiter felt his training wash over him and he remained calm, poised and waited for his moment to strike. The conversation started off bad, as expected. They wanted his money and his shiny little necklace, a gift from his wife. When he refused, the situation became worse as the ruffians displayed an assortment of knives and pistols.

Lassiter knew he was in serious trouble and prepared to attack the men, starting with the leader. He paused in his plan when he began to feel an odd tingling sensation in left arm. The tingling slowly intensified, and then he saw the time bubble forming about ten feet away behind the self-identified gang leader. The leader turned to the source of new light and his expression changed from menace to fear.

Assassin 46 stepped from the bubble. His face went slack from surprise at the scene around the fountain, especially at the young man in the middle of the circle who had a striking resemblance to Apprentice 101. The young man's eyes showed determination, but also confusion. No amount of training could prepare someone to face six-on-one odds.

The gang leader partially turned and stared at the man who had appeared and at the disappearing bubble. “What the—”

Three of the gang members ran off into the darkness, one of them tripped as he tried to run and was knocked out cold when his head hit the fountain. The remaining three, the two with the pistols and the leader, stayed where they were, waving their weapons from one assassin to the other in near panic.

Lassiter saw the panic and confusion in the gang member's faces and knew that they would start shooting at any moment. Mission first, he looked at Assassin 46. “I was sent to tell you—”

The thunder of the first shot echoed in the still night. Lassiter heard it as biting pain filled his chest. He stumbled backwards, into the fountain water, as the bullet tore through his heart. He died instantly.

The man that had fired had not even realized he had pulled the trigger. He stood in shock at the smoke drifting from the barrel of the pistol. Before the echo died, Assassin 46 pulled his Glock 9mm from his waistband and, in rapid succession, shot each of the gang members in the head, including the one lying unconscious by the fountain.

Assassin 46 then knelt by the body of Apprentice 101 and searched for anything about his mission. He found nothing; no data crystal, no retrieval beacon. There was nothing on the body to identify that this was Apprentice 101.

Sirens wailed in the distance.

The Assassin stood, said a few words, and then disappeared into the darkness.

* * * *

"Uh, oh."

The comment, spoken aloud, broke the tense silence in the conference room. For the four men sitting around the small table, it was the first thing spoken in several hours.

"What, 'uh, oh?'"

"Lassiter is dead."

"What? How? How do you know?"

"Memories."

Blank looks from the crowd encouraged Assassin 46 to continue. He pointed to his head. "I had just arrived in Boston, on the Commons, and found a young man that resembled Apprentice 101...er...Lassiter, surrounded by several men, criminals, from the looks of them. He started to say something to me and they shot him."

A few moments of uneasy silence filled the room before Tomlinson motioned for him to continue. "And?"

"And, I killed four men. Two others ran off. I completed the mission and ended up here."

"Mr. Lassiter skipped two hours ago," the Administrator said, checking his portable computer. "The Controller states the machinery worked perfectly and there were no problems."

"There were no problems from this end, Administrator," the Assassin said sadly. "He was just in the wrong place at the wrong time.

"I couldn't find a retrieval beacon on him. I'm sorry. I had no way of returning his body here."

"Retrieval Beacon?" asked Mayweather, writing everything down in his notebook.

"It sends a signal back to the control room. The technicians then open a skip bubble and the assassin returns."

"We obviously have a lot to learn from you, Mr. Gabriel," the Administrator smiled. He saw a promotion in all of this and he was almost giddy. "Perhaps you should stay."

Mr. Tomlinson was the first to cut in. "No. He must go back to his timeline. We must undo this. Billions of people died who didn't have to."

The Administrator frowned, he was hoping for a little support from his assembled group. It appeared he was not going to get it. He looked at each in turn, and then finally gave up. "Fine! But, we've already lost one Assassin on this. I don't want to try to meet up in the Commons again."

Mayweather looked thoughtful. “Where did you go after the fountain incident?”

“To a staging area about five miles south of the Commons; a position close to the Dent house.”

“That is where we will send the next intercept.” Mayweather smiled and clapped his hands together, as if it was a very simple solution to an even simpler problem. “Our assassin will approach you, tell you the mission is cancelled, and everything will be corrected.”

“Is that all?” the Assassin laughed lightly, almost believing the simplicity. “What do you need?”

A pause and a smile. “Do you have the address?”

* * * *

Assassin 94 stepped from the time bubble and almost fell from the second story of a dark green house in the suburbs of Boston. She stopped one-step short of a twelve-foot drop into—she looked below her—holly bushes. She shook visibly, both from the feeling of cold the skip left her with and the thought of the scrapes she would have received from a fall through the bushes. She felt the electric tingle of the skip bubble and turned to watch it fade and finally disappear into the night.

Nice sound, she mused as she knelt and waited for her eyes to adjust. It only took a minute and then she made her way silently down from the roof, across the dark yard and into the shadows.

She moved from shadow to shadow toward her slated rendezvous. Her mind was everywhere but on the mission at hand. So distracted by her thoughts, she stepped off the curb and into the path of the one car out at midnight. She managed to jump out of the way and took a moment to slow her heart rate and get her mind back on her mission, which was more difficult that she wanted to admit for several reasons.

First, Assassin 94 had met with the man from the other timeline before she skipped and took an instant disliking. He had instantly recognized her as Apprentice 97, the girlfriend of Apprentice 101. He later found out that they were married in this timeline. He apologized for her loss, made the usual consolatory remarks, and then gave her meeting instructions. She left with a feeling of remorse, a tingle of excitement, and a strong desire to kill the man who allowed her husband to die.

She was instructed to meet the assassin before one o'clock in the morning local time and to stop him from killing the Dent family. Meet, deliver her message and, if everything went well, she would be returned to her time, but she had other plans.

She wanted revenge.

Second, she had just made history as the first woman to ever skip. She had been preparing for this all of her life, ever since she gave up her rich inheritance to make her own way. Her family had disowned her, but that was fine. She had the Guild, her friends and her husband. She wondered momentarily about her twin in the other timeline. Was she as happy as Apprentice 97 had been?

She shook her head and focused on her mission. First and foremost, she had to prevent the War of 2032. She knew exactly how she would do that, but what would happen to her? Would she simply fade away, or transport back to her timeline? She had been ordered to correct an error that could wipe out her very existence.

Time travel definitely gives you something to think about, she mused as she kept to the shadows.

Her heart rate slowed, she continued the remaining two miles to the rendezvous undetected. She saw the assassin before he saw her. He squatted beside a tree a half a block from the Dent home. Deep in shadow, he watched the house. Assassin 94 continued to move slowly toward him. She was within two hundred yards when he turned, saw her, and froze.

He made it apparent he was armed by opening his jacket and showing his pistol, but she kept approaching. She kept her hands out to show she was unarmed, and he allowed her to come forward. She halted out of arms length, still holding her hands up for him to see.

"I am Assassin 94," she introduced herself. "I was sent here to tell you the mission is cancelled."

"Assassin?" he mused, keeping his hand on his holstered sidearm. "Yesterday, you were only an Apprentice."

"In your timeline, perhaps," she smiled. "But in the timeline you create here tonight, I am an Assassin."

"The timeline I create?" He paused, looked thoughtful before he turned his eyes back to the woman. "What happens here tonight?"

"You succeed," she said with finality, "and the world changes."

He smiled. "Master Li sent you, didn't he?" Assassin 46 shook his head. "That son of a bitch. I'm a veteran of a dozen missions, and he still insists on testing me. Damn it!" He looked at the woman again. "You go back and tell that Chinese bast—"

"I don't know a Master Li," she replied. "But I do know that you must not kill the Dent family tonight. If you do, you start a timeline where billions die."

"Billions?"

"Just activate your retrieval beacon and go home," she ordered. "I will not allow you complete your mission."

"You won't allow—"

Assassin 97 shot him mid-sentence.

* * * *

The conference table was stacked with coffee cups, various unread reports and two portable computers. Assassin 46, Tomlinson, Mayweather and the Administrator sat around it in silence. The four men looked worried, but said nothing, each one dealt with the anxiety and waiting in their own way. The Administrator mentally went over training schedules for the Guild, Tomlinson considered prototype testing of a new memory crystal, Mayweather assembled a schematic in his head of the skip beacon, and Assassin 46 simply stared at the flashing lights of the control consoles. The technicians around them glanced at them occasionally, but did not interrupt.

"She has been gone three hours," Tomlinson finally broke the silence. "She should have made contact by now."

"Do you have any new memories?" Mayweather asked of the Assassin, who sat unmoving.

"No," came the distant reply. The Assassin gulped, grabbing his head. "I...I don't feel so good." He screamed and fell to the floor. Everyone in the room turned to watch him writhe in agony.

The Administrator was on his feet. “What the—”

Tomlinson yelled at a nearby technician. “Get the Doc!”

Mayweather rushed to the Assassin, trying to control the man as he clutched his head and rolled from side to side. Tomlinson stopped him, and pulled him away. “Don't.”

The Administrator joined the two men as they stood, helplessly watching the man on the floor. Assassin 46 suddenly let out a final, long scream and stopped moving. No one said a word as Assassin 46 simply dissolved in front of them. Tomlinson, Mayweather and the Administrator stood in stunned silence, exchanging bewildered glances. They missed the fact that six other people in the room dissolved as well.

The entire world seemed to dissolve into an opaque, disfigured shape of itself. The room morphed from the messy, disorganized, and open control room, into the sterile, organized Skip Control Room. Tomlinson, Mayweather and the Administrator also changed, but none of them realized it as the timelines merged together.

Tomlinson remained Tomlinson, albeit somewhat younger. His hair became shorter and darker, and his waistline lost a few inches. He stood calmly talking to the man to his left, oblivious to the changes as the world solidified around him.

Mayweather, standing on the left of Tomlinson, morphed into Master Li; the soft-spoken college dropout changed into the gruff Chinese instructor in mid-sentence.

The Administrator morphed into Apprentice 101, who stood with his arms crossed, listening to his two mentors. He looked and felt tired as the two men continued the now hour-long conversation.

"...and I'm telling you we need to pull the Assassin back, now. We have every reason to fear the completion of this mission."

Master Li simply shook his head. "I understand your concerns, but the Council has never been wrong. We should not doubt them now."

"The Council has never had this much pressure put on them," came the response. "This will not go well for the Council, or us."

The argument was cut short by a technician who hit the 'retrieval switch' that turned the control room lights from incandescent white to a dull, light blue. With that signal, everyone turned to their control panels and prepared for the arrival of an Assassin or a Cleaner Team.

Tomlinson consulted a small computer and realized they had nine teams out. He briefly wondered who was returning. He turned, with Li and Apprentice 101, to watch the portal.

The bubble appeared, opened, and unceremoniously dropped a lifeless Apprentice 46 onto the floor. The bubble hovered for a moment, as if contemplating what it had just done, before dissolving with a barely audible pop.

"Get the Doc!" Tomlinson yelled as he and Master Li moved to the side of Assassin 46. Apprentice 101 was a second behind them. They all noticed the chest wound immediately, but it was Master Li who found the note. He pointed to the slip of paper as he checked for a pulse.

Tomlinson grabbed the note inside the assassin's jacket, handed it to the apprentice, and went back to checking pockets until he found the memory crystal. Tomlinson grabbed the crystal and moved to a nearby table where he plugged the crystal into the reader and quickly scanned the readout. It showed that the Assassin had only been in 2011 for about ninety minutes. There was nothing about the mission or his death. Tomlinson returned to the side of Apprentice 101, who had the letter unfolded and was reading it.

The Guild Doctor arrived and pronounced the Assassin dead. Her staff placed the body on a stretcher and then she led them out toward the infirmary, which was conveniently down the hall from the mortuary. Once they were gone, Mr. Tomlinson motioned toward the apprentice and the letter.

"What does it say, Apprentice?"

"'I killed him. I killed him because he killed my husband. I killed him to prevent the death of billions.'" The Apprentice looked up at that, saw the concern in the other men's eyes, and continued. "'Do not kill the Dent family. It will destroy mankind. I've seen it. Do NOT kill the Dent family. Signed, Assassin 94, Rachel'"—he gulped "'—Sullivan.'"

"Assassin 94? Rachel Sulliv—" Tomlinson asked. "Who the hell is that?"

Master Li was searching for the name in his mind when he noticed Apprentice 101, who stood fidgeting. "You know this person?"

Apprentice 101 nodded. "So do you. Only," he paused nervously, "you know her as Apprentice 97."

Chapter Thirteen

THE WORLD SEEMED TO shift as soon as the firefight began. An unfocused opaque white film that shifted the world to the left by one meter and caused everything to shimmer; like the shaking of a minor earthquake. A time ripple as two timelines—two hundred years in the future—combined.

It only lasted a few seconds and shifted Rick Brewer to his left, out of the path of the automatic rifle fire from the door. It seemed to pause time for a fraction of a second, but only Brewer noticed. The rogue assassin took full advantage of the pause and shot each of his attackers. His pistol clicked empty as the last man fell to the floor. He reloaded and shot each man in the head—just to be sure.

Rick Brewer knew that time had changed via his déjà vu gift for temporal disturbance. He had felt the sensation several times in the past, but never anything as noticeable as a physical shift of the world. That ability was one of the reasons he had applied for the Guild in the first place. He did not know what had changed, but knew that it was in his lifetime before the banishment. There were no more temporal aftershocks, so he reloaded his pistol again, grabbed his 'go' bag, and left the now shattered apartment.

He joined the crowd on the street and moved away from the apartment as sirens began to wail in the distance. He saw three more of the thugs waiting in a parked car across from the apartment and thought briefly of lobbing a grenade in their direction. He dismissed the thought as the first of many police cars entered the block. He melted into the crowd then turned to observe the activities. Twenty minutes later, as the onlookers became bored with watching the police, he again blended with the crowd and left the scene.

As he stood in the crowd, he thought of the time wave that had disrupted the brief firefight. What had happened...and when? Since the world only shimmered, instead of morphing around him, he realized that whatever had happened had been corrected. He might have to take the next assassin that came after him alive. He needed answers.

The Assassin had another safe house across the river. He needed to regroup, and to plan his next move. Rick Brewer had a mission to complete and enemies to deal with.

First things first.

* * * *

President Martin Luther King, Jr. sat in the residence wing of the White House watching the Nightly News, flipping through all of the major networks that said virtually the same thing. He leaned toward the television and listened to the stories that his administration had told to the media. Not all of it was a lie, but enough of it was.

The news cut to a clip of Vincent Harding, the Press Secretary, saying that US Forces were still in preparation for deployment due to the forty-eight hour deadline imposed to the Russians almost forty-two hours earlier.

In reality, he had already ordered all forces mobilized and dispatched both the Atlantic and Pacific fleets to prepositioned locations within striking distance of Russian forces in Europe and Africa.

The Press Secretary also said that the Russians still denied involvement in the attempted assassination, which was true. However, the Press Secretary also said that the Soviets had stopped advancing through Africa, which was an outright lie. They were advancing. The only thing slowing them down was the vanguard of US Forces dispatched to the African Continent even before the assassin's bullet killed Secretary Abbott.

The President sighed heavily. He was in deep trouble, and he knew it.

There was a knock and the door opened. Defense Secretary Ralph Abernathy and Attorney General Clarence Jones entered the living quarters. Both men wore expressionless masks on their faces.

“Evening, Mr. President,” Abernathy commented.

President King nodded as the two men took up positions on either side of the President, sitting in overstuffed recliners facing the television. Both men watched the rest of the spokesman's comments before speaking.

“Think America will believe that the Russians stopped in Egypt, Libya and Tunisia?” Jones began.

King nodded as he glanced over at AG Jones. “Yes, for now.” He sat back on the couch. "And when we let it known that they have started advancing again that will be our catalyst to enter World War III.”

“It's the best way, Mr. President,” Abernathy said, arms crossed and sincere. “We waited too long to get involved.” He held up a hand as he got an accusing look from King. “I know. My mistake.”

He stared at the President, not quite making eye contact. “My advice was wrong. We should have intervened on our ally's behalf sooner. Much sooner. But now, with your ultimatum, and the official statement that the Russians have stopped advancing, we will have an excuse to get involved.”

A knock on the door interrupted the conversation, followed by the phone ringing and a television news reporter in Kenya reporting heavy fighting as the Russians advanced through Africa.

* * * *

Rick Brewer wondered absent-mindedly if he would survive through another war.

He stood in his third safe house in Arlington, Virginia, cooking a small pot of pasta over the stove. In the two weeks since he had killed the Treasury Secretary, he had witnessed the Russians damn near conquer all of Africa, US forces engaged the enemy in their first major battle, and America suffered its first defeat of the campaign. An entire tank division, over thirteen thousand men, had been either killed or captured. The world was in turmoil and no one could stop it. Now, he was ready. It was time to kill the President and push the world over the brink. Again, he wondered if he would survive.

He ate dinner in silence, splitting his attention between the television and its endless monologues about the Russian advance and listening to see if anyone set off any of the early warning devices outside his condo door. It was a relatively peaceful dinner, until the phone rang. No one had the number for the condo, so he was expecting a wrong number, or a salesman. He was surprised as he cautiously answered the phone.

"Hello?"

"Mr. Brewer?"

"Yes."

"My name is Jonathan McKindrick," began the caller in a calm voice that immediately triggered the fight or flight response from the banished assassin. The familiar voice continued, "I have been sent by the Guild to take you back to the Twenty-Third Century."

Mesmerized by the calm, matter-of-fact tone of the caller, Brewer replied, "Is that so? Why would I want to go back there? Last I heard they wanted to kill me."

"True, Mr. Brewer," replied the chilling voice, "but there are many ways to die."

Rick Brewer felt fear for the first time in decades. Fear studded perspiration erupted over Brewer's body. This fourth assassin, sent by the Guild, evoked spotted memories, but it was the voice that set him trembling.

"Have we met?" Brewer managed to ask.

"Briefly, once," confirmed McKindrick. "I was using the name Newberry at the time, although I doubt if you knew that. You shoved me out of your way the day you escaped into the time stream."

Brewer had a quick flash of memory: punching a guard, shoving a man from the door, hours of agony in the time stream. He shook visibly, and then regained his composure. "Hope I didn't mess up your mission."

He made sure to stay away from the windows as he grabbed his 'go' pack and made his way to the door. He checked the peephole, ensuring the area was clear.

"There were a few problems, but nothing of your concern."

The conversation dropped into silence.

"What kind of death do you have planned for me?"

There was a faint laugh. "Mr. Brewer, I'm not here to kill you, even though I am authorized to do so. The Guild wants you to return so that they can study you. You've been stranded in history for almost two hundred years, as near as we can figure. The Guild wants a firsthand account of that history. They also want to know what you've done to change it. And, probably most importantly, they want to study why you haven't aged."

Brewer checked his pistol. "Guinea Pig?" He shook his head to no one. "No thanks. I'll take my chances."

Across the street, Jonathan McKindrick, aka Assassin 73, sighted his German made Sniper Rifle through two windows of the intervening building, at the back of Rick Brewer. He adjusted the aim until his crosshairs were on the back of the assassin's head.

"As I said, there are many ways to die, Mr. Brewer."

The banished assassin stood silent for a moment, unaware that his head was in the sights of a hair-trigger less than four hundred meters away. With the scope he had, McKindrick could not miss.

Brewer moved his hand away from the doorknob. “I'm not saying I'll go back, but I will agree to a meeting.”

Across the way, McKindrick released the tension from his forefinger and moved his eye from the scope. He smiled threateningly. *If I can get close enough, I'll take us back together*. Two people travelling together in one skip beacon was risky, but it had been done successfully a few times before. He did not want to think of the dozen or so times it was not so successful.

“When and where, Mr. Brewer?”

Brewer thought quickly. “Three days from now. The Air and Space Museum at the Smithsonian. Three pm. North entrance.”

“Why the delay?”

Brewer turned, looked through the window directly at where McKindrick was watching, and smiled. “To give you time to enjoy the sights.” Brewer turned the knob and disappeared from his condo.

* * * *

The Presidential Podium stood in the center of the makeshift conference room. Technicians, aides, and pages ran around frantically in an effort to finish the last-minute details as guests started to arrive. Although in the center of the room, the podium appeared to be in a corner due to the large blue curtain that divided the room. Select Senators, Congressmen, Cabinet Members and other dignitaries entered the auditorium and took their seats, packing the Museum's Auditorium. President King stood in the wings, doing a final rehearsal of his speech. He allowed himself a minute of reflection. How had the world come to this point? Was it something he had done, or something he had failed to do? Was it simply bad timing? Or, was it that the world just was not ready for a black man to be in charge of the greatest nation on Earth?

The last thought troubled him the most. He had hoped that in the fifteen years since the Civil Rights Act that the US and the World had grown out of its bigotry. He now feared the worst. The United States had come a long way, the election proved that, but maybe the world was not quite ready.

Now he had to ask Congress to go to war.

The choice of venue was an odd one to some, but the President liked the history and the hope that the Smithsonian symbolized. The curtain behind the podium, when parted, would display the Enola Gay, the plane that dropped “Little Boy”; the first of only two atomic bombs ever used in conflict. He hoped that the symbolism would help him with his next task.

Vincent Harding took to the stage and made a short statement. It was a short recap of the Russian aggression, the assassination attempt, the ultimatum, and finally, the continued Russian advance. It was a short history lesson that led to today's Press Conference where everyone expected the President to ask for a Declaration of War.

A brief question and answer session followed. Mr. Harding did his job well and gave the media what they wanted.

* * * *

Jonathon McKindrick stood off to the side, in amongst the tabloid media. He did not ask a question. He did not need to. He was there for only one reason: kill Rick Brewer.

The Assassin had received updated mission information via a Skip Bubble the day after he had talked with the renegade. The Council had reconsidered and now Brewer was to be terminated. The Council felt they could gain some information on aging and history from his corpse. Brewer was too dangerous to leave alive.

McKindrick did not agree, nor did he care. He wanted them to make up their minds. It would have been so much easier to kill him three days ago.

McKindrick had written off trying to kill Brewer today, too much security, but he did want to keep the meeting. The Assassin knew that by keeping this meeting, he would get another chance.

The Press Secretary finished his portion of the brief and introduced the President. McKindrick was genuinely interested in this conference. He had studied the King Presidency and was genuinely impressed by his intelligence and his attempt to create peace in the world. Too bad it did not work. McKindrick shifted to his left to get a better view.

President King approached the podium and forced himself into a calmer state. He needed to show America and the World that he was calm and in charge of the situation. He looked at his notes and began a history lesson about the world at war.

* * * *

Rick Brewer lay motionless in the ductwork high above the crowd at the Smithsonian; hundreds of people stood thirty feet below him. He scanned the crowd through his riflescope and marked potential 'McKindricks.' He did not quite remember what the man looked like. In his defense, he did only get a brief look as he threw himself into the time stream.

Brewer identified seven people in the room he thought could be the futuristic assassin. He made a mental note of where all seven were, moved the weapon around in the close confines to ensure he had a shot on each and then doubled checked his weapon and camouflage. As the President neared the main part of his speech, Brewer refocused on his primary target and waited.

Brewer had lain prone in the ventilation duct for almost two days, ensuring he was secure in his location before the Secret Service secured the building. The ductwork was high overhead and near impossible to get into, so the Secret Service ignored it. Brewer had turned it into his sniper nest.

As his Dragunov was now in the hands of the FBI, the renegade assassin turned to a Yugoslavian Zastava M-76 with a specialized suppressor. The weapon, built to be very similar to the Dragunov, was made for him by a gunsmith who tragically died in a fire that engulfed and destroyed his gun store in Maryland. The weapon had a range of over eight hundred meters. Brewer was less than a hundred meters from the President.

President King finally got around to the point of the speech, asking Congress to declare war. Brewer sighted on the President and waited for the cue to open the curtain to reveal the Enola Gay.

* * * *

Jonathon McKindrick, also known as Assassin 73, watched as the President motioned behind him. The curtain slid apart to each side and the auditorium opened up to include several aircraft. Behind the President sat the SR-71 Blackbird on the far left, the Wright Brothers prototype plane was suspended from the ceiling and in the middle of the new open area, sat the Enola Gay, the B29 Super-fortress that began the end of World War II.

Something was wrong. It was a sense that had saved his life a dozen times in the ten years since he had graduated the Guild Academy. Assassin 73 slowly scanned the room. He saw the elected officials, the Secret Service and the police, and all of the history behind and around them. He finally looked up to scan the ceiling and, for the first time, saw the jumbled mass of support beams and ventilation ducts. His eyes settled on an air vent in time to see a small flash.

* * * *

Rick Brewer watched as the curtain opened and the crowd let out a collective gasp by the spectacle behind the President. Brewer took the opportunity to scan his seven secondary targets again. He had been in Kill Devil Hills when the Wright Brothers had flown their plane in December of 1903 and had worked as an aircraft mechanic on the B29 Bombers in World War II, so the site of the planes did nothing to awe the assassin. During WWII, he had even received a commendation for fixing a fuel line issue that would have prevented the flight of the Enola Gay. Of course, he did not tell them he had caused the fuel line problem in the first place.

The Assassin ticked off each of his suspects until he got to number four, who methodically scanned the ceiling. *Gotcha*, thought Brewer as he changed position slightly, aimed and pulled the trigger.

He did not even wait to see if his target went down. At this range, it would have been almost impossible to miss. He simply shifted his aim back to the President and fired again as someone in the crowd screamed. Brewer watched the President drop as his first bullet hit King in the chest. He fired a second time at the President, just to ensure that the man was down and then slid back into the ventilation duct out of sight.

Brewer heard the sounds of chairs shoved out of the way, people stampeding, and the yells of the Secret Service scanning for the shooter. He even heard two shots as a security guard killed a man who grabbed his chest as he had a heart attack. The Assassin ignored it all as he moved some ten meters from the opening and then slid into place a false panel. Anyone checking the ducts from the opening would see a solid wall and a ventilation duct system that had not been tampered with.

Now, it was time to wait.

* * * *

Four days is long enough, Brewer thought.

The sounds of the search had long since faded, but Rick Brewer still lay where he had hidden himself after the assassination. He had planned for a two-day stay, stashing enough food and water for that duration, but stretched his rations as the Secret Service had lurked around a lot longer than he had anticipated.

Now, he was ready to move.

He started to move the false panel aside and thought briefly of the last time he had looked out of his hiding place. The Secret Service had set up a series of cameras and recorders that criss-crossed the entire museum. He had reluctantly moved back to his cramped space. That was two days ago. He hoped the surveillance equipment was gone.

Finally, the noise died, and Brewer slid the panel aside. He breathed a sigh of relief as the cameras were gone and he was free to exit the building. He moved from his hiding place, leaving four days of wrappers, bottles and other debris.

The Assassin made his way through the maze of ventilation ducts. It took him almost an hour to make it to the basement. It felt good to be moving.

He stopped twice during the hour as he heard voices: security and janitorial staff roaming and cleaning. Both groups—or was it the same one—bypassed him without incident and he finally exited the ductwork. He paused, changing his rank clothes for a new set of janitor's overalls he had hidden in an adjacent vent. He carefully made his way from the basement.

He whistled softly as he walked up and, without missing a step, began pushing an abandoned cleaning cart toward the back of the museum. The cart was loaded with mops, brooms, and other cleaning supplies that added to his coveralls disguise. He proceeded down the corridor and made it all the way to the janitorial office before security challenged him.

Brewer entered the outer security foyer and saw three agents sitting and watching security camera footage of the grounds. Secret Service Agent Bart DiMario rose from his chair, his face asking the question, *Who the hell is this?* as he looked at the other two men stationed there with him. "Afternoon," was what he actually said.

Brewer nodded, looking at his watch. "Evening. Long day?"

The other two men stood as well.

"Where is Frank?" DiMario asked. "I didn't know there were two of you on this wing."

Brewer almost looked over his shoulder, figured that would look awkward, so he kept pushing the cart and simply shrugged. "I don't know. I've been working in the basement and haven't seen him in over an hour."

"ID please," ordered one of the other Agents, holding out his hand.

"Sure," the assassin replied, but knew his next move would be the most difficult.

Brewer had anticipated everything up to this point, but he had no way of knowing how much additional security would be here waiting. Three-on-one odds were actually better than he had anticipated. He slowly moved his hand toward his wallet. That was when Frank and another Agent entered the room.

The older, gray haired man with bloodshot eyes and two-day stubble looked confused for a moment. His eyes darted from side to side and his lips moved as if he were actually carrying on a conversation with himself. Finally, his eyes straightened at Brewer. "Who are you?"

Several things happened at once: the Agents went for their weapons, Brewer pulled his pistol and pulled the trigger in the general direction of DiMario, the world began to turn a milky white, and Frank the custodian pissed his pants. DiMario felt the bullets as they missed his head by less than an inch. The other three Agents paused, drawing their weapons, as they sought cover. Rick Brewer hoped he lived long enough to see the new world as this timeline began to morph.

Brewer dropped his pistol and raised his hands. “Don't shoot!” he yelled as Agent DiMario finally got a solid bead on the man. DiMario felt his finger tense before he could stop, and felt the weapon recoil. The white, opaque world engulfed the assassin before the bullet could travel the short distance and Brewer closed his eyes to let the maelstrom overwhelm him.

He felt the usual brief dizziness that accompanied a timeline change, but this one was not brief. It was like the time skip that had thrown him back to 1783, two hundred years earlier. He wondered if the Guild had discovered a way to retrieve him against his will. He did not like that thought.

It was replaced by the memory of the agony of the vortex he had traveled in before. There was no screaming this time, just electrical pinpricks all over his body that kind of tickled the assassin. The noise in his opaque sphere made him think of a waterfall, a noise growing louder. The loud rush of sound spiked and overwhelmed him. He doubled over as if hit in the solar plexus. The cramp faded quickly and he stood back upright, but kept his eyes closed against the white light outside of his eyelids. The noise eventually subsided, replaced by the sounds of a quiet day. The roaring wind of the time stream replaced by a cool, gentle breeze of what felt like an Autumn day.

He opened his eyes as the white, opaque world slowly came into focus.

Rick Brewer stood atop a windy hill in Washington D.C., staring intently at the Marine Corps Drill Team practicing for their upcoming Veteran's day performance. One unfortunate Marine dropped his rifle and received a verbal onslaught from his superior. Brewer simply smiled in the cold late October air, happy the days of answering to higher authority were over.

He had a vague sense of déjà vu, but ignored it as footsteps turned him to see a fat man in a heavy brown trench coat, hands thrust deep in his pockets and a scarf draped around his neck, approaching from a parked limousine. The man made it to the top of the hill, his breath visible with each rasping gasp. It took him several seconds before he could finally speak.

"Mr. Brewer. You understand that this meeting never took place and we never met today." The man used the end of the scarf to wipe a bead of sweat from his forehead.

He's going to die just walking up here, thought the tall, lean man. The sense of déjà vu grew stronger and Brewer knew he had been here before. Exactly here. He remembered the slacks, the gray turtleneck sweater and the deep brown leather jacket. The same leather jacket that now had holes in it from the apartment ambush. He ignored the man for a moment while he inspected the jacket. There were no holes. He turned back to the new arrival and his brown eyes studied the man for a few seconds before responding. “I understand. What is it you want done?”

“My employers do not like the path this country is taking,” came the reply, the raspy breathing replaced with a smooth, politically persuasive voice. “They seek a regime change, if the election next week does not go in their favor.”

Rick Brewer turned back to watch the Marine Drill Team, now performing flawlessly as the unfortunate youth was out of the formation, doing pushups in his dress uniform. The sense of déjà vu grew stronger and he began guessing what would happen next. He was correct every time.

“Regime change,” he gave a slight grunt. “Fancy way of saying ‘Assassination.’”

“Perhaps, Mr. Brewer, but it has a more polite ring to it.”

Brewer, his back still turned to the man, mouthed the words along with his visitor. The fat man took a large manila envelope from his jacket and took one-step toward Brewer's back.

“If the election does not go our way, and you agree to accept the assignment, then your pay will be considerable.”

Turning back to face the fat man, Brewer took the offered envelope, like he had the last time. “It will have to be. No one assassinates a President and simply walks away.”

The Fat Man turned and walked back down the hill, pausing at the limo door to collect himself before his driver opened the door and allowed him to enter. Brewer watched with an overwhelming sense of déjà vu as the limo took off toward the freeway.

He'll be dead in a week, he thought with certainty.

Finally, alone, Brewer closed his eyes and searched his memory for the source of his sense of déjà vu, finally found it, and relived the last three years of the previous timeline in an instant.

"What the hell happened?" he said aloud as he tore open the envelope.

The face in the dossier was different from the last one the Fat Man had given him. His memory drew a blank on this face and Rick Brewer knew that history had been changed. It had been changed and he realized, with a sudden tinge of fright and excitement, he had no idea what the future might hold.

* * * *

Apprentice 101 closed his microcomputer that held his outline and rested his hands, clasped together, at the top of the podium. He rested his elbows, leaned forward and made eye contact with his fellow second year classmates. His blue robes swirled as he took a long drink of water.

"In that timeline, we know that President King was killed in early spring of 1982. His death sparked a war with Russia that ended in the nuclear destruction of much of the Middle East and half of Europe. The Western third of Russia, including Moscow, was obliterated, and the Eastern Seaboard, to included Washington, DC, was destroyed. Millions died and the Western World dissolved into chaos.

"We also know that it took less than ten years for the Chinese to overthrow the rest of the world, not by force, but by pure economics. They came through the war unscathed and had all of the resources needed to take over; and take over they did. It was another two hundred years before the Chinese Hegemony was destroyed from within.

"In the unaltered timeline, it was only thirty years ago that our current world government was founded from the ashes of the Western Culture and the Chinese Hegemony."

The Apprentice checked the clock on the podium and realized he had been talking for over an hour. It was supposed to be a thirty-minute presentation. He glanced nervously at Mr. Donovan, who smiled and motioned him to continue, but he tapped his watch as a reminder that he was, indeed, out of time.

"The Guild decided to intervene when a timeline variant presented itself. It was the first, and only, time that the Assassin's Guild killed by proxy. A Cleaner Team contacted a prison inmate named James Earl Ray and promised to free him if he would kill the then thirty-nine year old Civil Rights Leader. This would have been almost fifteen years before he had even considered a run at the Presidency.

"Ray accepted the deal and killed King in Memphis, Tennessee. Ray made it all the way to London before being caught. Upon his return to the US, he pled guilty and was sentenced to life in prison.

"His guilty plea was also part of the Cleaner Team deal. They promised to break him out of prison a second time if he pled guilty. Once he was convicted, the Guild, of course, recalled the team and left Ray to his fate.

"I know I'm out of time, but are there any questions?"

Apprentice 89 rose. "What conspiracy theories are there surrounding this assassination?" He was a squirrelly kid with thick glasses and a very bad mustache.

Professor Donovan smiled as he thought the Apprentice would end up as a specialist in the 1970s.

"Good question," Apprentice 101 said. "There were actually two variations of one theory, and both involve the Cleaner team:

"The first theory is that James Earl Ray had accomplices, a team of assassins sent by the government to assist him. Easily disproved as he confessed that he acted alone; no government assassins helped him. Even though our team did break him out of prison, he planned and executed the assassination on his own.

"The second theory is that he was, in fact, just a fall guy for a team of assassins. This one gained a little more momentum as he was seen talking to our Cleaner Team from time to time. The brief mention of a small Army Unit added fuel to the fire and took our team out of the spotlight.

"The Army Unit alluded to in a few eyewitness accounts, was researched and accusations made, but there was never any proof of this unit's involvement, so the accusations were baseless. Although, there were several investigations conducted into the activities of this military unit.

"As I have exceeded my time here today and apparently saved Apprentice 104 from having to do his presentation," —the apprentice looked up at the mention of his name, his face beaded with sweat, and smiled weakly, "—that will conclude my briefing."

Chapter Fourteen

THE ROGUE ASSASSIN SLOWLY closed the book and leaned back in the library chair. He exhaled softly and rubbed his chin thoughtfully. Almost twenty years of history, from the Kennedy Assassination until two weeks before the Presidential Election of 1980, Rick Brewer had spent the last three days studying it all.

Most of the events were the same: Nixon and Watergate—that he missed because he was stuck in a Turkish Prison—the Moon Landings, and the Iranian Hostages. He was not familiar with the new set of politicians: Ronald Reagan—some kind of actor?—or Jimmy Carter, an honest to God peanut farmer? The research showed the economic and world situations seemed almost identical.

His thoughtful musings were interrupted by a sudden realization and he grabbed a book off to the side, flipped it open, and began scanning the pages until he found what he was looking for; the death of Martin Luther King, Jr.

He read the history book quietly, his lips moving with the words and his voice barely audible.

"King, his close friend Reverend Ralph Abernathy, and the rest of his entourage were staying in Memphis at the Lorraine Motel. They stayed there so often the room was dubbed the 'King-Abernathy suite.'" Rick Brewer leaned closer to the book. "At six-oh-one, as King stepped out onto the balcony, a single shot rang out. The single shot hit King in the right cheek and smashed his spinal cord before lodging in his shoulder.

"King was taken to St. Joseph's Hospital and was pronounced dead an hour after the shooting." Brewer sat back again. "He died fifteen years before he was elected President." He returned to the book. "Who was the assassin?"

He flipped a few more pages and found the information he was looking for. "James Earl Ray, an escaped convict, was apprehended at Heathrow Airport in London two months after the assassination. He was quickly extradited to Tennessee where he confessed to killing King. He later recanted his confession, but pleaded guilty to avoid a trial conviction and the death penalty.

"Ray claimed he met a man in Montreal, who called himself 'Raoul,' who was also involved in the conspiracy. Raoul was never found. Ray spent the rest of his life attempting to withdraw his guilty plea and secure the trial he never had."

Brewer sat back, thinking back through all of the names and faces of the Guild. After fifteen minutes he was convinced that James Earl Ray was not part of the Assassin's Guild, nor was there anyone named 'Raoul' in the Guild.

He half snorted-half laughed softly. "The Guild killed him through Ray." He shook his head. "Never heard of them doing anything like that before."

"Shhhh," came across the table from a fifty something woman.

Brewer nodded politely, left the table and headed toward the door. Perhaps it was time to send another message to the future.

* * * *

Apprentice 101 found himself standing in front of the Council for the fourth time, an unheard of feat for most Assassins, much less a mere Apprentice. He was no longer nervous standing before the five elders. He had learned to embrace the event and draw strength from the Council. It was something he was only vaguely aware of, but the Council, through the bi-annual psychological testing, knew he was now comfortable in the chamber and were impressed by it.

His light blue robes, with a red stripe around each wrist signifying his status as a Senior Apprentice, moved slightly as he swayed back and forth. He still did not know the reason why he had been summoned on the first day of class, but he had the distinct feeling that Mayweather had returned.

"Has Mr. Donovan been summoned as well?" He broke the awkward silence.

"Mr. Donovan is currently on a special assignment with Assassin 97," the lone female Council member replied. She gave a wry smile. "I believe you are familiar with Assassin 97?"

"Yes, ma'am," he replied. Apprentice 97 had graduated the Academy and was now Assassin 97, preparing for her first assignment. He did not know that Mr. Donovan was working with her. He pushed that information to the back of his mind to ponder later.

"Excellent," she replied, twirling her arms so that her robes wrapped around her wrists. "We need to discuss your between semester assignment."

He cleared his throat into his right fist, and took a moment to gather his thoughts. "I have narrowed down the best time to affect another attempt to kill or capture Rick Brewer. It is the early part of the 1980s.

"I did a little more research after my second year final thesis on Martin Luther King, Jr. I am convinced that Rick Brewer was the assassin in the other timeline." He expected the questioning look from the Council and continued. "The records were, of course, sketchy after the war, but what I did confirm is that our own operative, Assassin 73, was present at the event and was killed first.

"Then King was shot twice by an assassin who was never identified or captured. It took the Secret Service six months to even confirm where the shooter set up; in the ductwork above the crowd. By the amount of trash, water, and waste in the duct, Brewer has spent days in the duct waiting.

"Add to that the fact that James Earl Ray was not even alive in the other timeline and that leads me back to the man who, as we have confirmed, has a talent for Presidential Assassins."

"That is not a concrete confirmation, Apprentice," came the doubtful voice of the oldest of the five Council members.

“I've researched the renegade for almost five months now,” the Apprentice replied, standing tall and defiant. “I know it was him,” he finished, nodding.

The lone Councilwoman held up a hand to stop the retort of her colleagues. “Let's assume you're correct, Apprentice. What is his next move?”

“In my research, I've come across several memos and rumors that an Assassin was hired by a secret political organization to kill King. I am convinced that the assassin in question was Brewer.” He cleared his throat again. “That same organization exists in both timelines, and I believe that the organization will again approach Brewer in 1980 to affect either the election or the President himself.”

"And you propose to send a team to intercept him before he can interfere further?"

“That's the problem.” He shuffled his feet and shrugged slightly. “I cannot find where he was actually a part of the Presidential Assassination of 1981. Even if we sent a Cleaner Team or Assassin back, I can't give you a starting point to find Brewer.”

“What do you know about the Assassination?”

“I have just started researching those events, sir,” Apprentice 101 said, uncomfortable for the first time. “It will take me a few weeks, at least, to get a comprehensive timeline of the Assassination.”

“Stay on it, Apprentice.” The youngest man on the dais nodded. “And give us a report as soon as you can.”

* * * *

A few weeks had been an understatement.

It had been three weeks since he had stood in the Council Chamber and his knowledge of the 1981 Presidential Assassination was still minimal. He had details of that March day, but the back-story kept eluding him.

He sat in his room, back to the door, computer monitors, books and hand-written notes covering his desk. The room was in complete disarray: the unmade bed, clothes strewn everywhere and there was even a dirty tray from the lunchroom. All of that was against the Guild discipline policy. When the inspection came, as he knew it would, he would be in serious trouble.

Part of the reason the room was in such disarray was that he no longer had a roommate. As a third year—Senior, they like to say—he was entitled to a room to himself. He took advantage of that, for research privacy, but it looked like that might, in fact, be a burden. It also did not help that Assassin 97 was off on her secret assignment and had not come by in almost a month.

Apprentice 101 looked up from his monitor and into the mirror over his desk, rubbed his hands across his stubbled head—another Guild violation—and his face.

"I need a break!" he said to no one. He left the desk and began cleaning up his room.

It was less than an hour later that Apprentice 101, still straightening his now neatly folded clothes, realized what he had been overlooking, dropped his laundry, and ran back to his computer. He compared the killing of King to Reagan and knew that he had his answer.

* * * *

It was the last week of February 1981, President Ronald Reagan had been in office for one month, and Brewer was finalizing his plan. The Organization, as they called themselves, did not want another four years of Jimmy Carter, and had called a halt to Brewer's activities with the election of Reagan.

Now, they were unsure of the former California Governor and had growing doubts. The rogue assassin did not care about the Organization or their wishes. He felt cheated after the time merge and he wanted to kill someone. Brewer was not going to pull the trigger himself, not this time. He spent months searching for a proxy, and he had found the perfect scapegoat. John Hinckley, Jr. was a troubled young man and Rick Brewer was going to use it.

Brewer had researched the news for weeks before running across a story about Hinckley stalking a young actress named Jodie Foster. The news reported that this man had been arrested in Nashville, and had sent hundreds of letters to the actress, effectively stalking Foster across the country. The Secret Service had gotten involved when the troubled young man had been seen around Jimmy Carter on more than one occasion. He had even been within one foot of the President at one point before the Secret Service intervened. Brewer had revised his plan to include Hinckley. Now he had to approach the man and push him over the edge.

Rick Brewer sat at a coffee shop just off the campus of Yale University in Connecticut; a place often frequented by John Hinckley, Jr. The rogue assassin watched as the man entered the diner. Hinckley strolled past Brewer's booth, his unwashed medium length brown hair plastered to his skull. The Assassin thought he looked like a child, his slightly pudgy face and dark eyes belying the fact he was twenty-six years old. Hinckley sat in a booth and ordered a coffee. Brewer gave him a few minutes and quietly moved to the booth behind him.

Brewer opened a two-week-old paper to an article on Jodie Foster and said aloud. “Damn, she's good looking.” He read a few minutes and then let out another comment. “A talented movie star on top of her good looks, she'll go far!”

Hinckley was not paying any attention.

The rogue assassin turned from his seat toward his victim and tapped him on the shoulder. “Excuse me, but can I get your opinion on something?” Without waiting for an answer, he continued. “Don't you think Jodie is a talented actress?”

“Jodie?” came the mumbled reply.

“Yes, my cousin, Jodie Foster. I think she is going to make the family very proud.”

Hinckley turned to face him at the name of his obsession. “She's your cousin?”

“A distant cousin, but yes. I came up here to visit with her for a few days. I haven't seen her in years!”

“You know, Jodie?”

“Yes. Do you?”

“Not really,” Hinckley said cautiously. “But I've been trying to meet her.”

Rick Brewer knew he had his proxy.

* * * *

“He is going to use a patsy to kill Reagan.”

“A what?” ask the female Council Member.

Apprentice 101 once again stood before the Council, his robes swayed as he shuffled his feet nervously. He knew he was right, but he did not quite know how to convey it. He had also forgotten to shave the stubble from his head—he had already been admonished for that—which added to his nervousness. What else had he forgotten to do?

“A scapegoat. A proxy. Brewer will not kill Reagan himself. He is setting up someone to assassinate Reagan. That's why my research never could find him.” He talked fast, his words came in a rush. “He is working behind the scenes.”

“Preposterous,” replied a bald Council Member with a patch over his left eye. “He has never killed in this manner before.”

“And neither had the Guild until the King Assassination.

“Brewer is a student of history, like most of us. He killed King in the old timeline, all of which was erased when the Guild used James Earl Ray to kill King in 1968. I believe Brewer will use someone else in the killing of Reagan, just to show us that he, too, can adapt.”

"If what you say is true, then it will be almost impossible to catch him. We can stop the assassination, but not him,” stated the bald Council Member.

“Actually, sir, I think we can do both.”

* * * *

Mr. Donovan and Assassin 97 sat across from Apprentice 101 and the female Council member. It was a rare thing that a Council member would leave the chamber, much less come to the common area for a meeting. Rumors ran rampant about what was going on in the Guild. Mr. Tomlinson and Master Li entered the room and took the last two seats at the table piled high with notebooks, history crystals, coffee cups and several wads of crumpled paper.

"Gentlemen," Apprentice 101 began, "and ladies." He gave a nod to each of the two women present. "As you know, I have been studying the history of our rogue Assassin, Rick Brewer. I think, for the first time, we have a genuine chance to capture him without completely disrupting our own timeline.

"We know, unequivocally, that he has either been responsible for, or in the vicinity of, every Presidential Assassination since 1840.

"Harrison; elected 1840: looked like the flu; but, we now know it was a flu strain introduced by Brewer.

"Lincoln; elected 1860: killed by John Wilkes Booth but, Brewer was at Ford's theater.

"Garfield; elected 1880: killed by Charles Guiteau but, Brewer worked in the White House.

"McKinley; elected 1900: killed by Frank Czolgosz, but Brewer was in Washington at the time.

"Harding; elected 1920: died of a heart attack, but Brewer again was in Washington and I believe introduced a toxin he concocted that was undetectable at that time.

"Roosevelt; elected 1940. Roosevelt is the anomaly. He, too, died in office, but from a long illness. My research says that Brewer was there, on his staff, and actually tried to save him.

"Kennedy; elected 1960. We know that Brewer was in the crowd, but had nothing to do with the Guild sanctioned assassination.

"This brings us to Reagan; elected in 1980. History shows that he was shot two months into office by John Hinckley, Jr., but that is not what killed him. The autopsy on the President showed that the bullet that killed Reagan was fired from a high caliber rifle. Hinckley used a pistol.

"In my research, I discovered that the kill-shot was fired from an unknown woman from a building on the opposite side of the street from where Hinckley was apprehended.

"She was never captured and her identity was never discovered."

"A woman? You think she was working for Brewer?" asked Tomlinson.

"No, sir. I think Hinckley was his puppet."

"Hinckley? But what about the woman?" again from Tomlinson.

"Sir, I don't know how she fits in, or why she fired the shot, but..."

Distraught, Assassin 97 looked up from studying the reports in front of her. "I know who killed Reagan."

Everyone turned to face the woman as she fought to bring her emotions under control. She did not quite manage it.

"Look at this long range photo that shows the crowd opposite Hinckley. That woman, right there." She pointed to a shadowy woman barely visible in a third story window down the block. "That's me. I killed Reagan."

* * * *

Anxiously, Assassin 97 made her way up the stairs to the third floor of the building. The hallway was clean, pristine, recently refinished. Assassin 97 looked at the decor for a moment. *I hope I don't have to ruin it*, she thought.

Having spent the last three days with her cleaner team going over every aspect of the mission, she knew what to do, but this was to be her first true mission. Nervous sweat coated her hands and butterflies tore at her stomach. She thought back to her first skip to 1865, to try to calm her mind, but that was a recon mission. She had barely escaped capture by Brewer on the train. That memory did not help.

She checked her watch, 14:25. Almost time. She rubbed her hands on her jeans to dry them and unholstered her pistol. She quickly checked both ends of the hallway before attaching the suppressor. Touching the communicator implant behind her ear, she heard a single response and waited with her back against the wall, the pistol pointed at the floor.

At 14:30 she took a step from the wall, turned, and kicked open the apartment door. The door splintered and she followed the kick into the room. She saw one man, holding binoculars looking out the window. He turned at the sound of the door and reached for his pistol in his waist.

Rick Brewer and Assassin 97 recognized each other at the same time and both paused, sizing up the other. Brewer calculated his experience would carry him through the shootout and finished drawing his pistol. Assassin 97 felt a calm wash over her as she shot him twice in the chest. She checked the body, then the room before she picked up the rogue's sniper rifle, checked to ensure it was loaded, and took up a position overlooking the Presidential entourage.

President Reagan left the Hilton Hotel surrounded by Secret Service Agents. The agents formed a small corridor for him to move from the Hotel to the nearby Limousine. He was halfway to the limo when John Hinckley, Jr. burst from the crowd and opened fire with a small pistol. The would-be assassin fired two shots, hitting two Secret Service Agents, before Assassin 97 zeroed in on Hinckley and pulled the trigger.

It was Hinckley's third shot that hit Reagan and spun him sideways and into the path of the bullet fired by Assassin 97. She saw the impact and Reagan's collapse. She released her finger from the trigger, and she felt her body descend into shock.

"What have I done?"

* * * *

"That, Assassin, is why you will not enter the room and go after Brewer. You will remain outside and let him come to you," Tomlinson said as he turned to face the table as the image on the viewer faded. Assassin 101, Assassin 97, and Professor Donovan sat at the table.

"What about Hinckley? He still kills Reagan," Assassin 97 asked.

Apprentice 101 shook his head. He checked his notes from the various timelines from which he had compiled the report. "Hinckley's shots missed. Well, most of them do. We think Reagan survives."

"We think?" she asked, not liking the fact that her boyfriend was the one briefing her.

He nodded. "Yes, we think. Only a few of the timelines we have traced have him dying."

"The only thing we know for sure," Professor Donovan chimed in, "is that if you pull the trigger, your shot is the one that kills the President. That occurs in *every* timeline that Reagan dies. So you do not, under any circumstance, enter that room."

* * * *

That was three days earlier, before her skip. The memory replayed in her mind as she stood in the pristine hallway, hoping she did not have to mess up the decor. She checked her watch, 14:25. Almost time. She wiped her hands on her jeans to dry them before she unholstered her pistol. Assassin 97 quickly checked both ends of the hallway before attaching the suppressor. She touched her communicator implant behind her ear, heard a single response and waited with her back against the wall with the pistol pointed at the floor.

President Ronald Reagan, surrounded by a wall of Secret Service, left the Washington Hilton Hotel, and greeted the small, but boisterous crowd. It was almost 14:30, the sky overcast and John Hinckley, Jr. stood in the crowd toward the rear of the Presidential Limousine. He kept his hands in his pockets. His right hand clutching the twenty-two caliber pistol he carried. He truly hoped today was his day, and that he would finally be on an equal level of fame to win Jodie Foster's heart.

Reagan passed less than six feet in front of him, waving to the crowd, and Hinckley knew he would never have a better opportunity. He pulled the small caliber pistol and squeezed off six shots in less than three seconds before he was hit and knocked to the ground.

The first shot hit Press Secretary James Brady in the head, the second hit a DC police officer in the back of the neck. Hinckley's third shot flew high and Assassin 97 heard it ping off a window of the building she was standing in. She flinched but did not move. It was not time.

The fourth shot hit a Secret Service Agent in the abdomen. Even as he fell, he was pushing the President toward the waiting limo. The fifth shot ricocheted off the limousine's bulletproof glass into the sky. The sixth shot, the one that would have killed Reagan, missed its mark as Cleaner Team Leader Malcolm Davis shoved the man next to him.

The bystander, a man named Alfred Antenucci, slammed into Hinckley and knocked him down, sending the final bullet off its planned course. The bullet, instead of hitting Reagan in the head, ricocheted off the armored side of the car, entered through the left armpit and lodged itself in the President's lung an inch from Reagan's racing heart.

The Secret Service shoved the President in the car. The limousine, with its escorts, roared off down the street as a crowd of Secret Service, DC Police and citizens converged on Hinckley.

* * * *

Rick Brewer smiled as he watched the crowd through a pair of binoculars. The President made his way from the Hotel toward the limousine. He watched with a smile as shots rang out and people fell. Reagan had waved and smiled at the crowd until gunshots began popping. Reagan's face turned from a smile to a look of astonishment and wonder as the Secret Service shoved him into the limousine.

The rogue panned the binoculars from the limousine to Hinckley, or at least the pile of people on top of the would-be assassin, and back to the limousine. He tracked the vehicle with his binoculars as it roared off down the street.

He lowered the binoculars, let loose several choice words in a fit of rage, and turned his attention to the television.

Did Hinckley succeed? he thought.

Within minutes, the airwaves were flooded with reports that Reagan had survived the attempt. Then the news changed. A would-be assassin had shot Reagan; his status was unknown.

Brewer smiled, his rage instantly gone. His proxy had done the job, and he, for the first time, got to see it all. Not from a sniper scope as he had King, but from a distance with a wide-angle lens. He suddenly realized that he liked being the puppeteer instead of the puppet.

He stored the binoculars, and grabbed his small bag from the bed. He paused, his hand on the doorknob, and watched the news a few more minutes and his smile faded as the news reported that Reagan survived.

“Damn it!” he yelled, walked over and kicked the television off its stand before he headed back for the door.

The first thing he noticed in the hallway was the woman. She was of medium height, slender, but full figured, with short brunette hair. She stood casually with her back against the wall. Brewer took in the scene in an instant and his thoughts turned immediately to his hand-to-hand instructors at the Guild. 'Do not let emotions cloud your judgment, or your observation of your surroundings. It could cost you your life.'

She raised her gun and pointed it at his head. The woman stood far enough away that he could not rush her. Her stance, and the way she held the weapon, told him she was Guild trained.

"Mr. Brewer, I presume," she said softly. The voice triggered memories that he had not accessed in over one hundred years. He smiled involuntarily.

"You're the young lady from the train." He left the smile on his face. "Did you finish that Ivy League education?"

"Never made it," she responded with a shake of her head, the pistol never wavered. "I had to finish another degree first."

"I finished that degree. I just used more of a hands on method."

"So I've heard." Her expression changed from mild admiration to pure business. "Now, slowly put the bag on the floor and take out your pistol, *very* slowly."

Brewer let the bag slide off his shoulder and caught it in his left hand. He then bent and lowered it to the ground, never taking his eyes of the brunette. "I'm not armed," he said as he stood back up, his hands at eye level.

"Now, why don't I believe you?"

He smiled again as he slowly produced a pistol from his waistband. “Because you are well trained, assassin.”

He dropped the pistol on the floor. The pistol pointed at his head had still not moved. He silently began to worry that he would not make it out this time.

“Turn around! Hands on your head!” she barked.

“You're going to take me back?” He looked bewildered for a moment and his fear grew. “You're not here to kill me?”

“It's an option,” she replied. Brewer could tell she was moving closer to him. “But it's not my first choice. I would prefer to take you home alive.”

“Why?”

She did not answer as he turned around with his hands on his head. He stared blankly out of the third floor window in front of him as he concentrated on the woman approaching him from behind. He was so engrossed in listening to the woman's movements that he completely missed the man in the next building with the sniper rifle aimed at him—a dark silhouette against the brick building.

He heard her footsteps as she got within range, but he had to be sure of where her pistol was before he made his move. He felt her left-hand pat him down for another weapon and felt the knife removed from his left waistband. He still did not know where her pistol was.

“Hands behind your back.”

He turned his head slightly. “You can't send me back handcuffed like that. The skip would break my arms.”

His arms still raised at head level, he turned his head and noticed she had holstered her weapon in an attempt to apply flex-cuffs on him. Both of them realized the error at the same time. Brewer was faster as he launched the first attack by bringing his hands down in a vicious chop.

Assassin 97 jumped back, narrowly missing the down thrust of his arms, and launched her own kick attack at his mid-section. It connected and he doubled over slightly. The woman took a step back, assumed her fighting stance, and waited. She thought briefly about going for her weapon, but knew she would never draw it in time. Better to leave the weapon where it was rather than have it knocked across the hall.

Brewer placed his hands on his knees, took a deep breath, and regained his composure, taking that moment to size up his opponent. She was in one of the three Guild trained fighting stances. He had a pretty good idea of how she would come at him and he mentally stored the series of defensive moves he would use. It had been decades since he had fought hand to hand. He hoped the rust would come off quickly.

So much for the decor, she thought as she launched a kick to his head. He countered easily and landed his first blow to her mid-section. Assassin 97 staggered back, but stayed on her feet.

"Is that all you got?" she taunted.

Brewer launched his own attack: a series of punches to the face and abdomen, followed by a leg sweep. She countered the punches easily, but did not see the leg sweep until she was on her back. Brewer pounced on the woman and pinned her by the throat.

"You're number five. Did you know that?" Brewer asked. His voice became tense with the strain of strangling the flailing woman. "You are the fifth assassin sent back to kill me. Sad thing is you didn't even come that close."

Assassin 97 could feel blackness creeping around her, enveloping her. She grabbed his hands and tried to pull in a last effort to free herself, but he had gravity and strength on his side. His hands continued to tighten.

Assassin 97 felt the blackness engulf her and she succumbed to its warm, peaceful embrace.

* * * *

Assassin 73 watched the woman through his sniper scope. Her back was to the wall outside of the rogue's door. He heard the distant gunshots of Hinckley's pistol and saw the rookie tense momentarily. He was not sure if she was the right person for this assignment, but the Council had ordered him to provide oversight. It appeared that both he and the rookie had a past score to settle with Rick Brewer.

Assassin 73 watched as Brewer exited the apartment and was immediately confronted by the rookie. She had him covered from the time he opened the door.

So far, so good, the veteran thought as she disarmed the rogue and made him turnaround.

"Hands behind your back," he heard her say through the implanted communicator. Brewer obeyed and turned in Assassin 73's direction.

Then she holstered her weapon, produced a set of flex-cuffs and approached her target.

What the hell are you doing? he thought as she approached the rogue.

Brewer turned his head, saw she was unarmed, and attacked. Assassin 73 let it play out for a minute; some lessons needed to be learned the hard way. The rookie went down with a leg sweep, Brewer landed on top of her, and the sniper sighted in on Brewer's head.

His finger tightened on the trigger as he contemplated his orders. The Council wanted the rogue alive. After finding out that the rogue had killed him in an alternate time-line, Assassin 73 disagreed. His finger tightened more.

That is when Assassin 97 slumped unconscious.

"Damn!" voiced the sniper, adjusted his aim, and shot the rogue assassin in the ass as he continued to squat over the body of the female Assassin.

The shot startled Brewer and he moved away from his victim and leaned against the wall opposite his room. He gingerly plucked the tranquilizer dart from his rear as the world slowly began to collapse on him.

Brewer instinctively reached for where his pistol should have been and realized it lay in the corridor where he had dropped it. He raised his hands, showing the sniper that he was unarmed. Quietly, he wondered if the sniper had a real weapon, and how was he going to get from his perch to this corridor without losing his target.

Assassin 97 rolled over slightly, enough to draw her holstered pistol, and weakly raised the weapon in Brewer's direction. She fired two tranquilizer darts into Brewer's chest before dropping her hand to her side. She simply watched as his unconscious body hit the floor.

She lay on the floor, regaining her strength little by little. "Lesson learned," she said.

It was several minutes before she had enough strength to sit up. She rubbed her throat for a moment as she kicked the unconscious rogue further away from her.

She produced the skip beacon she had brought for her target and crawled across the hall to his unconscious form. She attached the beacon to his arm as her communicator sounded, “You okay?"

Assassin 97 looked up and through the third floor window and saw a man holding a rifle. She nodded to him. “Yeah, I'm fine.”

Assassin 73 took a moment from disassembling his rifle and waved to her. “Rookie,” he said, “there are much harsher ways to learn. At least you survived the lesson.”

She waved back weakly through the window and then bent back over her victim.

She activated the skip beacon and stepped back. She watched the bubble envelope the rogue assassin, kicking his foot one last time as the opaque white door opened fully. A minute later, the bubble, and Brewer, disappeared with a barely audible pop.

“It's done,” she said as she began cleaning up the area. “Did Reagan survive?”

“Yes, we changed history,” came the reply. Assassin 73 finished packing his rifle and other effects, “we won't know how much until we get back home.”

She nodded. “And the others?”

“The Cleaner Team is clear. I saw Davis skip back right after the shooting.”

“Good, then let's get out of here.”

Minutes later, they were gone.

Chapter Fifteen

REGINALD MAYWEATHER STOOD BEFORE the Council, looking up at the five people in their robes. Two of his top aides stood on either side of him. His normal garish red outfit had been replaced by a navy blue conservative suit and tie.

Apprentice 101, Mr. Tomlinson and Master Li stood off to one side, accompanied by two guards with instructions to keep the young Apprentice from tearing Mayweather apart. Tomlinson and Li created a barrier between the Apprentice and the man who had called him out by name. The two guards, dressed in dark blue uniforms stood on either side of the Apprentice with stunners at the ready, holding him at bay.

“I said that I do not want that boy working on anything to do with the Dent family,” Mayweather growled.

“Mr. Mayweather, we will, of course, listen to your recommendations,” the Council Chief said. “But we will make the ultimate decision as to who undertakes a mission.”

Apprentice 101 listened intently to the exchange. It was the first time he had ever heard the Chief of the Council talk.

“Mission? He is a boy...an *apprentice*! He isn't going on any mission for what, another year or two?” Mayweather turned to his assistant on the left, and procured a document from the case the assistant held. “I have a letter, signed by Senator Malcolm Sebastian, ordering you to do *whatever* I say! And I say I want the boy out of here and away from my case!” He pointed in the general direction of the Apprentice who stood behind his human wall tall and defiant.

“I have already talked with Senator Sebastian,” the female Council member said softly. An edge to her voice that no one had ever heard rang through the chamber. It was obvious she did not like Mayweather or the Government dictating to her. She took a deep breath. “I'll tell you the same thing I told him, ‘We will assign agents as the mission dictates.’”

She pointed at the nearby Apprentice. “That Apprentice is the most knowledgeable person we have when it comes to the Dent family tree, and he will continue to provide intelligence on any further missions dealing with that family.

“We do not want a repeat of the disastrous timeline change from the last ‘success,’” she said the last making quotation signs with her hands.

Mayweather let out a snort. “What disastrous change?” He raised his arms and made a show of looking around. “I don't see anything different!” He raised a hand to stop the Councilwoman. “I've read the report on your so-called ‘disastrous’ timeline, and I don't believe it one bit. It's just a pitiful excuse to *not* carry out the mission you've been given.

"Now, as you've already talked to Senator Sebastian, you understand that your Guild Charter is at stake." He eyed each Council member and waited until the Chief of the Council nodded before continuing. "I want Dent dead. I want that entire family dead, and I want it done today! No more delays!"

As the word 'delays' echoed in the chamber, he turned on his heel, gave a disapproving glance in the direction of Apprentice 101, and left the Council Chamber. The door slammed behind him.

"Options?"

"We have two options, as I see it," one of the Councilmen began. "We can ignore the threat and risk a possible Government intervention, or we can go back and eliminate someone in the family ancestry."

"The one thing we cannot do is go back and kill the entire Dent family."

The debate began as each of the Council members gave their input, each one except for the Chief who, according to the by-laws of the Guild, could not weigh in unless there was an impasse. The trio of men and the two guards simply stood and tried to ignore the process. The debate lasted less than ten minutes.

"Mr. Tomlinson, Master Li, please come forward."

"Prepare to send Assassin 80 back to eliminate a family member that is in the direct line to Mr. Mayweather's competitor. Use the Apprentice's research to find one that, hopefully, won't disrupt the timeline too much. I don't see we have any other choice."

Apprentice 101, still flanked by the two guards, stepped forward. “If I may. I think there is one other option.”

* * * *

Mr. Donovan, Assassin 97, and a squad of guards escorted a sluggish Rick Brewer through the corridors of the Guild Academy. The mixture of uniforms and colorful robes made the precession resemble a walking rainbow. Bound and shackled, the fugitive wore a pale orange, single piece, jumpsuit.

Brewer studied every door, every side hallway, every crosswalk, and every person he passed. Not only was he looking for a way out, but also he was flooded with memories and emotions he had long buried. He fought the rush of emotions and kept his face stoic. It was like swimming upstream against a strong current.

Assassin 97 walked to Brewer's left, keeping her right hand on his left arm. She had a red welt on her left cheek that continued to grow and a set of bruises around her throat that drew looks from everyone they passed.

Brewer, likewise, sported a blackened eye and still had blood on his face from falling when he was tranquilized. Since he wore shackles, everyone in the Guild knew who got the worse end of the fight.

The group arrived at a set of huge double doors that opened as they approached, running face to face with Apprentice 101 and his entourage. Everyone recognized Brewer immediately.

"So, you got him," Master Li said with a rare smile. "Not bad for your first mission. I told you that you would do great things for the guild."

"First mission?" Brewer said with a mixture of astonishment and anger in his voice. He raised his shackled hands and pointed at the woman. "You sent a rookie after me?"

Donovan smiled. "A rookie using intelligence gathered by an Apprentice."

Brewer took in that information, paused for a moment, looking the young man up and down, and then gave a smile to his former mentor. "That would be the only way to capture me, using novices. You always did have a thing for the young and impressionable." He turned to look at the Apprentice. "Beginner's luck." He turned back to Donovan and gave a little smirk. "You did get the bodies of the others you sent after me, didn't you?"

"Their deaths have been added to your list of crimes."

"You know full well those were my *only* crimes. You had me sentenced to death to protect what...your little mission to the past? I could have killed you in 1963. I should have. How did you manage to talk the Guild into allowing you to go on a mission, anyway?"

Donovan responded before thinking, "I never went on a mission in—"

A sudden silence engulfed the corridor. Brewer broke it after only a few moments. "So, that was the little meeting I saw. You were telling the Cleaner to make sure he brought you back. Now I know your secret."

"That will be a secret that you will take to your grave."

Brewer's features suddenly turned cold and his voice became ice. “Then carry out my sentence. You can only kill me once.”

“There are many ways to die, Mr. Brewer.”

“So I've heard.”

* * * *

“Mr. Brewer, you are charged with—”

“I know what I'm accused of,” Brewer interrupted. He spoke with defiance and just a hint of fear. “And I know what I've done and what I didn't do!”

He stood tall in the accusing eyes of the Council. He could tell they were already on edge, possibly because of the meeting before he came in. He knew he was walking a very fine line if he wanted to live.

“The question to you is; what are you going to do with me?”

He had never been in the Guild Council Chamber before and did not know if he should be impressed by the size and scope of the room, or disappointed that there was really nothing to it other than its size. He was not surprised at the raised dais and the five members sitting over their audience. Standard domination psychology was taught to all first year apprentices.

“That is indeed the question,” began the female Council member. She stood and made her way down the hidden staircase and appeared at Brewer's left. He decided he would be impressed with the room and the Council.

“You stole history archives,” she counted the accusations off with a finger for each.

"You know I never stole—"

"You committed unsanctioned assassinations over a two-hundred year period," she continued despite his interruption. "You killed three members of the Assassin's Guild—"

"Four. I killed McKindrick in the other timeline. But, you must admit, those were self-defense." He smiled softly. "You did, after all, send them to kill me."

"—and you created time ripples that had such a disastrous effect on the timeline that we had to correct your interference."

"So, you did send someone back to kill King. "He nodded. "I knew it."

The Councilwoman seemed to stop at that remark. She stared at the shackled man for a moment. "So you *can* feel temporal disturbances?"

The prisoner stood perfectly still, weighing the significance of the question. He responded with a simple nod.

The Councilwoman looked at her colleagues, received a curt nod from the Chief of the Council, and turned back to Brewer. "I think you just saved your life, Mr. Brewer. However," she stepped forward to make sure he understood, "if you give this Council or anyone in the Guild, any grief..." She left the threat unspoken. "Cooperate, and live."

Brewer paused before answering. He wanted to live, and if they were willing to give him a chance to live, he would take it. At least, he thought, until he could escape again. He looked distraught and defeated, lowered his head, and then nodded his compliance.

"Mr. Tomlinson," she faced the Time Skip Chief, "take him to Professor Van Der Bleen in Temporal Studies. Have him begin his research.

"Mr. Brewer, just so that you understand your situation," the Chief of the Council said from the dais. His voice was growing weak and feeble. He would have to be replaced soon. "Professor Van Der Bleen can study you, or your corpse. Of course, the readings and information would be much better if you are alive."

Brewer smiled. He was going to live.

Epilogue

REGINAL MAYWEATHER STEPPED FROM his limousine into the frigid tundra of the Guild Mountains. The blowing snow and howling wind instantly chilled him, even through his several layers of clothing.

"Out of my way!" he yelled at his driver who held the door open. Mayweather shoved the man aside and then made his way up the mountain trail toward the training entrance to the Assassin's Guild.

He trudged up the hill slowly, his cane adding a bit of leverage to aid him with the steep incline. The wind whipped the red hat off his head twice during his ascent. He retrieved it each time, slowing his progress. He was nearly frozen by the time he reached the large, wooden gate.

The long trek up the mountain gave him time to ponder what he was doing. He wanted his competition out of the way and killing him now would cause too much grief with the authorities; grief even his Government contacts may not be able to counter, but would the Guild balk at such a request? It is not every day you ask someone to go back in time and wipe out an entire family!

He pushed the gate open and immediately spotted two boys, standing perfectly still in the blowing snow. They had apparently been there for a while by the ankle high snow piled around them. Mayweather would have thought they were frozen solid except for their ragged breath.

He issued a grunt, found it a bit unnerving that he could actually see the grunt as it dissolved in the cold air, and made his way to the huge double doors that opened into the Guild training facility.

He used his cane to rap heavily on the door, the sound nearly lost in the howling wind. He looked over his right shoulder at the two boys. "Still, I'm doing better than those poor bastards."

He turned back to the double doors and knocked again.

At his third knock, he felt a hand grab him from behind, pull his head to the left and a needle puncture his neck. Mayweather looked behind him to see one of the two boys lying face down in the snow. The other obviously had him in his grasp.

"Let me go!" He struggled as he felt a warm liquid enter his neck.

"You arrogant son of a bitch," sounded the reply.

"Who are you?" Mayweather asked as his body began to heat up.

He suddenly felt great, better than he ever had, but it only lasted for a few seconds. As rapidly as the euphoria hit him, he began to feel a sense of weakness that rapidly consumed his body. He slumped from the arms of the man holding him and fell into the snow at the foot of the Training Facility doors.

The Assassin looked him in the face and said nothing. He watched the businessman slump into the snow, twitch twice, and then die at the steps of the academy.

The young man walked over to the candidate still lying in the snow, checked for and found a pulse, and smiled.

"No hard feelings," he said and shook his head sadly. "But you weren't going to make it anyway."

He moved off to the side of the courtyard, near the simple wooden gate, and actuated his retrieval beacon. He heard the giant double doors open and someone yell for a medic. *No broken nose this time*, he thought as he stepped into the semi-transparent bubble.

The man, once known as Jason Lassiter, now known as Assassin 101, entered the time skip bubble and disappeared.

The Adventure Continues In...

Chapter One

ASSASSIN 101 STOOD, right arm stretched before him, his hand held toward the white opaque void of the time stream. He moved his hand in a small circle and the sensation of crawling ants assaulted his fingers and palm. He pulled his hand away, rubbing it to rid himself of the static tingle. His eyes stayed focused on the static currents of the vortex as they discharged and swirled.

He turned to the Control Room Director, Mr. Tomlinson. “A little stronger than usual, isn’t it?”

Mr. Tomlinson, dressed in his usual yellow, full length smock, adjusted his glasses and typed a query into the data pad held in his right hand. He stole a glance at the open time portal and the slight swirl of the maelstrom beyond as he typed. He vaguely heard a technician across the room state that the mission was a go. The pad beeped and displayed the results of his query. Tomlinson’s brows arched noticeably, and he whistled softly. “Sunspot activity is creating a sharp increase in static charge.” He smiled weakly as he focused on the Assassin. "You could make the skip today, but you'll definitely feel it."

"Hell, I feel it every time." Assassin 101 gave a half-hearted smile, feeling less nonchalant than his remark. He again held his right hand to the Time Skip Door. A small, blue bolt of electricity leapt from the vortex and pricked his finger. He jerked his hand back, shook it, and then sucked on his finger to kill the pain. He failed. "Damn."

"It's your call, Assassin. We can postpone this until the sunspot activity has decreased." Tomlinson typed in another query on his pad, received a response and looked up at the Assassin. "Seventy-two hours."

The Assassin took a deep breath. "No. We've had four delays already and the Council is anxious to get underway." Assassin 101 straightened his leather jacket and ran a hand through his hair. "We finally have a location and, sunspots or not, we need to take care of the situation."

Pointing at the door with his left hand, Tomlinson replied, a little more condescending than he meant. "This is a door to time. He will still be in Ecuador in seventy-two hours."

Assassin 101 smiled. "You're not the one being called into the Council Chambers to be asked 'Why haven't you left yet?'" He sighed, shaking his head. "Sunspots or not, I'm going. It'll be worth the pain just to get away from the Council for a few days."

Tomlinson looked at the pad again then back to the Assassin. He turned the pad to show the readout. "Are you sure?"

Assassin 101 studied the pad, sighed again, and then shifted his vision around the room for a moment of reflection. The yellow painted walls surrounded the horseshoe shaped time-skip control consoles. Tomlinson's office sat atop a set of stairs at the base of the horseshoe, the office's large bay window presenting the Time Skip Director a commanding view of the consoles. Control monitors covered one entire wall, several of them showing historical events; other missions currently underway. The Assassin paused and watched the monitors for a moment.

"Yeah, I'm sure." He smirked and turned to face the door again.

The Assassin took a deep breath, straightened his clothes in anticipation, closed his eyes, and stepped into the vortex. A waterfall cascade of air washed over him as he entered the time stream. The wave of air quickly changed to tingling electricity as he picked up speed; freefalling through time. The static discharge consumed his body; a million ants crawling along his skin. Assassin 101 exiled the sensation to the recesses of his mind and the electrical current faded, temporarily subdued. His mind focused on the time skip and he opened his eyes.

The white, opaque tunnel of the time vortex assaulted his vision. Blue electrical current leapt from the tunnel, pricking his skin and clothing as he skipped.

Something's different, he thought. He extended his arms and wiggled his fingers to play with the blue bolts of electricity. The currents danced around his fingers. He brought his arms forward and watched as the electricity arched from his fingers and into the void. No pain, no crawling ants, Assassin 101 felt only the soft, caressing hands of time.

Smooth, he thought. The skip was not the usual whirlpool of buffeting waves that characterized a trip against the flow of time. *This is more like I'm moving with the flow.*

That thought snapped him from his reverie as an exit door appeared in the distance. The black dot grew in the white void. It *shouldn't be this soon,* he thought. Something was wrong.

The dot grew larger, morphing into the shimmering oval that ended a time skip. The pressure of deceleration pressed against his body and he prepared for the inevitable stop. His momentum slowed to a crawl as he approached the oval, allowing him a moment to peer through the door in to the darkness beyond. Blurry images moved in dark fog. The moment of truth at hand, he released the breath he did not realize he held and stepped through the door.

A chill engulfed his body. The Assassin stood shivering and rubbed his arms to increase circulation. He blinked hard, adjusting from the bright light of the vortex to the dim light of the chamber. His eyes focused on his new environment and he froze.

Assassin 101 stood in the Guild Council Chambers. He turned and saw the same dark, concave walls, giant double doors, and small beam of light that fell from the ceiling that he had seen a dozen times. His eyes focused on the dais and a group of three men and two women that he did not recognize: The Council. He turned again, acknowledging the three guards to his left. Each guard carried a small, wicked looking weapon that the Assassin had never seen before.

One of the Councilmen, dressed in the traditional black robes of the Council, rose from his chair and slowly made his way from the raised dais down a hidden staircase to appear at the Assassin's right. Assassin 101 watched him but did not move.

The Councilman extended his hand. "Welcome, Assassin 101. Welcome to the Twenty-Sixth Century."

The Assassin took the offered hand. The grip was firm, strong. It belied the wrinkled face and deliberate gait of the old man. Two of the guards nearby moved to stand on either side of the Councilman. The third remained a few meters away, out of range of the Assassin.

"My name is Vargas," the Councilman smiled. "I am afraid I must ask that you turn over your weapons. I assure you that no harm will come to you." He waited a moment for the Assassin to acknowledge, received a curt nod, and then motioned for the guards. He never took his eyes off Assassin 101.

The guard's methodical search of his person revealed his .40 caliber pistol, two extra magazines, pocketknife and small lock pick set. One of the guards examined the lockset and the knife. He held them up for Vargas to see. The Councilman gave a nod and the guard handed them back to the Assassin. The guards never uttered a sound.

The removal of his weapon helped to alleviate the mild shock the Assassin felt. He stole a glance around the chamber before landing his gaze on the old man and asking the obvious question. "Did you say, 'Twenty-Sixth Century?'"

"Yes, Assassin," replied the Councilman. He scratched his nose absentmindedly. "We have brought you three hundred years into the future." Vargas paused, scratching his nose again. "We need your help."

"My help?" Assassin 101 studied the man. The other Council members, the guards and the room itself also received the Assassin's scrutiny. The Council Chamber appeared to have remained unchanged for three hundred years. He had enjoyed the notoriety of being one of the few Apprentices to have visited the chamber and remain in the Guild. As an Assassin, he had been summoned to this chamber more than once. This time, standing in the spotlight once again, he felt the same sense of dread he had as an Apprentice.

The Councilman lowered his voice slightly in embarrassment. "We have a rogue Assassin." He shook his head. "Nasty business. We have had teams researching and pursuing this rogue for two hundred years. We can't seem to catch him. We believe he is lying low while he plans something that will disrupt or destroy the Guild." The Councilman smiled hopefully. "We need your help to find and capture him."

Assassin 101 turned his eyes to the elevated platform where the remainder of the Guild Council sat. They remained silent, as did the guards. The thought of activating his emergency retrieval beacon crossed his mind, but the Assassin dismissed it. The guards could mistake the movement as hostile, in which case he probably would not survive stepping into the Skip Bubble. The Assassin turned his eyes back to the Councilman standing before him. "Why me?"

"We were told you have experience researching historical files and tracking rogue agents. You know how to track anomalies." The Councilman met the Assassin's gaze. "We need that kind of experience to lead our research and retrieval team.

"We must find this rogue before he does something else to undermine and harm the Guild."

"Something else? What has he already done?"

Vargas grimaced slightly. "Three of our Assassins have been killed. Two government officials have disappeared. The once stable European Union has fallen into disarray.

"All of this is contrary to what our archived history says should have occurred."

Assassin 101 took another quick peek around the room, partly to verify where everyone stood and partly to give him a moment to think. A voice from the dais interrupted his musings and drew his attention to an old, white-haired woman seated above him. Her wrinkled face smiled down at the Assassin.

"You can relax, Assassin," she smiled, recognizing his conflict between fight or flight. Her voice took on a soothing tone. "We have no wish to harm you. If you wish to return to your Guild, you may do so. We only brought you here to ask for your assistance, nothing more."

The Assassin nodded his understanding but could not relax; too many unknown factors...and adrenaline. His heart pounded. His mind raced and tried to define and categorize all of the new information. He needed more time, so he forced his body to relax with a deep breath, nodded again and smiled. "Since I'm already here, I might as well look around," he said. "I'm happy to help."

Two guards escorted Assassin 101 through the rich mahogany paneled corridors of the Guild. The Assassin absently noted that the corridors had remained relatively unchanged through the centuries. *Tradition or apathy?*

he wondered. In either case, the familiar backdrop served to relax him. *Perhaps that's why they haven't changed, to provide familiar surroundings when someone is brought here from the past.* Assassin 101 smiled at the thought but shifted his focus back to his current situation.

The Assassin studied the two guards ahead of him as they moved through the halls of the Guild. Each man wore a black, skintight, one-piece uniform under dull black armor that slid over the shoulders and covered their chest and hips. The Assassin could not see any rank or other identifying insignia. The guard's uniform was complete with low profile combat helmets that sported reflective, full face visors, and a pair of mid-calf boots. They carried small, compact rifles that the Assassin had never seen before. *At least some things have changed.*

The two guards led him through the labyrinth of corridors, through the central hub of the complex and down the path to the residential quarters. The Assassin's instincts and habits took over as they entered the residential area. He turned left and stopped at the first door on his left; the quarters he shared with Assassin 97. He twisted the knob and found the door locked. The jiggling of the door handle alerted his escort that the Assassin no longer walked with them. One of the guards walked back to stand next to the Assassin.

"Sir, the VIP quarters are this way." The vocoder in the helmet could not mask the humor in the guard's voice. He held out his left hand to direct the way.

"Sorry," the Assassin replied with an embarrassed smile. "Habit." He took another quick look at the door, raised his left hand to touch it, closed his fist and started back down the corridor.

The three men continued down the winding corridors and finally stopped at a large, finely crafted and ornate wooden door. A nameplate on the door read *Donovan Suite*. He turned around and read the door opposite: *Tomlinson Suite*. Assassin 101 smiled as one of the guards opened the door to the *Donovan Suite*.

Holding the door open, the guard motioned the Assassin inside. "Sir, the Council has asked that you not go unescorted in the Guild. They wish to keep your presence here as quiet as possible."

Assassin 101 nodded his understanding and stepped into the *Donovan Suite*.

"We will return in a half hour to escort you to the library," the guard said, and the Assassin automatically checked his watch. The man pointed a gloved hand at the scarlet robes neatly folded on the bed. "We have provided more suitable attire for your stay." The guard closed the door, leaving the Assassin alone with his thoughts.

Assassin 101 ran his hand along the top of a finely crafted bureau as he walked through the room. The suite sported a meeting area, kitchenette, a work desk nook and a king size bed filling almost half of the main area. The room was easily twice the size of the quarters he shared with Assassin 97. Fine mahogany paneling covered the walls except for the wall to the Assassin's right, which appeared to be made of a large entertainment screen that served as the entire wall. The light fixtures consisted of a luminescent design that the Assassin had never seen before. He studied everything.

His eyes drifted back to the bed and the stack of scarlet robes sitting on the end next to the changing bench at the foot of the bed. He sat down on the bed, placed his feet on the bench and ran through the last hour of his life.

Was it really sunspots that caused the extra static in the vortex? he wondered. *Or was it the Twenty-Sixth century retrieval beacon?* He shook his head. *Irrelevant, since I'm now here.*

The mission: find another rogue agent. Was that his legacy? His mark on the Guild? He had joined the Guild to study history, not become part of it. He smirked again. *But, I'm already a part of history.*

His mind drifted back to his days as an Apprentice. Three years of Guild training, the tracking of a rogue Apprentice and the turmoil of Reginald Mayweather's plot to take over the world. Apprentice 101 had skipped back in time and killed Mayweather on the steps of the Guild, stopping the plot before it had even begun. His first kill, removed from his record for political expediency. In the annuls of history, Reginald Mayweather died of a heart attack.

That kill may not have been on his official record, but it gave Assassin 101 the confidence and the experience he needed to carry out his first true mission. Two months after graduation, the Assassin had skipped to 1938 Britain to prevent an assassination attempt on Winston Churchill. Assassin 101 and his team succeeded, but not unscathed. He received his first injury—a knife wound—that kept him in the infirmary for several weeks. He also lost a member of his cleaner team in that knife fight.

He recalled the cleaner, a stocky, balding man in his late thirties named Wilson. As he threw himself at the three men that had the Assassin cornered, Wilson knocked them all down in one charge. One of the men with a knife fell into the Assassin, hurling the Assassin into a wall and dislocating his shoulder. The man left a jagged cut down the Assassin's left side as they fell. Another knifeman turned and stabbed Wilson through the heart before he could stand. Wilson saw the knife, grabbed the man's head and twisted as they both fell. The cleaner killed the man who killed him.

Assassin 101 had little doubt that the cleaner saved his life. The Assassin killed the other two knifemen after they mistakenly thought him too hurt to fight. The threat to the Assassin, and to Winston Churchill, ended in a back alley in Liverpool, England. He wept at Wilson's funeral a week later. The Assassin learned a valuable lesson and vowed that he would never lose another member of his team due to his inexperience or negligence.

His next two assignments were observation missions. He skipped as part of an observation team to 1881 to witness a shootout in Tombstone, Arizona. The three-man and one-woman team stood on the wood plank sidewalk and watched as Wyatt Earp, his brothers, Virgil and Morgan, and the charismatic Doc Holliday strode past them. The Assassin, still a young man of twenty-two, watched in awe.

"The Gunfight at the O.K. Corral," he had whispered to his team leader. "I read about this as a boy." The Cleaner nodded absently but said nothing. The Assassin received a reprimand upon his return: failure to control emotions. He spent the next two months in the classroom teaching the first-year class the importance of emotional control.

His third mission took him to June 1944, this time as the leader of a cleaner team. The team sat, over a mile from Normandy Beach, watching the allied forces storm the beach. The thunder of incoming artillery gave way to the steady sound of machine gun fire in the distance. The Assassin raised a high-powered pair of holo-binoculars and watched the invasion.

"Now that is bravery," he commented. "All of that armament on the beach and they still just stepped off the boat." The Assassin shook his head. "Incredible."

"Maybe," his second in command remarked, his voice awash in arrogance and boredom. "But we change history."

The Assassin lowered the binoculars for a moment, watching his second. He raised the glasses and watched the invasion. "So did they," the Assassin replied, watching as thousands of men stormed Normandy Beach. "So did they."

His fourth mission, a skip to the lunar colony in 2196, presented the Assassin with his first failure. His mission to save Katherine Drake, the Governor of Moon Base Armstrong, failed when she died at the hands of a shadowy figure that Assassin 101 never found. Her death prevented the colony from declaring Independence and maintaining its neutrality in the Fourth World War. The Indonesian Consortium destroyed the lunar colony in 2212.

He closed his eyes. Almost two years later and he could still see it vividly. He had stood to the left of the Governor as she sat in the cafeteria. Politicians, courtiers, sycophants and citizens all gathered for a moment of her time. He thought he saw a shadow move and looked toward the upper catwalks that supported the lunar dome. He could remember shielding his eyes, but there was nothing but the lights and the catwalks.

He had turned to look back at the Governor when the first laser bolt slammed into the table to her right, exploding that section of the table with the force of its blast. The Assassin ducked as a second and then a third bolt hit the table; each one closer to the Governor. Katherine Drake died when two bolts slammed into her chest, knocking her backwards and sending the cafeteria into a panic.

Assassin 101, behind cover, searched for the sniper, but saw nothing. He broke cover and ran for the catwalks. No lasers tried to hit him. Within minutes, he was on the catwalk, weapon ahead of him, scanning. No one was there. He had spent three days searching for any sign of the sniper, but found nothing.

There were two other missions in his four years since graduation, successful. The Council considered Assassin 101 a full-fledged, skilled and successful assassin, very different from the timid child who had stood in the freezing cold a few years earlier.

Seven years ago, he had met the Council for the first time after he had killed another Apprentice in unarmed combat. Fear that the Council would execute him over the affair had made him a nervous wreck during that meeting. Apprentice 101 returned to his curriculum after being justified in killing the other student in hand to hand combat. He had four meetings with the Council before graduating.

His Council meetings were now so frequent that the Assassin never felt nervous. *Most assassins never meet face to face with the Council*, he smiled, *and I've been offered my own seat on the dais more than once*. Of course, he knew those offers were in jest, but Assassin 101 felt that one day the offer would be formal.

He shook his head. That offer was years away. He had to focus on the here and now—the Twenty-Sixth century. *Did they really bring me three hundred years forward to track down a fugitive?* he mused. He checked his watch and saw that twenty minutes had past. *I guess I'll find out soon enough.*

The Assassin stood up and changed into the provided robes, replaying the Twenty-Sixth Century Council meeting in his mind. Shock, not nervousness, had clouded his senses during the initial meeting. *That was something they never taught me at the Academy,* he mused. A single wish that Assassin 97 was with him flitted through his mind, but he dismissed it as quickly as it arrived. She would get a full report of it when he got home.

A knock on the door signaled the return of his escort. Assassin 101 crossed the spacious apartment and opened the door. He found a small, heavy-set man with thick glasses, wearing a wrinkled suit, standing nervously in the hallway. The stranger startled as the door opened. He glanced up the hallway before retrieving a handkerchief and mopped the sweat from his brow. Without preamble, he quickly moved past the Assassin into the room and motioned for Assassin 101 to close the door.

Nervous and jittery, he half bowed. "Assassin, I don't have much time," he wheezed slightly as he spoke. His words flowed unnaturally as he forced himself to take several deep breaths. "I have come to warn you. Things are not as they appear in the Guild. You are in danger if you..."

“Wait a minute,” the Assassin interrupted, holding up a hand and shaking his head. “Take a breath, calm down, and tell me who you are.”

“There is no time,” the man replied. He wrung his hands, nervously fumbling with his sweat soaked handkerchief. “If they find me here, I’ll be put to death,” he paused, “as will you.

“Your mission here is a lie. I don't know what they told you, but I will tell you it’s a deception.” He paused, wiping his forehead again with his handkerchief. He looked around the room as if expecting the walls to come alive before he continued. “They brought you here to...”

A knock on the door interrupted the man and he froze in terror. Assassin 101 looked around the room for a place to hide the babbling man. “Yes?” he called as he opened a closet on the other side of the room.

“It's time, sir,” came the muffled reply from behind the door.

“One second, still dressing,” the Assassin replied. He pushed the terror-stricken man into the closet, wondered briefly if the man was insane, and closed the door.

He quickly made his way to the door and opened it while straightening his robes. “Sorry,” he smiled.

Two armored guards, perhaps two of the same that had escorted the Assassin to his quarters, flanked a third man. The man stood at least two inches taller than the Assassin, dressed in a well-tailored suit that matched his well-groomed dark hair and a goatee. An acne scarred face surrounded his small nose. Piercing blue eyes and a toothy smile greeted the Assassin. The man extended his hand.

“Good afternoon!” he said cheerily. “My name is Michael Lassiter, and I'll be your liaison while you’re here.”

Also from Jumpmaster Press

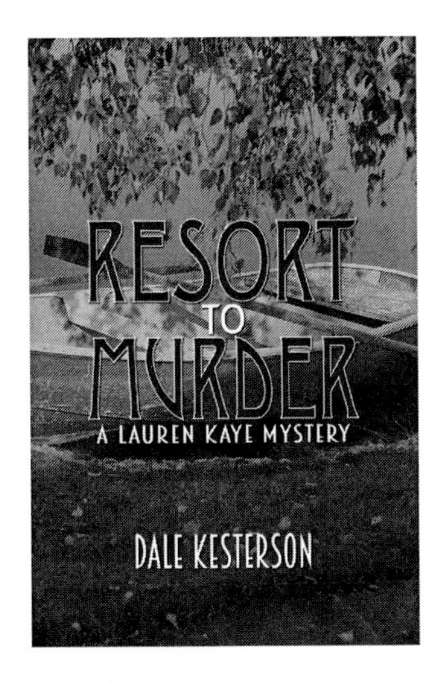

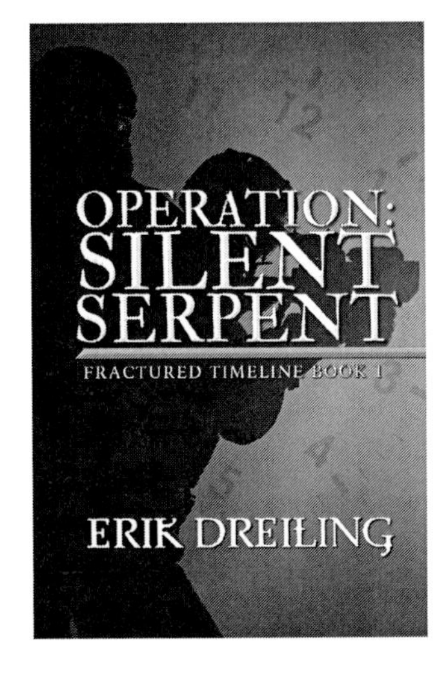

About the Author

With a face for radio and a voice for silent movies, writing was his only recourse.

R. Kyle Hannah is a self-professed geek and lover of *most* things sci-fi. He began writing in high school as an outlet for an overactive imagination. Those humble beginnings, combined with real life experiences from a 29-year career in the Army, have spawned a dozen full-length adventures and short stories.

His 2019 release, *Harvest Day*, won Best Sci-Fi Novel at the 2000 Imadjin Awards.

He was named One of the 50 Great Writers You Should be Reading by the Author's Show in 2016. He is also the winner of two Pinnacle Book Awards (*Time Assassins* and *The Jake Cutter Conspiracy*).

"Reminiscent of Arthur C. Clarke" is how Writer's Digest describes his first novel, *To Aid and Protect*.

He is a founder and Vice President of Jumpmaster Press. www.jumpmasterpress.com.

He is married, with two children, and lives in the suburbs of Birmingham, Alabama.